D0193991

ATOMIK
AZTEX

ATOMIK AZTEX

by Sesshu Foster

CITY LIGHTS · SAN FRANCISCO

© 2005 by Sesshu Foster
All Rights Reserved

Cover and interior photographs by Ignacio Bravo
Cover design by Yolanda Montijo
Book design by Elaine Katzenberger
Typography by Harvest Graphics

Library of Congress Cataloging-in-Publication Data

Foster, Sesshu.
  Atomik Aztex / by Sesshu Foster.
      p.   cm.
  ISBN-10: 0-87286-440-5
  ISBN-13: 978-0-87286-440-5
  1. Aztecs—Fiction.   2. Indians of North America—Europe—Fiction.
3. Imperialism—Fiction.   4. Colonies—Fiction.   5. Europe—Fiction.   I. Title.

PS3556.O7719A95 2005
813'.54—dc22
                                                        2005000899

Visit our website: www.citylights.com

City Lights books are edited by Lawrence Ferlinghetti and Nancy J. Peters and
published at the City Lights Bookstore, 261 Columbus Avenue, San Francisco,
CA 94133.

ACKNOWLEDGMENTS

Grateful acknowledgment is made to the editors of publications where portions of this book were first published in different form: *the Amerasia Journal, the L.A. Weekly* and *Salon.com,* and also to the late Frank Conroy of the Iowa Writers Workshop for the James A. Michener-Paul Engle Fellowship which aided these investigations. Kosmic thanks to Juliana Koo, Sunyoung Lee, Elaine Katzenberger and Karen Yamashita for your terrific support. Karate bows of deep thanks to you, my colleagues, students, and family.

For Lisa Chen, Rick Harsch, Warren Liu and designated drivers

Note

This is a work of fiction. Readers looking for accurate information on Nahua and Mexica peoples or the Farmer John meat packing plant in the City of Vernon need to *read nonfiction*. (See Michael Coe and Miguel Leon-Portilla.) Persons attempting to find a plot in this book should read Huck Finn. Also, in this book a number of dialects are used, including the extreme form of the South-Western pocho dialect, calo, ordinary inner-city slang, and modified varieties of speech from the Vietnam era. This is no accident.

> Step out of history
> to enter life
> try that all of you
> you'll get it then.

> —Charlotte Delbo, *Auschwitz and After*,
> translated by Rosette C. Lamont

I AM Zenzontli, Keeper of the House of Darkness of the Aztex and I am getting fucked in the head and I think I like it. Okay sometimes I'm not sure. But my so-called visions are better than aspirin and cheaper.

Perhaps you are familiar with some worlds, stupider realities amongst alternate universes offered by the ever expanding-omniverse, in which the Aztek civilization was 'destroyed.' That's a possibility. I mean that's what the Europians *thot*. They planned genocide, wipe out our civilization, build cathedrals on **TOP** of our pyramidz, bah, hump our women, not just our women but the Tlaxkalans, the Mixteks, the Zapoteks, the Chichimeks, the Utes, the Triki, the Kahuilla, the Shoshone, the Maidu, the Klickitat, the Mandan, the Chumash, the Yaqui, the Huicholes, the Meskwaki, the Guarani, Seminoles, endless peoples, decimate 'em with smallpox, measles and shit fits, welfare lines, workaholism, imbecility, enslave 'em in the silver mines of Potosí, the gold mines of El Dorado & Disneylandia, on golf courses & country clubs, *chingados,* all our brothers, you get the picture. The Spanish — I could explain this to you in a Mayan coffeeshop with full orchestral accompaniment (replete with yowls of anguish, agony, gurgling, choking from the Victimology Choir) — had this Sword and Cross strategy, Bible in one hand gun in the other, in other words fuck us over royally with their bullshit ideology, propaganda, the whole nine yards, massive media blitz, disinformation campaign, low self-esteem, dysfunctional self-image, voodoo ekonomix, war on drugs & terrorism, prison-industrial system, the whole works. . . . The Europians figured they'd wipe us out, *Plan A,* enslave our peoples down at the corner liquor store, crush all resistance thru germ warfare and lawyers, lie, cheat, kidnap, ransom, burn our sakred libraries, loot our kapital, install Christian theokratik diktatorships, slaughter us by the millions, **MILLIONS** (my emphasis), then claim it wuz all accidental, just their luck — they'd pretend they just happened by on their way to India to buy some cardamom, some nutmeg and spices — like you'd just *accidently* happen to decimate Whole Civilizations and Worlds just to set a nice breakfast table — hot coffee, cinnamon toast, chiming silverware; furthermore *just by chance, as luck would have it* they'd enslave our native brothers and sisters of *all other* Red Nations as well. Could we let that happen? Of course not. Did we care if they had a Plan B? Hell, no. Cuz in no way does that fit our *aesthetic conception* of how the universe is supposed to run. It's just plain ugly. To think that they want to foist that vision of Reality on the rest of us. That's the *insult.* Barbarik, cheap aesthetik based on flimsy Mechanistik notions of the omniverse as a Swiss watch set to ticking by some sort of Trinity. The Spanish believed they had superior firepower with their gunpowder, blunderbusses, crossbows with metal darts, steel body-armor, Arabian horses, galleons built in Cádiz. All that wuz true. But we Aztex had our ways and means. We have access to the meanest, nastiest, psycho Gods through voodoo, jump blues, human sacrifice, proletarian vanguard parties, Angry Coffeehouse Poetry, fantasy life intensified thru masturbation & comic books, plus all our armies, Flower Warriors, Jaguar Legions, Eagle Elite Units, Jiu Jitsu and of course the secret weapon. In a nutshell. The Spanish didn't have a chance. *Sure, the Spaniards rowed up in their quaint canvas-rigged galleons ready to conquer the world. The vicious leathery little rats crossed the Sargasso Sea come to find out indigenous peoples already had their number. We welcomed them to our land. They were not heard from again.* And after the Spanish fell to our advance forces, who was gonna stop us? The Italians? Come on! They don't even make second round of the World Cup.

The rest is history. One big fucking headache, I'll tell you.

Luckily we Aztex believe in circular concepts of time, cyklikal koncep-tions of the universe where reality infinitely kurves back upon itself end-lessly so all that has existed does exist and will always exist and so forth into infinity. It's the only POV that makes sense in the end. Which is the Beginning. (Don't worry if you don't get it the first time, it all repeats, as you shall see. This happened to you already & it will happen to you again in the future.) I mean, how else to go forth fearlessly into battle, vanquish our enemies on a global scale for generations and offer millions (and mil-lions) of still-beating hearts to the sun, the six thousand five hundred and seventy-four sacred steps to the top of the Pyramid of the Sun awash with layers of black blood, making the sharp granite steps slippery for the priests? We Aztek warriors can face our own death with komplete kool, knowing full well that on some plane of the spirit we go on living forever and ever, knowing that whatever torture, torment and travail the present finite moment brings us we exist simultaneously in all the happiest moments of our lives and these go on shining forever like the stars, as Mayan pop singer Juan Lennon put it, "Instant Karma's gonna get you. We all shine on. I wanna hold your hand. Yeah, yeah, yeah." Who could've said it better? No matter what horrible fate awaits us at the hands of some momentarily vik-torious enemy, we have altered the space-time kontinuum of the universe through our Aztek sciences and teknologies so that we shall emerge victo-rious on one level or another sooner or later, something which causes our enemies no end of anguish and horror once they realize that their own hearts are the key, the crucial item in the orchestration of our mastery of the time-space kontinuum. This great faith in the science and teknospiri-tuality of our ancestors the Tolteka, who invented the Heart As Engine of Urban Renewal, the revitalization of Reality, while the Europian savages were scurrying around inventing toylike items such as the Wheel, the Cannon, the Stirrup, etc., and moderately interesting items like Macaroni, the Can Opener, Suicide, and so on, which explains of course our triumph at the present stage of History, the full flowering of our reign in the Aztek hemisphere. So goes the usual telling of that tale, of course. You should take everything with a grain of salt. I'm fairly liberal as these things go. I'm willing to grant the Spanish and other subjugated peoples their kultural values and so forth. I mean, they all have their place. I'm not saying that you have to think Spanish food is worth eating, I certainly don't, well maybe some *paella* every once in a while, but I've listened many long hours to my Spanish slaves explain to me their quaint customs, their Katholicisms, their folkloric belief in the Linear God who is transfixed above them on the surface of the Heavens as they mope about the globe worrying about something they call Sin, and things of this nature. I am quite willing to grant Christianity konceptual validity in the marketplace of ideas; simply because they are Subjugated Peoples I don't entirely diskount some of their insights into the obdurate and kraggy face of existence underlying the human condition. I think our own high priests would acknowledge that there are some fundamental questions of human (that is, Aztek) existence that qualify as unresolved and open and therefore perhaps within the tentative purview of alternate visions of the universe such as might fall under barbarian superstition. Not for nothing do our major universities have radikal departments of Barbarian Studies where savage, exotik, paranormal worldviews are revisited. Everybody knows that atavism and savagery make the world go round. Certainly the professional ikonoclasts of the universities cause dangerous disruptions, explosions and lesions in the visible world, causing occasional death, destruction and even sometimes subversion of basik space-time elements of this, the Sixth World (or Sixto's World, as I sometimes think of it), but so what? That's the whole purpose of teknospiritual advancement anyway, isn't it? That's why we cut out millions of hearts every year, and a kostly boring bloody business it is, too, isn't it? That's why we're the best at what we do, isn't it? Cuz we have to. Cuz it puts everything right in this world, in the universe as it stands. Isn't that right? Of course it is. So we can afford to have some egghead professors, four-eyed poets and bozo spiritualists getting red-faced, goggly-eyed and spastik about the Linear God, the pot-bellied Chinese man, the Muslim Scriptures on Numerology and Women-Do-What-Yer-Told. So what if these innovations kost lives on a daily basis? We can afford it. That's why the Aztex rule, cuz we gotta do what we gotta do. If it takes a zillion hearts per anum to set the world right, we'll raise our blades. If we got to cut out all the hearts to keep the world turning, we'll cut out all the hearts, that's the way it always has been, that's the way it will be. The sacred ancestor Toltekas diskovered it for us. They laid the groundwork for the present munificence of global civilization ruled by Aztek science, Aztek teknospirituality and kommunist economiks. Life is good. Because of the applied Aztek Sciences of the Human Heart. There's a world of things we're doing something about; if it takes all the hearts in the world, we'll do it. We'll cut out all their hearts, we'll cut out our own hearts. So the world can go on like this, in its Glory.

The Wurlitzer of the Universe is packed with 78 rpm realities side by side. Get ready to drop your dime.

Heads pile up on a wet concrete floor. Bloody meat slaps the wet concrete. The blade spins, zinging thru the air till its tiny teeth bite into the pallid skin, the circular blade sinking out of sight underneath, descending to the bone, rubbery thick skin wrinkling and leaking fluids with a wobbly flatulence.

The frosty little window of the chilling room. Put your nose to the glass, you can make out what is hanging inside. It may look like the meat's moving, mottled red and white carcasses jostling for position in line, but it's just the overhead track oscillating, a hum in the freezing fanblown air.

Most days I worked the Farmer John killing floor with 3Turkey, Ray ("CIA agent in a former life," he told everybody, "you heard right, a company man"), Zahuani ("Pirate"), and a short thick guy, Nakatl, a black Central American Taoist happy fat man. Usually I paired off with 3Turkey. We switched off; whenever one of us got tired of cutting throats with the big knife, he'd take the "electrolethalizer"—the zapper—from the other, or if we were at the next station, eviscerating the hogs into a rolling vat, we'd trade off as a team, move a hog into place, situate the vat in front of it, then push it on to the next station where somebody (maybe Nakatl, maybe Ray) worked the saw, the other one "shagging"—hook the hog's rear leg, insert the hook through the flesh, snug around the ankle-joint so it won't tear thru & pull loose, cause that 400-pound pig to land headfirst and flip ass-backwards on top of somebody, hit the red button to lift it off the floor, stabilize it mid-air for the sawyer, get the head out of the way when it comes off, just before the carcass gets lifted thru the air, lickety-split, to the skinner. The line moves all the time. An overhead conveyor drags the hogs forward and up, each on a hind leg, swinging thru the air at 300, 400 pounds, still sort of alive, twitching, newly naked flesh shuddering with convulsive reflexes, jerking as it moves thru a wafting steam, clouds billowing around us, vapors emitted from newly opened body cavities, blood spattered on your plastic goggles, mists swirling in the air-conditioning that regulates the inside of the plant at 50 degrees or lower. Big hogs swinging at you, one after another, hour after hour, you had to swing with them, like a dance, a rhythm you cannot break, you can't stand around or daydream—keep your wits about you—you couldn't get too chilly or tired or slow, otherwise you might get hit. You don't want to get body-slammed by a 350-pound hog and fall on your knife or the spinning circular saw with its yellow spring-coiled electric cord, or bump somebody else with the knife or saw. USDA inspectors came thru checking the line once in a while, four signs on the wall say, "THIS DEPARTMENT HAS WORKED 154 DAYS WITHOUT LOST TIME. AVOID ACCIDENTS ON THE JOB. SAFETY BEGINS HERE" in English, Spanish, Chiu Chow & Vietnamese. Thru the big plastic doors the line workers push empty vats onto the kill floor, taking out tubs of heads or guts, internal organs, wheeling the vats of hogs' heads off the kill floor into one room, internal organs into another. None of it is thrown away, including the blood flowing into the grating, sticky, viscous and black under our rubber boots. All of it is sold.

(I supposed, standing atop the steel grates that get hosed down at the end of each shift—still a bit treacherous because stainless steel, slippery underfoot, and your sweat-soaked feet also shifting slippery *inside* the waffled boot itself—I was thinking of how the gunk sloughing off down the drain is dried somehow, I really don't follow all these details so I couldn't really tell you for sure, but these thoughts occur to you, standing on the kill floor all night, *I bet [Whoa! Fuck! Nakatl came too close, watch out!] all this blood is dried out and packaged, sold by the metric ton to some feedlot outside Bakersfield, fed to all those milk cows under the dairy sheds perfuming the breeze along Highway 5 with a momentary stench as you drive by.*)

The kill floor's hard heavy work, but I'd found out I couldn't do other jobs with the finesse and speed required farther up the line. I cut myself and fucked up department safety statistics when they put me in sausages or hams. Other crews wouldn't want their holiday bonuses reduced cuz I cut myself & screwed up their record. But mama raised a big boy, she fed me well, so I can wrestle whole 375-pound hogs all day better than any, while those unassuming women, boys and old veteranos on the disassembly line just can't take it. Each broadback hog descends toward the kill floor through a chute with its huge head first, the sides of the chute pressing and holding it as 3Turkey zaps 'em in the neck, delivering massive voltage direct to the spine. He hits a button, and the chute opens, dropping the hog to the floor. 3Turkey steps over it & hooks a leg. It swings upright (trusting he hooked it fast), I reach my left arm around the hog's shoulders as I lean into its girth, the warm, grizzly skin prickling worse than your old man's two-day stubble, I give it the last firm goodbye hug, pressing the knife into its throat at the same time, drawing it diagonally down, slicing the carotid with one motion, then on out the other side. The blade comes back at me soft as sliced cornbread. It's a one-two movement, that dance step. Convulsively, sometimes the animal kicks or jerks, shuddering as it rides up the chain. Sometimes the electricity hasn't really put the animal out, and the whole time it's been squealing that shrill high-pitched porcine shriek, but I can't bother to notice stuff like that any more. You got to keep your wits about you. In the fog of fatigue, the warm moist red air we're always wiping off our nose and mouth with a sleeve or the back of our hand, you got to keep a mental fix on the location of the guys next to you, blades in hand, somebody stepping in with the saw nearby, the general outline of the hog swinging up and away from you. I step back, out of the spray of the sheet of blood. It doesn't spurt out of the neck like it would if you cut a limb off, it doesn't drip or run out; it jets out in a black sheet. It's like turning on a pressured jet. It splashes my rubber boots and my black apron. Lofted on the chain, the hogs tremble, some aimlessly running in space, blood frothing and spattering as the whole hot heavy mass ascends to hog heaven. The heads come off as the line carries them to the chill room where umpteen twenty tons of hogs chill for 12 hours. There's a little hose if blood gets on your hands; you can't afford to fumble the next ones with a slippery grip. Every motion—leaning in, hugging each hog to me, then the cut—all of it has to come at once, without a thought—sure, quick, exact. I have to be able to do it in my sleep. Soon as I stand back, ready, steady, go: 3Turkey hits the button for the next one.

When we switch, I do the same for him.

Blood flows thru the floor grating.

This is where my days (my nights) go.

Where you think your bologna sandwich comes from?

Try to tell your kids that. My daughter works for the county probation department, spends all her time hanging with white people at some church in Glendale. When I show up, they all act like I'm covered in invisible blood from head to foot. They're very polite & cold, those people. "I'm glad they're polite! Imagine if they weren't!" my wife would say, tall plastic cup of wine in her hand. She said you got to expect that with girls, going off with boyfriends, getting married, ending up in somebody else's household. But my son and I used to be real close. When he was little we did everything together. One year somebody hit me with a saw, took out my knee, I had to stay home for six months, I took care of him 24 hours a day 7 days a week. I even took him to my physical therapy sessions at Kaiser. He was only four, and I'd be working a machine and he'd sit on the floor or on a chair nearby, talking to me the whole time. The nurses' assistants would cuddle him, coo, say what a beautiful kid he was. He really was beautiful, too, a round-headed dark-eyed boy. The nurses fell in love with him. He showed such a good heart, and he was open to people. He and I talked all the time, about everything. People told me they never saw a little kid only four years old, a boy especially, so well behaved. Whatever that was between us, it got lost in the past four or five years. He won't say anything real to me these days, or when he does, half of whatever he says turns out isn't true. He doesn't want anybody to know what he's up to, his hair cut off his head like a hardboiled egg, running the streets all the time with his so-called homies. Last time I saw him, I pulled up to a stoplight in my van and I looked down, there he was, sitting in the passenger seat of some little car with his buddies. I watched him there, sitting in the car, talking & laughing, the music playing so loud it rattled my van; he didn't notice me watching. "Hey!" I shouted. He turned his head fast, with a hard-mouthed look, a rough look, who wuz the motherfucker who dared to say 'hey' to his ass? He saw it was me, got a little half-smile and gave me a nod. We looked at each other for a second. What the hell was he thinking? I was gonna ask him what he was doing these days, then the light changed and the car took off. That was it. I was thinking, that's my boy? All the years I spent raising him, for that? That's it?

Some time later I went to the supermarket and filled two boxes with every Farmer John product I could find. Bologna, salami, head cheese, footlong hot dogs, ballpark franks, pepperonis, summer sausage, Polish sausage, breakfast sausage, Italian sausage, hot links, canned ham, sliced ham, honeybaked ham, ham hocks, ground pork, bacon, you name it. I stuffed two boxes full. I tossed in other stuff too, stuff that comes from the same animals under a few other brands. Chicharrones, pickled pigs' feet, smoked pork chops, even a little handstitched souvenir football I found by the check-out stand that said Raiders. That's pigskin, you know. I put all this stuff in boxes and delivered them one night. Neither of the kids was home, of course, cuz I didn't call ahead. They're never home, anyway. I just left it on their doorstep with their names on them. The boy doesn't bother to call and say anything, of course, so you don't even know if he ever got it. My daughter called and left a message on the machine; she said thanks. Maybe she was puzzled. But I could tell neither of 'em got the message.

Way it started, I was walking along the kanal outside Xochimilko, down along a sort of empty lot reeking of human excrement and tropikal vegetation exhaling humidity in the heat. Across the kanal was the kapital, bustling multitudes on raised causeways, jam-packed subways and crowded avenues into the city, haze of cookfires rising above the residences, market-place din and everyday rumble of the metropolis. In the distance, the immense pyramids peach-tinted by the early morning light hovered above the smog. I had been driven out of my house at an early hour, driven to distraction by my confusions and whatnot, lost in thot, or what passed for thot for me personally, wandering about preoccupied, late for an appoint-ment with Clan Elder Ixquintli, one of the kalpulli administrators I am answerable to, who was about to, in spite of my objections, recommend me for a spot of brain surgery, Kranial Boring to release Xtra spirits from inside my head. It had saved the sanity of hundreds of thousands, I was to be told. Just the thing for headaches! It improves your looks and your disposition, your chances of winning the lottery, experts verify in report after report. Ah, well. So be it. If they wanted to take a flint drill and puncture my skull at one or two precise points they must have their reasons. It would cure the headaches and they promised it would solve my continual problem of unwanted visions attacking me at all moments rendering me overly thoughtful inhibiting my spontaneous bloodlust and subsequent poetry. Who needed unwanted visions of vast concrete rooms, scrubbing them down with buckets of disinfectant and high-powered hoses, plastic & steel vats of flesh & body parts pushed up against the wall? And so it was that I was wandering that morning, lost in thot . . . I watched a snowy egret fly-ing off over its reflektion toward the Tezkakoak Gate across the kanal. I tried to think of a good excuse to get out of Aztek brain surgery, tho I knew it was in my best interest. ("Drugs," I'd insist, "drugs are available. Medicinal cures, ayahuasca, yage, kurare, cokaine, peyotl, Rainbow Rocket kaktus, the thorax of krushed stink beetles, psylocibin mushrooms, red & black ants known as Short People, mota, tobacco, great stinking funguses of the Rain Forest, mezkal sweetened with the tears of Spanish children, I can have all of these brought to me and I will eat them all." "Zenzón, my son, you and I both know you've messed with these cures your entire life. They didn't do a thing for you! You're the same as you always were, worse even.

You spent years engaged in painful sex rites with raving captive Catholic Spaniards, curative exorcisms with Mixtek googoo-eyed Maria Sabinas and her various disciples, the kult of Jaguar Squadrons where you rose to blood-thirsty prominence as one unequalled in imbecilic fury in pitched street battles against the Tlaxcalans and the Apaches, I know about all of that. I know all your former komrades and friends flee when they see you coming and I know why. I know you've worked assiduously, tried all kinda hokey cures including burnt peach pits inserted into your nostrils as you chant Afrikan songs by Stevie Wonder, you've gone down all routes into the Dark Places looking for ancestral spirits who flee like everyone else when they hear you coming. I know you've done your part, and now it's time to let us do ours. I don't have to warn you what the consequences might be if you fail to heed the whims of our burgeoning bureacracy." "Fucking Spaniards, chingao! This is what they've done to us," I grumbled. "They've reduced me to this for participating in the destruction of their flimsy Messianic worldview and the elimination of their so-called civiliza-tion from the Index of Possible Worlds. I can understand that. I accept all manner of smaller sins, incisions into my foreskin, aches and pains, rheuma-tism at my age, parasitik maggots hatching in my scalp, various other indig-nities because of it. I understand there's a price to pay for doing one's part for the People. But is this the thanks I get from my own brothers and sis-ters, the Great Aztek Socialism? Shit, I mean, really?" "Oh, Zenzón," my Clan Elder murmured, "I know that part of you will enjoy it. You may even get a few last-minute visions out of the whole affair which will make you even more beloved among the musicians, amputees, Mayan defectors, los-ers and slackers hanging out in the pulque bars along the alleys behind the Eastern Market." "Great. Just what I need," I whined. I knew that whining was mighty low on the list of Aztek attributes and only the fact that my previous actions *(which paradoxikally would take place in the future)* had endeared me to the Clan Elder and allowed him to look upon my snivel-ing with clear dispensation. But I was disgusted with Myself. So I expected to kapitulate to the brain surgery koncept with a shrug (as the old buzzard knew I would, becuz he recalled how the future wuz gonna turn out), even as I fretted, "You know, my wife's grandmother went loko, tried to run away with some Spanish explorer, was sadly dejected when they brought her his head to use as a pillow, and they tried this surgery on her, those self-elekted surgeons. You know what happened to her? Her damned head swelled up and her hair fell out so that her skull looked like some kind of French pastry with chocolate icing flaking off, pus squirted like egg kustard out of all the orifices in her head, including the new ones, her whole body swelled up like an inflated pigskin and then she died screaming French prose poetry, trying to swim north out of a puddle of her own piss like a beached dolphin. I don't like French literature. I don't want to end up in the same afterlife with her, Clan Elder. I don't deserve all that Baudelaire & Mallarmé." "Ha ha ha. Nice story Zenzontli. Shut up now and leave. I gotta toke a little mota and recombine elements of the sixth universe into new utilities to produce better trade with the EZLN in Chiapas." "Gee, thanks, Chief." "You and me, babe, you and me." "I'll be back afterwards, my Clan Elder, afterwards you can feel the phrenology. I'm sure I'll be getting new interesting dreams out of the whole affair." "You can tell me about it later. I knew you'd see it our way, my son. We depend on you. I did tell you we're sending you and your unit to Russia, didn't I?" All of that was to come later in the day.) I had a full day ahead, even as I wandered along the tepid Southwestern kanal lost in pseudo-thot. I was wondering if some possible rekombination of elements, like the extraktion of the stoic sexual appetites of a Jewish-Arabic-Andalusian princess delivered to me while parts of my foreskin were burnt on the balcony by one of the priests who still owed me supernatural favors, along with jug and klezmer musik played by Chamula renegades would allow for some relief. If not, I could insert Chinese fortunes I had written myself into incisions in my torso while breathed on lightly by Conquistador eunuchs who'd had their eyes removed and replaced by large Amazonian sapphires, while masturbating in several separate realities in a treehouse overlooking the sea. But then I realized I'd tried all that several times already. Just then some big black dusty ratty looking contraption of a bird flapped over my head—a raven I guess—flew by as I wuz humming. I sang out: "Who's the dick making all the chicks?"—

then a big shadow flew over me & away, ragged black wings swishing audibly through the unmoving heat. "*Shaft!*" the big bird squawked before it disappeared. What the hell wuz that supposed to mean? Sure, it did seem like a signifying augury of awesome import. I looked up in the general westerly direktion of the disappearing bird, trying to avoid falling forward into the greasy green waters of the kanal as it fell on my head again. Like a black curtain of rain. Another Vision.

Oh, Maria.

Oh, this wingéd world.

I catch Cuzatli (Weasel) giving me the eye sometimes around the taco truck—especially since he only has the one left, which he usually likes to keep fixed on the voluptuous chavalita in the skin-tight shirt, particularly while she's leaning her chest across the counter to hand someone their order thru the little window over his head, maybe at night time with vapors rising into the night from the smokestacks lit from below here and there by spotlights, steam rising from styrofoam cups the men stand around holding on break, steam issuing from their mouths like feathered plumes of speech in Aztec codices. Generally I choose not to believe in paranoia, per se, I don't go for Ray's conspiracy theory of the universe that says everything is the result of three jokers meeting in a hotel room in Miami in 1961 and the rest is all just domino theories, Gerald Ford's presidential pardon after the fact, smoke & mirrors. But there is something in Cuzatli's glance that gives me pause, "Fuck you, Weasel, what I got that you want?" I'll be thinking while smiling at la Sonia, who's handing me the paper plato de carnitas con guacamole, which I'm careful to keep level lest it drip the grease down my front and make me look even more like another used-up hardworker motherfucker in front of la chula teengirl, who's handing me a fistful of change with an unnerving dark-eyed smile that seems to recall something more important to be remembering than any of the rest, but I step over to the picnic tables provided for this 3 A.M. repast with a last glance at Weasel;

in fact he is nonchalantly watching me as he leans against the truck like he's taking his sweet time to order. As I sit down I nod to him, as if I do appreciate his support in our bid to certify the pinche union, sure — here's to you, Cuzatli — and I tear off a bite of savory crisp pork flesh, tortilla soft as the skin of a woman's belly in the moonlight, with aromatic picante roasted chile salsa filling my sinuses. At 3 A.M., you'll find nothing will ever beat a bellyful of heart-attack carnitas topped with smoky hot salsa, swallowing hot coffee if you have to head back to the plant and go another eight-hour shift. What do I know about Cuzatli? He's an okay worker, works hard and fast but sloppy, so they're always shuffling him around jobs that can't be screwed up too bad, or pairing him with someone more reliable. Maybe somebody's looking out for him; certainly if I had his rep I'd be looking over my shoulder. In the glare of the roach coach fluorescents against the absorbant dark, Cuzatli lifts his face to jive la Sonia, and any passersby peering thru the plant gate not too far away wouldn't see any distinguishing marks, even at that distance, nothing to set Weasel apart from the rest of us, no matter the grinning patter of witticisms, a raffish charm that had 3Turkey, Nakatl and even Pirate you could say on his side, stiff black hair in a boyish spiky cut, only the dark scar rising from an empty eye socket indicating a bit of trouble in his past. That indication, too, almost exactly like any of the rest of us — you can't go this distance and come this far without a scar of some kind. *So what if you knew,* heard he kept women with families on both sides of the border, lost the kids from one when he gambled his way into a debt with gangsters on the lookout to kill him till this very day, so he told his friends and relations that he was going to commit suicide, then ran away, never to be seen by anyone again? Then here he is in a blue Farmer John jumpsuit, looking just like any one of us.

Apparently some passersby pulled over in a couple kanoes to make sure I didn't slide into the muddy waters when I slid down the embankment, foaming at the mouth with my long hair in the kanal and, after a moment, peed in my shorts. When I came to some ten minutes later (they tell me), I rested there a moment with the blood flowing to my head because of the angle, a flock of children being kept back by an elder using the flat of an antiquated Spanish saber and by the stern demeanor of two warriors who no doubt knew who I was, standing above me but at a certain distance, looking off toward the smoke and din of the Eastern Market and no doubt konversing about more pressing matters, as if taking no notice while allowing their svelte, befeathered presence to have the necessary Effekt, as a group of Women of 3 Generations, grandmother to granddaughter, knelt at my side and used their clothing to wipe the mud out of my right eye. As I blinked with confusion, I recognized instantly what had happened, it had become so commonplace even in the mental fog and haze such spells would leave me. The younger women leaned over me so close that I could smell them, their sweet breath and slight perspiration (a soaplike fragrance) in the Teknotitlán heat and humidity, the tips of their long hair brushing my face my neck and my chest where their elders had loosened my tunic. Their eyes were fixed either on my mouth or on some point off to the side as they awaited with bated breath my first words (which were accorded immense currency among certain circles of young, rebellious or confused Aztex who fastened upon such words and treated them with even greater gravity than their elders did the latest Central Committee gossip). I wished they'd all go away, flee instantaneously, in spite of the vague gratitude I felt to them for keeping me from sliding headfirst into the kanal muck. I struggled to breathe, to free my tongue from the roof of my mouth, to oxygenate some part of the curlicues of my brain murky as the depths of the canals. "A big black . . . black . . . bird . . ." (They listened, rapt.) "Who's the private dick who's got all the chicks? Shaft . . . John Shaft." ("Ah!" one teen sighed involuntarily. An old woman clucked, "Shush!") Out of a failing sense of gratitude, I muttered a few words about the vision, "I saw . . . saw a highway . . . a highway like these that run the courseways into the capital . . . it was jammed with trucks and cars, horseless carriages of Europian and Asiatik style . . . they were being mercilessly strafed and bombed by jets and helicopters . . . all the way from one country to the next stretched a string of burnt-out vehicles driven motionlessly by the stinking, smoking charred corpses of an entire army . . . The horror, the horror! . . . This occured on 1 world in 2 places simultaneously . . . In the hilly mountain towns of another country, tiny sticklike Afrikan children, insectile in the heat but with hideously human movements pursued each other through the streets, hacking and beating each other to death, roving mobs organized for the purpose . . . on this same world (what a place!) entire Mayan villages were razed and everyone wuz slaughtered . . . people were packed into town halls and churches and the buildings set on fire . . . anyone attempting to escape the burning buildings was shot or hacked to death . . . marketplaces packed with milling shoppers were fired upon by snipers, by mortar positions . . . entire populations were packed into trains and trucks, taken into the woods and shot or funneled into prison camps of barbwire where they were tortured to death or extermi-nated en masse . . . men, women and children, entire families and clans and communities were slaughtered, disappeared from existence without cere-mony, proper ritual, or sacred prayer! . . . The Indonesian army fired point blank on funeral processions in a cemetery, machinegunning them as they ran . . . East Timor . . . East Oakland . . . while this happened, entire pop-ulations of Spanish-style nations went about their daily business like sleep-walkers like zombies . . . conscripting leftover children of the dead and raising them as ghosts with no ancestral knowledge . . . the children shoot-ing each other, parents murdering their own children and committing suicide in existential agony . . . in centuries of Darkness, death and destruc-tion, junk food in styrofoam boxes . . . an age when This World in ques-tion was being slaughtered and the people were to wander its surface like ghosts in hell perishing in their sheepish Desires . . . This was the civiliza-tion those Europians sought to bring us . . . this was the reality they sought to invoke upon our land . . . and while it all was happening as they deliv-ered it across the world they would have watched it replayed in movies to musical accompaniment! *Auschwitz, the Musical! Mauthausen Off-Broadway!"* The older women were weeping. I was weeping myself, overcome, I could no longer speak. The teenage girls, sickened and shocked, stepped back a few paces. I was secretly relieved. I was, in fact, becoming used to the extremity of the Visions. I knew they shocked and sickened your ordinary, normal, healthy Aztek. In fact, as the women stood me on my feet, used cloth purchases from the market to clean my hair, my face, my hands, as the warriors stood off a ways pretending not to notice, as an old man explained to a knot of kurious children the nature of my visions, I knew what was going to happen to me. It had already happened to me in the future.

Your usual busy morning. Power breakfast with Clan Elder. Yummy cactus salad, nopal, green beans, rings of red onion, Mayan corn chowder, Inka fried potatoes with krispy golden fried guinea pig, octopus ceviche on cabbage, numerous delicacies which I failed to appreciate but ate anyway in a self-preoccupied funk. Clan Elder, he says, you gotta go get a hole in your head. I say, yes yes of course. Clan Elder Ixquintli [Hairless Dog 21] says that he will convene a Blue Ribbon Commission of scientific experts to slay hundreds, offer the pure hearts of Spanish warriors and virgins to whichever gods go well with cokaine, along with the upcoming possible dates for my surgery, and they'll consult the kalendarial gods, figureheads and scary items that appear in the sky whether we like it or not. Clan Elder Ixquintli offers me and another guest—I never caught his name, a 300-year-old Olmek spirit who looks like an Afrikan Buddha wearing a leather helmet of an Aztek flying ace—to each of us a Spanish slave princess for sexual favors as dessert, specializing in manual or podiatric manipulations to the tasteful accompaniment of a panoply of singing parrots and rainforest birds, but I'm so full. Another time, Clan Elder. (The Olmek spirit tries to get in on the conversation, but the konnection is no good, he's breaking up, even if we understood his dialect it's all garbled, so Clan Elder Ixquintli and I just nod and laugh, cuz we don't want to piss this spirit off since he's been so kind as to show up for breakfast three centuries later. I'd just realized that the Clan Elder had said that I was being transfered to the Russian front as special candidate for War Hero against the bad Nazis, liaison to our anarko-syndikalist allies, causing me to choke and to cough up coffee thru my nose.) *Some things are more scalding than bitterness drowned every morning with coffee. I told as much to the Clan Elder. "I protest! I request re-assignment to another Theater of War, someplace with coffee shops, sidewalk cafes, cultural events, a hap-*

pening night life, efficient and affordable public transportation, a higher quality of life, better schools, a few remaining shreds of civic pride. According to my research, that's either San Francisco or Paris! I respectfully request, sir, that you send my Jaguar Unit to Paris! We shall invade Paris, drink wine, learn to paint like a Cubist, look like Picasso, read Celine, hang out on the East Bank with North Afrikans, boogie in jazz clubs with expatriot Negroes, write manifestos, walk along the Seine, acclimatize ourselves to French cuisine with a view toward preparing ourselves to become ready to strike a death blow into the heart of the Nazi War Machine at the first possible Opportunity! Sir! Who said James Joyce has a lock on interior monologue?"
"What did you say, Zenzón? I wasn't paying attention to your dismal chatter." "Sir, I respectfully request that you prevail upon the Council of Tlatoani to re-assign us to the Europian Theater, out of the Eastern Front where from all accounts casualties are extremely high — due to limited intelligence provided for us — it seems entirely likely that you are sending us on a suicide mission." "Now Zenzón, I won't deny this is a suicide mission. . . ." "Run that by me again?" "There's nothing wrong with a suicide mission every now and then. It's good practice." "Sir. I wish you'd consider Paris." "Fuck Paris, Zenzón, have you ever seen any French movies? Have you? There you have it. French civilization in a nutshell. It's not worth discussing. All talk, no action. Cream sauce, high calories and fatty foods. Mayonnaise on their sex clubs. They love complicated syntax; they don't have any sense. They couldn't be direct with you if you nailed their dick to a Bikini atoll and set off an atomik bomb." "A what, sir?" "Nothing, Top Secret, don't mention I said anything about it. Forget I mentioned it." "What about the famous pussy they all talk about? Even Celine mentions it." "Paris? Listen, Zenzón, we're not opening up a second front in Europa till the major cities have been reduced to rubble, prices are lower, and whole suburban populations starving across the continent can be bought for cases of nylon pantyhose, bushels of watercress, cilantro, celery, cartons of Mohawk tax-free cigarettes." "Sir, are you suggesting that the lives of my men, the lives of millions of innocent civilians on three continents, entire cities and the ancient cultures embodied in them are to be forfeited simply so that you and elite councils in power in our nation can enjoy cheap if not free access to untold masses of slaves?" "That's a fact. Which is why I expect you to do your damnedest, cuz it's god damned important to me and my personal well-being, my stock portfolios, my investments, my umbrella of business

enterprises sheltered by statute, legislators & a phalanx of high-paid attorneys." "I think I could be of some use to you in Paris, sir." "I'm quite willing to consider it, Zenzón, I assure you. But **after** Stalingrad. Not before. Perhaps if you survive Stalingrad, we'll have opened the Second Front in Europa by then and your unit can rotate thru the Western Theater on their way home." "Let me say then, sir, for the record, that I voice my objection to the whole strategy, to sending my men and me to die on the Eastern Front for the chance that your portfolio returns may increase a point or two, that the Aztek slave trade be expanded to a few more two-bit ignorant underdeverloped countries." "Two or three percentage points? Are you kidding Zenzón? I'm looking for a double-digit increase at the very least! If the gaping vortex of chaos and apocalyptik disaster continues to widen, we won't be just talking about horseshit little nations in the Balkans, Albania, Scandinavia, the Arab Emirates & shit like that! Our plans will make the Belgian Congo look like a tea party! IMF Bailouts will look like continental breakfasts! The Annexation of East Timor will look like Lox & Bagels! Argentina's Dirty War will look like low-cholesterol eggs & tofu sausage! The Rape of Nanking will be fresh as ground roasted coffee! The Final Solution will look like half a grapefruit! We're talking major markets, entire civilizations, worlds of opportunity beyond your imagining." "Wish I was in on it," I sighed. Then I brightened, "Whatever did happen to my life savings, that nest egg I had you invest for me in the Burmese opium trade, the Golden Triangle? What happened to that company, Air America, the CIA front?" "I'd been meaning to bring that up with you Zenzón, so I'm glad you finally mentioned it. Unfortunately—I can explain it in fairly simple & straightforward terms in a second—that entire fund was lost. That company went down the drain. Zippo. All your money's been lost. Completely, totally, just like that!" Chuckling, Clan Elder Ixquintli snapped his fingers, grinning sadly, shaking his head at the terrible suddenness with which these accidents do sometimes occur. "You just got fucked on that one, my boy." "But, Clan Elder, you said you could explain, at least. I mean, if I recall correctly at the time, you said that investment strategy was 100% guaranteed." "Oh yes. Let me see now . . . How to explain it to you . . . Let me put it this way . . . Well, let me see if I can put it in terms you might understand . . . Do you know much about the Index of Leading Ekonomic Ko-efficients & the Marcos-Suharto Guaranteeship for Investment Maximization?" "Can't say I ever heard of 'em, no sir." "No? Amazing. Astonishing, really. Zenzón, how could you suggest that we put your life savings into the heroin trade when you don't know the first things about the mysterious Oriental Paths to True Investment? You must read Daisetz T. Suzuki on IRAs, 401 & 402(k)s, three-tiered mutual funds & money market transfers. Obviously, you've been led astray by the turmoil of your day-to day desires, bamboozled by the dark clouds of your inner emotional conflict, made mince-meat by the your lack of Chinese Wisdom when it comes to keeping tabs on the hard cash, **loko!** I bet you never consulted a Taoist certified investment banker at a rep-utable feng shui brokerage firm in your life, have you, karnal? Have you bothered to have tea made out of your lapsed insurance policies so that you could read between the lines & find out what it says in the small print inscribed on the astrology of your financial plans? No? I thot not. See, that's your problem right there. Thanks for com-ing to me with your problems, tho, son. It always does make me feel better somehow. It's always good for a chuckle. I don't know why. I guess I just like you, that's all. Somehow these things just can't be rationally explained. I don't give a fuck how super-intellectual our scientists think they are." "But in regards to Stalingrad sir—" "That's right Zenzón. You and your unit give 'em hell at Stalingrad for me! If I could only be there! I know you'll do great things there. It'll be a hell of a time! By the way, come over here and shake an old man's palsied, pasty, noodle-limp, jerk-off hand. I may never see you again and I wanna remember you the way you are, head-ing out my door for good, one last time, I hope." "Thank you, sir." "Don't thank me yet. Thank me when you're out on the street so that you don't take up any more of my time. Ciao, kid. Been good to know ya."

I mean, sometimes the Aztek fetish for feathers even gets to those of us who take pains to be the most Aztek of all; it just dulls the appetite hic-cupping & spitting out the feathers of tiny species. I left the sumptuous winter dacha of the Clan Elder, joined by my bodyguard 3Turkeyvulture, who'd been playing mumblety-peg with household children in the court-yard entranceway. I was not surprised that 3Turkey had found me after my epileptic peregrinations of the day, since that wuz his job, but I was pleased to have him accompany me. Terrorism by the subject peoples had been limited of late, the main bombing targets being Federal Buildings & Twin

Towers, having the politikal effect of incensing our well-educated Aztex, with the effect of further discrediting the cause of dissident Mayan sects, Chumash, Hawaiians, Taino, etc. I appreciated 3 Turkey as a man who could take time out from his numerous duties as my Chief of Staff, instead of take himself overly seriously, engage in public displays of martial arts performance and practice, kill low-ranking passersby in fits of low self-esteem, reek of unwashed blood for weeks, etc. All that professional military caste behavior so stereotypical and tedious. 3 Turkey was easygoing, he could be counted on for kongenial company and advice, something I desperately needed in my time of solitary flights of lunacy. "3 Turkey," I could say with a straight face, "I've been dreaming that I kill pigs. And I am not talking *one or two* pigs. I've been dreaming of cutting the throats of tens of thousands of pigs." "Let's do it!" he'd say. 3 Turkey could both make light of my fits and seizures and make sense of my visions according to the lights of his somewhat limited education. He was not well-read, it's true, preferring the exotica of modern European romances to classical Codices, but he was always honest forthright and direct. Like a breath of fresh air, as they say. Not that I, however, paid him any undue attention passing through the courtyard and out of the entranceway, moving down the steps as he took up a semi-watchful position beside me. It's not merely that I greatly outrank my guard, nor that I'm a generation his senior, but simply that I left the Clan Elder's quarters feeling overfed, dazed and strangely expectant. You know the way life is, a little torture and the risk of death in the near future is probably a good thing. Sometimes one even envies the Spanish their cults of Katholicism and Inquisitional self-flagellation, which is why you can see such ideologies have been adopted as part of the stage persona of various wannabe rock stars and teen groupies. Still, even in my muddled state I found pleasure in the summer's afternoon, the day mellifluously perfumed by the hanging garden of the Clan Elder as we descended the steps in dappled shade to the level of the sun-kissed street. You've seen it in pictures, I'm sure, even if you haven't had time to visit our kapital in person, so you know that neighborhood streets in Teknotitlán are strictly limited to foot and animal traffic, with most of the mass transit on waterways, subways &

Ho Chi Minh bike paths hidden under the trees, therefore, every neighborhood retains an appearance of lively tranquility, thriving pedestrian community interspersed with animals of all types who are our brothers, our nahual spirits, feedstock and pets. Which is to say, the dust in the street had the tang of llama dung, the afternoon resounded with the squawks of peacocks, cooing of doves, chirps of geckos, not unpleasant given the tremendous perfume of surrounding estates and their lush foliage. Occasionally, too, the throaty growl of big cats could be heard above the quotidian rumble of the vast kapital. Such pets were common among the well-off; I myself happened to live in a more modest, mixed neighborhood, because, though I wouldn't admit it to the faces of my elders, because their aesthetik sense is reputed a sign of spiritual status on more planes of reality than this one [*a whiff of—could it be?—pig shit? the fear of pig sweat broiling inside transport trucks?*], so you can't mess around with it, but I often find that and other Aztek orthodoxies and strictures to be dull when carried too far.

Then someone tried to kill me. At first I didn't notice a thing. Typically, I was descending the steps, worried about myself, weighing the concerns and consequences of empire, wondering how to get out of this existential fix I was in (maybe those Doktors could work wonders, maybe those Metaphysicians could actually release my soul one way or another from its own entrapment, somehow, in some Other world, *quizás*) when I noticed the commotion—vaguely—as a blurred motion in my peripheral vision. "Fucking 3Turkey," I started thinking to myself, "some woman—" but 3Turkey wasn't chasing the fleeing woman down to speak to her, berate her in the street for some personal indiscretion, past affair or what have you as I first thought; he didn't try to talk to her at all. The woman ran with the inspired swiftness of holy terror, and she was carrying something like a ball under her arm, weaving and dodging through the pedestrians who parted, and turned to see—as I myself finally had turned to see, 3Turkey kill her. I suspect he meant to slow her down, as he later protested when I berated him for his stupidity, but he outweighed the woman by 150%, overtaking her amidst the parting of the crowd, some of whom had to fling themselves backward out of the grand elliptical motion of his arm as he brought down the war-club onto her cranium, which cracked like a hummingbird's blue egg under your thumbnail at a state luncheon, and the woman flew headlong, face-first into the dust like a puppet whose strings had been cut as she swung. She looked like a pitiful girl as 3Turkey de-accelerated over her, huffing in his furious adrenal rush, glowering and hefting his thick dark heavy-flanged club and casting glances on every side as the crowd fell back, not wanting to come within striking distance, not wanting to be the next to lie—as everyone in sight become suddenly aware—still and dead as this thin, middle-aged, long-haired Aztek woman. *"Pulpo en su tinta,"* whispered a passing Spanish slave. She was obviously dead, face half-rolled in yellow dust, mouth pressed open into the dirt as if caught in partial attempt at swallowing the actual world, jaw slack and eyes half-open, glazed over, her long black hair spread around her like the night of the underworld, as 3Turkey knelt to rifle her bag frantically. I strode up nonchalantly, as if indifferent to the frantic cursing of my bodyguard, who turned to me as my shadow fell across him, his face upturned in anguish, crying, "It's not here! It's not here! She had an accomplice! Zenzontli-Master, you've just been assassinated!" I knew what he was looking for, dumping the contents of the Guatemalan bag on the paving stones as the murmurous crowd looked on—the Kodak Instamatik Camera was not in her possession. I scanned the crowd for any telltale signs in any of the faces, but there was only the polite inquisitive Aztek diffidence in the face of sudden death. *It wasn't them this time.* So it goes. I had some professional role to uphold, I felt, and admonished 3Turkey with caste-hardened severity, "Shitbird! How dare you kill her? What the hell were you thinking?" My bodyguard rose, useless papers from the woman's bag fluttering away from his body as he stood before me, his perfect horror all-apparent as was his wish that it would have been him instead of me, as he gestured with supplicant hands empty at his sides, mouth open, crying inside himself as he stared at me with a tumultuous empathy. I could read it in his eyes. The woman had snapped my photograph and passed it on to an accomplice in the chase, in full knowledge that she would be captured, tortured and killed. It had been a suicide mission like others in recent months. The photograph would be posted on milk cartons and post office bulletin boards in hellish underworlds throughout the universe, and my end would be swift, rank and horrible. My visage would be duplicated and plastered across shit holes and low-rent barrios in the worst alternate parts of the known omniverse; assassins would emerge from the woodwork, they'd descend upon me like flies to the the moisture of an open wound. 3Turkeyvulture knew this already, he grieved for me even as he contemplated his own failure as my bodyguard strewn at his feet, and so did I. I'd just been assassinated.

I could've sworn I saw someone looking at me out of the corner of my eye. I was leaning around the side of a carcass, stamping the rump, suddenly I stopped doing what I was doing and stood and looked up and down the line. No way somebody could duck out, instantly, like that, disappear behind the racked carcasses into the shadows in a corner of the room! I don't think. . . .

It was a common method of assassination. In fact, it was the fashionable rage of late. Moktezomah 4, whose skin became transparent as his flesh turned to pink translucent jelly, his bones to chalk, his greenish nerves dissolving in puddles as he perished in screaming delirium; Tlotzin 2's entire body wracked with fever & chills and swaddled in blankets as he lay in bed, his purplish torso swelled up to twice its previous size and rocked violently from side to side, his mouth finally peeling back to emit a huge vile cloud of poisonous black wasps leaving his corpse an empty sack speckled with larvae, causing the evacuation of fourteen city blocks; the well-respected Minister of Edukation and Kulture under Kuatemok 5 led blind and keening from place to place until one late afternoon when his rotten head literally exploded and kollapsed in on itself, his once-proud pale body lying in the courtyard of the house beside a pile of greasy rotten fruit, like the emptied white sack of a frog's skin after molting. Of course, it was a method of assassination the Aztek High Command had authorized against the Nazis in World War 2, when General Rommel's photograph was purchased from a French agent in Morocco for 200,000 Aztek Tzotzils, and the

General found himself suffering from one of the most unspeakable cases of genital elephantiasis unlike anything Saharan Afrika had ever seen, such that when his death actually occurred when his Daimler-Benz staffcar was fired upon by an Aztek Imperial fighter, the General would have been able to save his own life had he been able to exit his vehicle at all without the help of two personal aides pushing the small wheeled cart containing his delicate sexual apparatus alongside the General's own specially designed folding gurney. As it was, the Germans buried Rommel's boar-sized genitalia at an oasis outside Tobruk with great pomp and ceremony, meant to impress their Italian, Moorish and Vichy allies with the long history of Aryan sacrifice on the Dark Continent; and for the home audience, the rest of Rommel was buried in his hometown, the spiffy northern kommercial city of Brandenburg, far from his heralded desert campaigns. . . . Which the Azteks under Kuatemok 5 overran anyway, six months later, from the west, as hordes of their allies, the Anarkist Forces under Russian Generalissimo Makno took Berlin from the East. Some similar ill fate was in store for me—*all that was in the infinite future, so much vaster in its prospekts, Good and Bad, than the Limited Present.* Even now, my photograph, that image of the human soul, was making its way to the hands of my Enemies, whoever they were. I didn't know who they might be, but obviously I was doomed. I was history; that's what I saw in the harrowed stare in 3Turkeyvulture's eyes. I was a ghost already. I could see he held himself together through main force as he assembled the woman's possessions and held them ready, even as he scanned the crowd in renewed (if belated), redoubled effort not to let anyone else assault his Master. "Shitbird, you fucked up, I don't even appreciate it," I thought to myself. But outwardly, I muttered, "Don't worry about it, 3Turkey, this could befall any warrior of reknown, these days. We live in dark times. Enemies of our way of life are everywhere. You did well," I lied, and told him, "I've been expecting something like this, anyway." 3Turkeyvulture stiffened, his face brightening somewhat, as he searched my face to see if it was true. "I've already got some people following the accomplice, to find out who these enemies of the Aztek State are." He wasn't fully convinced. I nodded, "That's right. We'll take care of them. You shouldn't have killed her, though. We needed her alive." His head fell in shame, momentarily, and then he stiffened, recalled his duty and began alertly scanning the crowd once again. I sighed. "Oh, you Shitbird," I thought, "I wouldn't want to be you when my wife hears about this." As the crowd dispersed, excitement over, and we waited for the konstabulary to arrive and secure the scene, the fluted melodies of a Mayan ensemble wafted through the air. Somewhere in the neighborhood, Mayan musicians were being paid to entertain a wedding reception or a gathering of some kind. Fucking Mayans, I thought, they're everywhere. Their own civilization collapses and so they come to take over ours. That's the problem with the Aztek way. Our generosity amounts to the sin of self-indulgence, we civilize the world and the get the dekadent dregs of failed civilizations like the Mayans and the Spanish—people who didn't have the heart(s) to appease the Sun and therefore never had a batshit chance in a hurricane wind of surviving as a kulture. Now everywhere you go you find Kakchikels, Tzotzils, Mams, Pokomams, Kiche, and Kekchi. Even now, there were Spanish slaves among the passersby watching my every move. The Mayan music was airy and transparently elegant, as many of the Mayans are themselves. But on the eve of my own assassination, I considered the music a bad omen. Mayans, with their affected nobility of bearing, affected homoeroticism, affected Bay Area high culture, affected stylization of the sakred game of football. It was all so disgusting, that and the poverty of their jungle-infested pyramids, mocking our stately kapital. The flutes soared sweet over soft percussive bongos, making me wince. Mayans give me the kreeps.

2

IN the early morning hours, the week before the rear end in my van went
out, I was driving home after pulling two straight shifts, the streetlamps
going north on Soto splintering on my windshield as if the glass itself was
shattered in a massive web and then falling out of my peripheral vision like
burnt-out flares. I was totally exhausted after a week of pulling back-to-
back shifts, not just the hauling of the hog carcasses for 16 hours straight,
but the filth, and most of all the noise. I worried about my reaction time, I
didn't want to hit them when the two girls walking thru the warehouse district turned around in my headlights, I didn't know if I was seeing real people or shadow images projected from the back of my mind or from
headlights coming in the opposite direction; this in an industrial area where
you never see pedestrians day or nite. For good reason. The women stuck
out their thumbs, and the van bounced across the railroad tracks as I
swerved to the side of the road, a couple of semis blowing by. I leaned across
the passenger seat to unlock the door & push it open. I turned down the
radio. "Hey!" the shorter, lighter one said, "Where you headed? Give us a
lift?" "I'm headed to the 10. I can give you a lift to town." She hesitated,
craning her neck to scan the darkness in the back of my empty van. "All
right!" she barked; I could see she was at least in her late forties, thin brown
hair cut short, though she looked like she might be fifty or more. Her face
was lined and weathered around the bright blue eyes as if she'd spent a lot
of time outdoors. Like her companion, a dark-haired dark-eyed twenty-
year-old (whom she told, "Climb in the back"), the older one was dressed

in Levi's and a t-shirt. They didn't have anything in their hands that I could see. "Where you going?" I turned to ask the younger one; she didn't answer, casting me a suspicious, fearful glance. Maybe the younger one didn't speak English. "Hollywood!" the older woman answered, "We're going to party up in Hollywood!" I nodded, pulling out onto the avenue, heading north. I hadn't gone a block, stopping at the next light, when the older one, raspy in her harsh, smoked-out voice said, "You like to party? You wanna party with us?" I looked back at the younger one in the rearview mirror, her dark glance bouncing off mine with a nearly audible crack like a billiard ball, as I said, "I don't think so. Not tonight. Just pulled a double shift at work, you know, kinda tired." Not to mention that I smelled like shit—that mix of smoke, blood, pig fear, pig excrement and death that coated your skin after a single shift inside the plant, not to mention two shifts back to back. I wouldn't even want to piss or drink a glass of water until I showered. Then, I knew, I wouldn't feel like moving at all. The older one studied the side of my face as I drove. My hair was plastered against my temples by grime and sweat. "Come on," she urged, trying to put some purr in her gravelly throat, "People tell me I give the best head they ever had in their life. Nobody can do it like I can. Why don't you pull in somewhere up here where it's quiet and we'll get down?" I wasn't going to tell her she looked so turkey-necked mean and tough that the thought flashed thru my mind that maybe she was a cop, the kind of cop who would shoot you in the neck & plant a cheap pistol on your ass if you told her she wuz too ugly. To make conversation, to go the distance, I made small talk, stuff like, "How much you want?" "Twenty." When I cast the girl in back a glance in the mirror, she was studying the passing street like none of this had anything to do with her. "Ten then," the older woman said. "Too late in the month," I had to say, "I'm broke. Don't get paid till next week." "Come on," she said, "You sure? I'm really good." "That's okay, thanks," I said, "but can I give you my phone number? Maybe if you're around here again, we could make a date. I work nearby at the Farmer John plant." "I could tell that. Believe me I can tell," she said. I wrote out Max's name and phone number on a piece of paper and passed it to her. She looked at it like it was no use to her. "I'm a foreman at the plant; you call that number any night and ask for Max. I got a private office upstairs, and if you come to the main gate, just ask the guard where Max's office is. What's your name?" She hesitated a beat, "Vicky." "All right Vicky, I'll be waiting for your call, sometime soon, okay?" "Not tonight?" "Not tonight, sorry. But come by the plant another nite, Vicky," and I met the gaze of the girl in back in the rearview mirror, "Bring your friend, too."

1 A.M., or whatever it was, I emerged from the tunnel near Union Station and turned into the Terminal Annex parking lot, the post office open all night, let out the two prostitutes I'd driven out of the City of Vernon. Worried they might get in trouble, I told them they could get a ride in front of the train station and pointed out the taxi stand on Alameda, they nodded and walked up to the corner. I turned my van in the blackness under the big dark eucalyptus trees and went right at the light. The women had crossed Alameda to Sunset, so at least one of them knew the town. A few cars followed me thru the intersection and in the rearview mirror I saw the older one, the smaller, stick her thumb out. I drove up thru Chinatown to my apartment building at the foot of Chavez Ravine. The streets of Chinatown were of course empty, black & reflective in the wet, everything smelling damp and fresh thru my open window. It's a great thing, that fresh air after you pull two shifts back to back in the plant. I could smell the scorched blood on my skin & clothing, but I kept the window open as I drove, driving into the fresh chilly edge of the wind. Chung Mee's was closed as I went up Alpine Street (they told me the card games in the back went on till morning, I don't know, I can't play Chinese poker), but the lights were still on. In front of the open door, a guy in a white apron swept the sidewalk as I went by and I caught a steaming whiff of rice porridge that roused a sharp hunger. I dwelled on that hunger as I drove up the hill. I expected I'd find old leftovers in the refrigerator, something I would wolf down cold or heat in a frying pan. Failing that, I always had one last can of chile beans in the cupboard. I parked the van with the other vehicles behind the main building and climbed the rickety back stairs to

my apartment over two garages where the owner kept old cars and construction supplies. I paused midway up the stairs, not becuz the stairs shook against the clapboard side of the building like they were in danger of collapse, that was nothing new, but because something wuz wrong. My sense of familiarity felt wrong in some way. These old steps, I'd run up them a million times, so what? I scanned the silent parking area, but nothing moved, not even a mouse. Or a cat. No lights in any of the windows, no one moved in the shadows. Had I heard a noise? What was the source of the sudden difference I was feeling? I turned & ascended the stairs, listening. I heard nothing in particular. Inserting my key in the door I stepped into the kitchen, and it came to me. This was my old place, the place I'd lived in some time ago. I don't know how many years previous, but it felt like a long time. How was it I had returned? I closed the door behind me. It rattled in the familiar old way as it closed, as if trying to irritate the silence of the dark apartment. My hand hovered over the light switch, hesitating. This feeling of deja vu, maybe it was just a feeling. Just a symptom of redoubled fatigue. Just a figment in the mind, like gaping holes you can see in the road after driving all night. That must be it. This deja vu was just an illusory feeling that came from working too hard. I turned on the light and it flickered, as always, before it fully came on. On the kitchen table in the pale glare, a plate of cold chicken and potato salad, silverware on a napkin. An empty glass, a pitcher of iced tea. But how long had it been since I'd come home to dinner waiting for me? How long had it been since I'd come home to someone else sleeping in my bed? I walked quietly across the ugly linoleum into the hallway and leaned into the nearest bedroom. The children breathed softly in their beds. I smelled her presence as I walked into our bedroom. This was the way the apartment had smelled when the wife was living in it. It made the air alive, her inhabitation of it, and I realized she was there, nestled warmly under the covers. "Did you see your dinner?" she murmured sleepily. "Yes," I said, a hoarse whisper I barely heard. "Take your shower then and come to bed," she said. "I will," I said. What do you know, I'd gotten home again somehow.

Sometimes you can wake up from such a deep sleep, exhaustion so deeply embedded in your bones that it's hard to move, and there's a momentary confusion. As usual, the late morning or mid-afternoon sunshine filled the curtains with idle heat. The vague memory of my own snores buzzed around in the stillness like forgotten flies. My throat was dry, almost sore. My legs ached for no apparent reason.

My children's young faces, school photographs in school uniforms, smiled with sweet blankness from the frames my wife had placed atop the dresser. The smiles swam through my yawning, and as I groaned, dropped fast through a ragged sigh. I had swung upright, meanwhile, my feet on the carpet, as my knee made snap crackle pops like Rice Crispies, as it did every morning. The shiny crescent scar itching like it does first thing, as I scratch, and it is apparently 1:22 P.M. by the clock. Better not to consider what it is I might look like, stumbling from the bedroom, rubbing my head, splash water on face.

Reassurance of a ceramic cup, cold coffee in hand as I emerged shirtless from the sliding glass door. I wasn't sure how to deal with the overwhelming glare of sunshine on this new day; there's the impulse to go back to bed, but I kept moving forward. Probably there existed some shade, some protection. I paused to sip at the cool caffeination, squinting to get my bearings.

After rubbing my eyes, I got a view of the backyard, the density of bright lawn, avocado and eucalyptus trees hanging semi-bedraggled from the slope above the yard, brush as thick as chaparral on the hill above the retaining wall, chain link fence up top. The flower beds my wife had planted along the foot of the wall and in every corner of the yard projected electric hot pinks, affirmative yellows and red-oranges into the daylight. Some colors so hot I expect they would reflect warmth onto your skin if you held out your hand to them. In spite of their brilliance, she was on her hands and knees at the edge of the lawn, and one of the beds had been literally turned over, laid to waste, dark soil exposed in a new furrow. Her thick dark hair was coiled in a bun at the back of her head that shook gently as she chopped at some roots.

I stifled a yawn, trying to speak, "What are you doing, Xiuh?"

Xiuh drained her plastic cup and placed it on the grass without speaking. This time of day, she favored Chilean wines, as she worked her way through Trader Joe's imported specials. Xiuh liked South Africans better than the Australian stuff, but Chilean, she said, was about as good as Californian. She went back to work with the spade, and I thought she didn't hear me.

"What's the matter?" I asked. "The flowers look good."

"Yeah, like you know something about it," Xiuh said.

"Just seems like a waste to rip them out when they're still looking good," I shrugged.

"Look," she hissed, too furious even to look in my direction, "I don't bother you when you're having a good time."

"All right!" I said jovially. "Would you like me to get you a refill on whatever it is you're drinking?"

She didn't answer, but turned to pull out another plant, leveraging the roots with the spade in her left hand and when they snapped free, she shook off the dirt. She tossed the plant onto the pile and shifted slightly to her left. For some reason her empty plastic cup called to mind a time years ago, an empty plastic cup she used to leave on a formica kitchen table when the kids were still living with us, long ago, when we all lived in a rickety apartment with one of those ice boxes always so frosted over that nothing could be put into it or taken out of it, in Chavez Ravine, above Chinatown. Once upon a time we lived in a rickety clapboard apartment the wind rattled on stormy nights in Chavez Ravine, in sight of the bridge for the 110 freeway, and in those days when the kids were small she rode herd on everyone with the tenacity of a sheep dog, writing unwritten lists of numerous things we had to do (I gave up trying to figure out when she'd be done), insisting we attend lectures, meetings and forums in a communist bookstore downtown, at the same time she was attending PTA and school council meetings at the kid's school, on weekends making picnic lunches so we could all take the bus to the beach or hike in Elysian and Griffith Parks, then when she made friends with a fisherman in the neighborhood, besides getting a yellowtail or barracuda out of the deal once every couple weeks that was the freshest fish we ever ate since we cleaned and cooked it ourselves that same evening, we used to go out sometimes on his boat or borrow his poles and fish from the pier. We had to work the plot in the community garden, or failing to gain access becuz of a bureaucratic rule, make windowbox planters. Why read that trash; the library card was useful for checking out how-to books. She had friends who were musicians we'd go hear play at auditoriums or open air concerts sometimes at benefits for campaigns or political causes, and sometimes she sang as she worked around the house. Funny how Xiuh always used to be the one pushing us out the door to do new things and see what these people were up to and now—*nothing; no more interest in any of it.* Her empty cup reminded me that I hadn't heard her sing like that in fifteen years. It took us decades and many thousands of miles to get here, and apparently she's over it. Nowadays if you mentioned there was Chris Hani speaking about South Africa or Dolores Huerta talking unions on the avenue, or a community meeting in the church basement, she'd shrug and give you a flat stare. If you pressed her on it, she'd become annoyed. Things that had tickled her in the past, now made her upset and angry. If you suggested an outing to the pier, she'd sneer ("Ride the bus all day to come back tired, sunburned and sandy? Hang out with those wacky whities at the dirty beach? The water's polluted!"), or mention a hike at Elysian Park, she'd complain, what was wrong with me— wasn't I tired enough from work already? I certainly was. Where had the intervening years gone?

Recently I seemed to have dreamed a dream about it.

In vast lots under corrugated tin roofing behind the plant it smells like the county fairgrounds at 4 A.M., semi after semi entering row after row of sheds, ramps deployed with a clatter as thousands of hogs are unloaded into the gated pens, grunting, squealing & squawking like sports fans, huffing & puffing as they descend heavily into the concrete pens covered in straw as I sat on the subway next to a sweat begrimed warrior reading the *Toltek Times* with the headline, STALINGRAD SURROUNDED, ASTROLOGERS FOREKAST DOOM FOR GERMAN 6TH ARMY. My kid brother was a military advisor to Makno's anarkosyndikalist forces, but I didn't believe anything I read in our papers about the war. The only thing they were good for was reading between the lines, massaging the temples and listening half-heartedly to fleeting wisps of your flagging aspirations on the patio while the radio played Duke Ellington, Satchmo, Mayan covers of Miskito kalypso and Central Amerikan blues. That's what I planned to do before my afternoon siesta. I knew my wife had other things planned for me, but if my maneuvers served, I'd soon voyage down kanals of dreams in the birchbark canoe of drowse. I got off at my stop and went through the turnstile, hardening my piglike eyes in my mask as a Warrior of Caste, which kept the riffraff half-Spanish Mexika, Zapotek and Mayan street urchins at a distance, my martial stride emboldened by a purpose that I no longer bothered to feel or even seriously consider but wore like a Clan Elder's feathered cape at some banquet in my honor, making my way through the disembarking throng without a glance either right or left. I stopped at a kart at the korner of my block and imbibed a pipette of coka krystal and two jolts of expresso, knocking back one after the other without regard to the possibility of kaffeine addiktion, and then a tobacco chaw to cover my breath as I took the back route into my house: north through the service alley behind the kompounds, in through a backdoor to the sunken garden where my sleek ocelots and mangy jaguars prowled, sleek as a shadow myself moving through the stinking, humid, lush jungle foliage, past my authentik replicas of gigantik Olmek heads whose gaze is fixed on the doorway to other levels of existence (admittedly, used largely for recreational trips to get away from the frenetic hustle of overcrowded Teknotitlán), to squat momentarily above the sunken cages where I'm required to tend the usual lot of ritual kaptives. As usual, they locked their eyes on me as I appeared before them in the carefully tended gloom, thinking (this I knew from interview and experience) that I was at once Angel of Death, Olmek were-Jaguar, barbarian lord of the underworld in the service of Satan, vicious slayer of thousands or—for all they knew—millions of their men, women and children, Executioner ("verdugo") sitting in judgment on their entire doomed civilization, etc. The Europian savages simply had no koncept of how much thought we put into their kareful selektion and processing as centerpieces for State Ceremonials. My own cages, for example, were equipped with the most up-to-date kontemporary stylings, with every modern convenience including running water (overhead sprinklers to wash down both cage interior and prisoners at the same time), electricity (for both lighting and nonlethal elektroshock training), scientifikally determined square footage per prisoner designed for maximum efficiency (derived from ancient texts of the Kalifornia Youth Authority showing how to keep juvenile individuals in personal cages in classrooms) in order to preserve the sakred human characteristics which were of immanent and ultimate importance in the teknospiritual festivities which preserved the benefits of Aztek civilization for the Western World. I knelt by each cage, skanned the upkast faces perfunktorily, making an approximate headcount to make sure the pathetic kreatures hadn't begun consuming each other or done anything contrary to the Municipal Code for the Preservation of Kaptives. I never liked to get tickets for speeding or slavery. The eyes of the slaves were uniformly light-colored for the most part, gray when the light caught their upturned faces, the vision in their eyes glazed with something like illness, which I took for ignorance in its purest form. Dust swirled in the darkness of their gaze and alighted on their unkept, shaggy heads. Among the adult cages, I thought I crossed gazes with some who evidenced a piercing intelligent hatred, who seemed in their pitiful barbarian krudity to wish they could will me inside the cage with them in order to tangle with me in kombat of some untrained and hopelessly inelegant form. That was always the best sign. No weeping, breakdowns and tantrums among such cages, where the kaptives were adept at plotting futile resistance that played right into our need for passionate Hearts. Such kaptives were of course prime quality and would bring me the greatest return on my account with the Clan Elders, among whom I was known to supply red-blooded Hearts, mostly of Europian stock. You want to enkourage such thinking by treating them with as much supercilious kontempt as you can fake — you must keep your affektions a secret. I passed by the cages of the children without stopping because I didn't want any noise in the garden to alert my faithful animals to my presence, as any sudden shift in the dreamy pattern of dappled foliage, sacred animalia, chirping jungle birds, invisible ghosts and other half-imagined presences in the garden might alert my wife to my arrival. I hoped to ascend to my hammock on the patio and fall asleep under my newspaper before she found me, knowing that she invariably left me alone when she came upon me napping. I had to give her that, but I was not above using that minimal generosity on her part for my own purposes. I should have avoided the children's cages entirely however, because something in my passing set off a keening among them which I knew would alert Beppo, my old male jaguar. Even though I was able to get to the switch for electric kurrent and give the row where the children's cages were situated a stiff debilitating zap which quieted them instantly (I paused for a moment to allow the kurrent to work its magic well into the bone, somebody's teeth set a-chattering), I heard Beppo's low cough. Perhaps my wife was otherwise occupied, was all I could hope. Feeble hope, I should give up such pitiful evasions; she and every other woman in my clan seem to be two steps ahead of any scheme I try and fob off on them. In fact, she lay kurled in my hammock herself, the leafy shade soft on her lithe chokolate skin, the big toe of one foot sexily thrust toward the skudding cloudcover of the day. In spite of my better judgment, I paused to take in the scene, and there it was, she had me; though she appeared to be sleeping, her head turned in my direction as if accidentally. A sekond sooner and I might have been able to fade back into the bushes, step behind the massive footing of a giant fig strung with lianas, but now I was stuck kontemplating whether she was asleep behind those sunglasses or not. *Not,* I thought. Sure enough, momentarily her upper lip kurled in a languorous inward half-smile. Was she pleased to see me, or pleased with herself? Both, perhaps. She cocked her head to one side, removing her shades with one hand and slipping a temple into her mouth, smiling at me as I came up out of the garden. I admitted defeat with every step, I was about to seek forgiveness for the plain bone-head prediktibility of my behavior. I had no right to be as dull, transparent and entranced as I was, in the presence of a woman of her character, and she knew it. She held her hand out to me.

Shuffling in the sticky black blood, shuffling in it, shuffling, singing your death song under your breath, klimbing the steps into the sun, it skours out your insides with light—she makes my heart race; floating out of the undergrowth like a butterfly; the sunshine radiates, splayed on her dusky skin—*shuffling in black blood up the steps, each sticky step mucking, mumbling mumbo jumbo to keep the mind's eye carefree, moving on automatik, sweating already, embracing whirling shadows inside an advancing doom*—her mouth is painted black, Aztek-chilango style, she smiles; her teeth flash behind the parting black lips of the married woman—*we've come out of the mountains of the underworld, underwater worlds of rain and misery in the submarine black light of no moon, new moon burning in water, endless roads of night with vultures inside vast emptiness of lost souls, drowning in flame, krucifixes in a death hand, wailing women who are happy for us*—touching her skin is relief from something, I don't know what, but it's sudden and all-enveloping like exiting from a canoe after a long period of confinement, a long endless canal, a liberty palpable in the paired eloquence of her hands; it's an awakening into a suddenly better place, one that had somehow been forgotten in all the hectic traveling of my big important days. Making love to my wife is always a beautiful thing. It's like stepping out into summer vacation after a long year of Aztek High School, you don't even want to know about that. But this thing with my wife, it's always been that way. I don't know why. It's not the same with other wives, other women. It's not like she and I have some perfekt wavelength, some perfekt rapport that makes it work right every time. I'm sure there are other women, probably I've koupled with enough of them myself, who are stronger funnier more imaginative krazier more delikate more this or that more scented with exotik fragrances more pronounced in some obvious way in sexual performance. It's not that obvious with her. The enchantment of her lovemaking is as subtle as the chiaroscuro along her jawline a twilight border that I like when it tastes of her salt. One of the top women in our society because of her tenured position and power in the Akademy of Sakred Aztek Sciences, my wife brokers her own social power with graces, charms and sexual relish. Sex with Xiuhcaquitl always rolls like a ride through the rapids on the river of one's own helter-skelter destiny.

Sometimes she chugs sluggishly like a river tug pushing a loaded barge (tacking back and forth slightly) up a muddy roiling jungle tributary; sometimes she's desperate, mean and short about it as a cat; sometimes she starts at it slow and she's a long, long time like she has to voyage a distance within herself and fetch something she'd forgotten some time ago. But her body's always a blessing when I come to it, a pissing warm tropikal rain, a waterfall into blue pools, flights of egrets across the central kauseway of the kapital on a good day; the benediction of her perspiration on my belly and thighs or calves is sweeter, a sweetness more substantial than the souls flying through the treetops on dark windy nights. She rides her own sensations into a kalm inlet, shifts over me or turns and lifts me above her, moving to increase the Effekt. She and I have been married many years and the sex has always been good. No matter how badly everything else goes in any other part of our lives, including kommunication with our ghosts or treatment of each other, when we make love it's good as it ever was. Even when we're not getting along, like nowadays. We've been in a slump for a year or so, not as bad as the time when she moved out and was living with some Tlaxklalan mercenary geek, martial arts nerd, skrawny methamphetamine zombie, but these days things weren't going very well for us, either. So what? So much for the ups and downs of life; I dispensed with these cares making love to Xiuhcaquitl. She rubbed herself against me; she perfumed herself with my fluids at the four points of the human kompass. Done, I left a glistening slime trail across her glowing skin like a meadow snail on a misty morning; Xiuh reklined, tracing little circles on my chest with her fingertips. Then she got down to Business. "Let me guess. The Clan Elder, that old monkey's flaming red asshole, he says it's a sure bet, this Operation. It's all there is for it. Wait a minute, wait a second, Zenzón, let me finish—that's right, he said it's just a matter of the best Aztek medicine can provide, teknospirituality at its finest and most precise, that grinning toothless fuck, and you hemmed and hawed and finally just shrugged and said, yeah, sure, why not? Eh? What? That's not exactly what you said?" She allowed for my reply. Then she continued: "So that's not *exactly* what you said. But that's sort of the way it worked out, wasn't it?" I didn't answer. I imagine I was staring at the kolor orange through my closed eyelids. "I knew it. I fucking *knew* it. I knew I should have sent your Double in your place. That old fuck would never have known the difference. I could have assumed total control of the Double's functions and negotiated the entire meeting. Like I did with the Tlatekatl Kouncil, you would have been in the shit with them, you would have been fussing with them, you would have messed up, you would have said the wrong thing, you would have told them things they didn't want to hear, they don't want your rationales, they would have demoted you, kashiered you, erased your pension, taken away your various insignia, stripped your name from the official accounts of the Europian Kampaigns, blotted your face out of the official stelae raised in the towns of stone monuments, assigned you to be piss-pot monitor at some third-rate Tlalok temple in Guatemala, Huitzilipochtli, I skatter jade before you, but they heard my words, *my* words coming out of your mouth, heard and were made aware of your kontinuing usefulness to the Kause of Our Socialist Imperium and furthermore to their own ascending prestige as Honored Faces Among the People. I saved your butt on that, you still have the sidelines of specialized slave-trade, you have your Unit intact, supporting you, you have a prosperous practice as Keeper of the House of Darkness, you have unkounted and unkountable blessings that you don't bother to even stop and imagine, and now you're gonna let some third-rate Clan Elder from your old barrio talk you into this new-fangled Operation just cuz success is going to your head?" "I'm not sure about this success, so-called success," I sighed, "I'm having second thoughts, third thoughts, strange ideas, funny visions, sideways apocalypses, nervous glitches, chicharrones, juxtapositions, pickled pigs' feet, moments of spasmodic nerdiness, cloistered hogwilditude, fornicated bowdlerizisms transposed on flights of fancy. I can't stand myself." "Just don't forget who you are and where you came from," Xiuh kommanded softly, her hand coming to rest gently on my forearm, "Remember that. And think of me, why don't you? Konsider what this means to me, for once. Huitzilipochtli! Think of what this kould mean for your children's future." "Actually, that's one of the things I have some doubts about," I began to say. "Oh!" she rushed a finger to her lips, her gaze rising into a middle distance, "I forgot to mention it, but you got an important phone call from Rixtl—he said someone's trying to kill you and all your men. Yep, he was pretty definite about that. He said he thought maybe it was someone close to you, yet somebody on a whole different world. He said Moquihuix was killed today and that it's only a matter of time before they kill you all unless you do something about it. So do something about it, won't you? Please." "Yeah, yeah," I sighed again. "Same old shit. More Party business, I'm sure. I was hoping they were just out for me. You better assign more guards over the kidz. Watch it when you take Ahui to soccer." "Well, you take care of it!" Xiuh urged gently, "It's your job!" "I will," I said. I thought the better of telling her about the rest of the day's events. She pulled her arm free from my side, chicken-winged and bent at a kramped angle in the hammock. One of our old slaves who'd amazingly escaped all Xiuh's fitful purges of the household staff had grown bored with watching us now that we lay quiet, and we kould hear him scraping the short-handled hoe in the garden. Our fluids had dried and stiffened like flecks of mica on our skin.

It wasn't easy for me to get a good job like this in the meat industry. I wasn't born working in a slaughterhouse. I crossed deserts to get here. I traversed the mountains of the Rumorosa & the Coast Range, skirting secret borders of forgotten history & identity. I sacrificed the Past, relationships & dreams of community. I tore open blisters & stubbed my toe on rocks. Empires lay in ruins along the way. I survived long odds, bad luck & bad trips as one of a select few. I negotiated with coyotes, rubbed elbows with travelers from everywhere, hung out under the watchful eye of the Migra. Lots of people—maybe most—don't make it this far. When the maroon Buick Riviera rolled over 4 times in the desert outside of Riverside, who do you think climbed out of the trunk & puked on a rock? When 19 other vatos were asphyxiated in a boxcar locked in the Arizona sun, who you think was the last left alive sucking air out of a tiny rust-hole? Who you think tried hardest to live & go on? Who you think kept walking across the desert with water in plastic jugs on both ends of a stick when the rest of them gave up, wandered off to die bloated & black under a bush? Those ain't my bones unknown out there, not my teeth scattered out there like a broken necklace. Mice ain't making a nest in my jacket elbow. Sow bugs ain't sleeping under what's left of my shoes. Blackbirds ain't playing tug of war with tufts of my hair. Rattlesnakes ain't sleeping in my last resting place. A cottontail ain't hightailing it from a piece of paper with my name on it blowing across a gravel wash. A creosote bush isn't wearing one of my socks. The wind isn't whispering my last words. I stayed alert at all times to every possibility in any given moment. I had to keep my mind alive to the multiple chances hidden inside every second. I had to feel the potentiality of the living moment, where every next step could lead to Death or to Life. There are secret worlds hidden in the air, secret possibilities that can keep you alive in the worst of situations. You got to find them or you may not make it. When the odds are all against you, you got to consider that there might be one possible thing you could do. Or one misstep to avoid. Your life depends on it. That's why I think like this. It's gotten me this far. I been waylaid, ripped off, lost & turned around, and still I made my way. I offer you suggestions on how to survive. You go thru all this, you too can get yourself a job in some industrial section like the City of Vernon slicing the heads off pigs with the circular saw descending from the ceiling, its yellow electrical cord recoiling overhead, hogs' heads rolling across the floor (with a helpful kick every now & then) as you reconsider behind dripping plas- tik safety goggles the fakt your wife really left you in spirit a long time before she departed in the flesh (you can see that now, as the saw bites thru the neck of the next hog, bits of skin shredding as you press the ripping business end all the way thru the spine), I concede I still owe my ex- mother-in-law two grand for a front end repair that didn't work, my kids who don't talk to me anymore are now gangbangers or evangelical chris- tians—now that they got it made in Amerika they disdain me, my values, everything I sacrificed & worked for. This thought alone might've killed me if I let it. Sometimes I did want to die. "Better watch yourself," I told myself sometimes when I caught a glimpse of myself, passing blurry by the little windows inset into the steel doors, I muttered to myself, "Sometimes your worst enemy is your self!" You heard that the suicide rate is 100% higher than the murder rate? That guy in the mirror, he was giving me some nasty looks.

Sometimes when 3Turkey's Apache pickup left the curb, I glanced back over my shoulder to see a little house nicely decorated with flowers, burning brightly.

3

3 TURKEY made a right turn like always, never acknowledging the dip at the curb as the pickup entered the employee parking lot. He's already spotted a vacant space and begun to swerve the front end of his crummy Ford Apache into it before I'm aware, sloshing coffee hot against my mouth as I raise the styrofoam cup, attempting to distract myself from my rising sense of dread. This sick fear not due to anything definite, certainly not due to the fact that today I will likely be fired. This sense of dread has been growing ever since, years ago, a decade ago now, I started on this job and didn't look back. I figured I needed a regular paycheck at the time. Now the bottom's blown out of my engine, the rings, rods & bearings are all shot, and I'm riding with 3Turkey because my van's burning two quarts of oil anytime I drive it anywhere, I'm two grand in the hole to my former mother-in-law, of all people, and there's no end in sight. Another work week was starting. It all happened like clockwork. I managed to drain the coffee. 3Turkey belched laboriously, sighing, "Well, fuck me," and he grinned exiting the vehicle, slamming the creaky door. The slamming door echoed down a corridor into the past, at least in my mind. Fucking Monday morning! I sighed too. "Pirate!" 3Turkey yelled happily at Zahuani as the hairy guy zipped by on his rice burner—I couldn't help but notice Max's Harley was already parked there when Pirate sidled up to the fence. Zahuani dismounted his Yamaha like a spider in my peripheral vision. Other figures emerged from parked cars like spirits rising from their cor-poral selves, but I didn't even look. I might have been seeing spots, there

might have been large blank spots in the world, I didn't care. It's the same every Monday, give or take a few details, a few hangovers, a few ghosts who would no longer hail us as we breathed deeply the slaughterhouse reek we no longer noticed. This shit-stink was the stench of work, my job—odor of death, pink burnt flesh, taint of dried blood and shit settling on everything like dust, all mixed up with the photochemical smog of the city pulsing around us. It's in our hair and our lungs and our eyes and I have long since gotten used to it. I did notice it once after I had been away for several weeks, having sliced off the tip of my finger. I noticed it when I returned, and it was like coming into work after first being hired, feeling that fear lock onto my soul anew, hardening inside me until I forgot about that, too. That's what I think people smell when they wrinkle their noses, catching a whiff of my work clothes. The Farmer John pork packing plant, dark blue with a wraparound porky pig mural you can see as you drive by, looming five stories above us as we walked into its shadow. It towered above us like the Pyramid of the Sun as we drove in on Soto from the north, hemmed in by semis as we emerge under the Southern Pacific overpass— I think we checked on it subconsciously, hoping somehow that some major disaster unknown to the public at large has destroyed the whole plant, the chill room where the mass of our work swings on a thousand hooks, and the cutting lines with wooden boxes full of knives, the sausage rooms and fetid wiener smokehouse, loading docks and animal storage pens out back, steaming pipes rising like conning towers above the yard where semis and 2 to 4-ton delivery trucks pull in and out, smokestacks above the offices and the front gate (with Bobo or Zack in his box, checking the trucks in). Certainly in L.A., where we've seen riots, fires, earthquakes, epidemix, crack wars and the disaster of our everyday lives, we would not be too shocked if somehow the entire City of Vernon was removed from the map over the weekend. Subterranean methane build-up, a refinery explosion, fuel leak in the sewer system, nuclear terrorism, something! But every Monday there it was, the blue mass of Farmer John rising above the L.A. River like a fortress anchoring a Chinese wall of fortified industry, its sheet metal and concrete arteries pumping pig blood into the vast urban sprawl—we got a clear view of it as we crossed the river on a Soto Street overpass, clouds scudding across a blue sky reflected in a river flowing without depth between broad concrete banks, the smooth surface of the water scummy with brown foam that we didn't have to imagine being partly the blood of 6,000 pigs dispatched between last Friday and today. We'd dropped down Soto on a beeline from El Sereno, we crossed the 10 when the radio reports a jack-knifed big rig has commuters backed up all the way to the 710, we had bypassed the commuter jam on the San Bernadino because that's the way we always get to work, 3Turkey telling me about another car wash he helped put together to benefit the family of some little kid from his street murdered in a drive-by a couple weeks back, "One teeny girl had legs like nobody's bizness and big chichis bursting out of a little yellow tube-top like party balloons, bizongas, melones man! She and her other teeny friends got into this water fight with their soapy rags, what a sight!" etc. "You gonna go to Arizona, man?" I asked, changing the subject to find out if I was gonna have to arrange another ride, since 3Turkey was forever threatening to join some armed American Indian Movement standoff against the federal marshals if he could find one in order to leave this life with a bang, leaving me stuck without a ride, or worse, driving myself to work alone with my shitty attitude unrelieved by his cheer. I was worried about myself, like always. "Zenzo," 3Turkey says, hitching up his pants as we jaywalk the avenue, "You should come with, Zenzo! We'll have traditional sweats. The elders will teach us about the Old Ways and our connection with Mother Earth. We"ll get fresh air and exercise. We'll learn you about Turtle Island. You need a break from this factory bullshit. Maybe Max will forget he's trying to fire your ass. Maybe you can come back and start on a new leg. Maybe you'll come back with a whole new insight on Life and Everything." "Start on a new leg?" I grumble, "Maybe Max'll get Auerbach to give me a parking space with my name painted on it. Maybe he'll stop assigning me overtime on the clean-up crew 4 days a week. Maybe someone will slip me Polaroids of him with two prostitutes atop plastic barrels of sausage membrane." We skipped up the steps and strolled the old unused loading dock. This was the point of no return. We'd be inside the plant in the blink of an eye. "Employees Only," the sign said, but we no longer saw it. Behind us, someone snickered, a noise like a hoot owl's diarrhea. "Fuck you," 3Turkey greeted Zahuani as he followed us through the side door. The door slammed as we ascended the steel steps, footfalls, backslapping and catcalls reverberating in the concrete stairwell. The rodent trap beside the first step was empty, I noticed without noticing. Pirate cackled, "Zenzón, you know right now Max is checking trucks out back. He's gonna oversee all the pigmeat offload. He's gonna see they're penned and get the downers up that chute before they die on him and cost 250 pounds of dick. Then Zenzón, while you're suiting up in the cloakroom, he's already thinking about you, working his way over to the killing floor, casual like. Like he's just making his usual morning rounds with his little FDA clipboard, just happens to have handy his little OSHA checklist, the little list of infractions he's keeping on you for the main office. He'll bring along that woman, Maria what's-her-name, la chula who's bucking for inspector. He'll be peeking over your shoulder as you cut the first pig's throat; just when that pig finds he can't screech any more cuz he's choked up on his own blood, there will be Max the Man trying to give you a kiss good morning. Ha ha ha ha!" They all laughed; it's common knowledge that I have to outfox Max at his own game and come out ahead by the end of the day, I've done it for years and that's what my rep's based on. I haven't let them down and that's why they all back me and that's what Max will never forget. Maybe if I had let him demote me just once without rejoinder, let him rip me off just once without payback in a major way, let him trounce me once publicly in the yard and have me give it up, then maybe he could have given me room and let some of my lip slide. But it was just one of those snap decisions I made and never looked back on, never give the ass-hole an inch. There was the time he'd reprimanded one of the local drivers for damaging the loading dock becuz the guy had bad brakes, and there he was up top of the load when I leaned casually against the bed—and what do ya know—the two-ton truck, load and all with "the Man" Max himself atop it, began rolling willy nilly across the yard and the driver— yowling—hopped up into the open cab and slammed on the brakes and who do you imagine did a somersault clean over the cab, bouncing on the hood to land hard on the asphalt yard? There was the time he handed me a pink slip because he asserted that it could only have been my clean-up crew that screwed up and fouled the steam unit with illegally disposed waste product, and then (how could this happen?) when Bob Handler— the day foreman—checked on the crew who went down into the pit and unplugged the stinking, filthy drains by hand they found a crushed plastic bucket clogging the drain, a bucket from the stacks of empties Max kept in his office with one of Max's gloves stuffed inside it. Even so, Handler probably wouldn't have rescinded the notification of dismissal except Maria, in spite of herself, put in a word for me about some little trick I'd done on the ham line to save the $7,500 computer chip that bakes the honey-golden hams. Then there was the time I met Max's good-looking sister Luisa at a Boyle Heights house party and introduced her to Zahuani. Even I regretted that one, but fuck it, these things happen between consenting adults. There was a string of incidents going back as many years, and there were about as many people rubbed the wrong way as were entertained by the whole thing. Max knew he could count on these vendidos in any situation where he or the other assistant foremen were laying down the law. Even guys like Cuzatli, "the Weasel," who chuckled at me mysteriously, "Hey, rebel," as 3Turkey, Zahuani and I suited up in the locker room. Guys like Weasel wanted to see me take the fall just cuz I'd been teetering on the edge so long. They wanted some action and damn the cost (no skin off their ass). Zahuani and 3Turkey gave him a sidelong glance as Cuzatli practically skipped out the door, heading up his ladder to a glass booth where he monitored computer screens and toggle switches controlling the big grinders that churn hot dog mix out of vats of pork, beef and pork fat. What was Weasel so happy about? He knows something, I thought to myself, zipping up my blue company jumpsuit. "Farmer John," the embroidery said over my heart. But who knows? Maybe, just maybe, it was the Weasel's way of telling me to watch myself today. Then I found the piece of paper someone had slipped into my locker when I put my street shoes down at the bottom. "Meet me across the street after work," it said, signed

"Nita" in a woman's neat penmanship. This was something new. "Te hua-cho, you sorry bastards," Zahuani said, slamming his locker door, "I gotta go work on my book, *Tighter Pussies I Have Known*, sequel to my best-seller, *You Don't Know What Love Is*." "Fuck it," I growled. I was in no mood to walk the line today, watch what I say, attend to every little detail and dot every i. This thing had gone on long enuf and if Max wanted to tangle with me, then let it happen. Meanwhile, let's go make some bacon. Six thousand pigs would dance down that chute today.

Once upon a time I had thought Max was a good guy. Big, black-haired, goateed, sharp-looking vato who seemed like he knew the bizness top to bottom, like he could run the whole plant in his sleep. Who would've known? You saw him out in the yard, standing out by the roach coach, eat-ing tacos de carnitas with the workers, joking with the health & safety inspectors. Just another one of the boys, you might think. Later, you saw him stalking thru the plant with his clipboard, scowling like he'd just woken out of a nightmare, hunched over in his white coat as if whipped by a furious unhappiness of some sort, his pupils so constricted he can't even see you unless he happened to look at you directly. And he wasn't smiling. He wasn't joking then, not when you met him one-on-one in a dank tunnel some-where in the smokehouse; you were just trying to get this job done quick, you'd been inhaling ammonia for hours swabbing down the corridor, he was walking thru the area you just finished, tracking across the wet, "Hey Max, I just did the whole floor—it's still wet . . ." you thought maybe he didn't hear you, so you said it again (and you figure later, maybe that's what really pissed him off, but who knows?), he just turned to you as he stalked by, slightly bent over, like I said, and thru his clenched jaw, he spit the words into your face (his face constricted—not the easy-going joker in the plant yard, the flirt with all the female line workers—mouth turned down at the corners), "See me in my office on your break." "All right," you said—he hadn't even paused midstep—he slunk off down the hall, bent like a shadow, disappeared around the corner, furiously clutching the clipboard to his chest. Down the corridor, his footprints slurred determinedly across the shiny film.

You always find out stuff like this about people on the job, of course. But with Max you had to marvel about the consistency of his schizophrenia. Unfailingly, he greeted you jovially in the yard, where he'd often have something nice to say about anyone sitting at the picnic tables and umbrellas set out by the roach coach where workers take their breaks, smoke cigarettes, eat their lunches, "Great time on that unit, this morning!" he grins, calls you by name, introduces a new line worker by the name of Maricela, "Maricela, better try out a pastrami from the taco truck by tomorrow, tomorrow being Friday; everybody only gets the first week before they get sick of the taco truck, then they got to make their own lunch," as Maricela smiled, she looked from you to him and back again, and you nod smiling too, knowing she'd find out about Max later, in the privacy of his office. Out in the yard Max was all bluster, everybody's buddy, he'd be loud, calling out across the yard to the old FDA inspector, returned after years of service elsewhere, he'd put thumb & forefinger in his mouth to emit a piercing whistle, yelling, "Whoa! Whoa, big boy!" at a truck driver who ignored Nacho at the gate—Max had stepped out into the path of the truck holding his clipboard up like a semaphore—the truck screeched to a halt; Max was pointing back to Nacho, who ran up to tell the driver to take it around to the rear entrance—but usually he prowled the plant in grim silence, clipboard at the ready to denote infractions, notate problems for your file, anything he can use for the caseloads of worker demotion or termination that he amassed, alone in his office, at all times. Out in the yard Max was all cheer, full of energy. But on the night shift, down the hallways and corridors and staircases of the plant, he was a sad man who hated his job, and he was looking for somebody to take the blame. He haunted odd corners of the buildings, coming out of a door in the shadows like a fiend. He was so unhappy.

Then there was his office. If Max's personality was patterned on Dante's Inferno, with inner circles providing special torment for the worst offenders, then the behaviors he revealed in his office were marvelous strange. At first I had paid no attention to rumors circulating about Max's office, especially among the line workers. Those girls fresh from the Eastside may not have had much experience in a slaughterhouse, they might be a little sensitive. Maybe they just wanted sympathy from the guys working the line. Then I started getting called to Max's office myself. Everything was very neat in his office, and if you've come across that before, maybe that's the first clue. I hadn't seen that too much myself, not being all that tidy. The first time I'd gotten called up there, the time I spoke to him in the corridor like that (I'd thought he was the same guy out there in the yard, asking me if I had tried the lengua burrito yet, the cilantro *rico!*), I noted the chalkboard behind his desk with annotations on it like leftover strategy notes from a football game, abbreviations, squares & arrows in red, black & white, his desk back near the board, facing outward, shelves behind it full of binders, county, state & federal codebooks, yellow pages, OSHA rules & regulations, company forms & reports, late afternoon orange haze blearing thru partially closed venetian blinds, dropped but aslant, the last afternoon light splayed across the wall broken by the door I entered thru. "Close the door," Max instructed. He waited till I sat, placing papers he'd been perusing into a desk drawer and closing it.

"What did you say to me earlier?" he asked quietly, leaning forward with his hands folded together in front of him on the desk. I couldn't think of what he might be referring to. It took me a second to recall anything that might pertain. "I guess I said I had just finished doing that part," I said. Max nodded understandingly. "I understand Weasel had to wait a quarter of an hour for clean vats?" Max inquired, arching an eyebrow. "Quarter of an hour?" I repeated, surprised, asking, "What's that? Five, ten minutes on the outside?" "That's thousands of dollars delay in the operation of the smokehouse," Max growled, "an unscheduled interruption, a delay in the whole operation of the smokehouse, FIFTEEN, 20 MINUTES! Why?" "I don't know," I shrugged, "maybe I was going back over an area I had already swabbed clean." Max's eyes had been fixed on me, and he stared at me like he was seeing something for the first time, he couldn't figure it out—but it was coming to him—he was nodding, eyes widening. He looked excited, almost happy—a total contrast to the guy who had passed me in the corridor looking like someone fleeing persecution. Max sucked at hairs on his upper lip with a smack & pulled at the whiskers of his black goatee with thick hairy fingers. He opened a drawer in his desk and leaned over & made a notation, grinning—grinning at what? "Ha ha ha!" he said, leaning back in his chair, "you might as well know next week you, Ray, Zahuani, and, uh" (he snapped his fingers) "3 Turkey, a couple others, you're all on double shifts! We got to pick up some slack and we need the man hours. Just thought I'd let you know, that way you got the weekend to relax."

I found out later, according to his annotation in my file, that I was responsible for a half-hour interruption of the smokehouse operation due to "dilatory exercise on clean-up crew." In fact, every time anyone was called to Max's office there was an annotation to their personnel file. Sometimes he'd have your file sent over to the front office or elsewhere so that other signatures and initials were made other than his own. He'd get someone else to sign off on something, some observation or schedule nota-tion—related to you or not. My file was in the front office one day, the secretary showed it to me—I saw next to various notes Max had made about the interruption in the smokehouse schedule (he'd gotten Cuzatli— "the Weasel" to sign off on the exact—according to them—times), he'd also gotten the other guard at the gate, Zack, to sign off on some note say-ing several trucks had just come in at that time. What the hell did that have to do with anything? With me, Max usually spoke very evenly, if incoher-ently, laughing occasionally at things that weren't funny in the least, but with other people, frequently groups of line workers who deboned, filleted or cut fat off the ham, Max could be heard screaming. He'd work himself up into a spitting rage. Some women would leave his office weeping. Other women, the young ones, he'd give them a good talking to. He'd talk to them for an hour or more.

At the end of the first shift on the kill floor I was working industrial cleanser across sections of the concrete with a push broom. 3 Turkey behind me, hosing it off into the grating. The chlorine in the mix was so potent it burned out your nose hairs & gave you a "night cough" (we were swaddled in overalls, rubber boots and gloves, with baseball caps or kerchiefs or rags on our heads like bedouin traders wrapped up against sandstorms in North Afrika), and as I poured out the industrial-strength mix, it splashed white on the cement floor, I shoved it forward with the broom, and when it hit a tiny piece of meat or chip of bone, the fleck of flesh or bone chip went white or gray. It bleached all the color right out of them.

We disinfected the kill floor in twenty minutes, coughing into kerchiefs tied around our faces, wiping our mouths on cloths like some gang of TB-stricken outlaws of the Old West, washed up rough riders with all the piss & vinegar beaten out of 'em by Life, good for nothing but pushing a broom around the bunk house — tossing nylon brooms, stiff brushes, long gloves and face masks into the clean-up cart and filing thru the steel door, dead at the end of the night. Except it wasn't the end. As we fell out on the steel stairs, muttering and spitting and groaning and shuffling down toward the door at the bottom, out of the corner of the building, we could tell the night was nearly gone. Light might be coming under the door at the bottom of the stairwell. When we emerged from the kill house into an atmosphere that ranked as pure fresh air to us, we paused. We stalled out in the yard, along the base of the high featureless concrete wall, catching our breath. One of the vatos might light up a reefer behind somebody's back, pass it around, the rest of us too beat to spit. Esophagus tracts raw from chlorine, we couldn't even smell the pall of pig shit, smoke flavoring, sodium nitrates, nitrites, carbon dioxide & blood floating over the whole plant. The sky might already be lightening, backlit that cool electric blue beyond the streetlights and halogen spots on smokestacks or rooftop walkways, and even as they talked about other things, I'd hear them thinking, this is the absolute shit. This is how the real shit begins. It starts all over again.

After a while, we would walk across the yard to the taco truck and buy a cup of coffee, no matter what it tasted like. Best to start the next shift with something hot inside you.

The next thing I knew the cold was shaking me awake as the plane shuddered over the frozen white wastes of the Russian steppe east of the

Volga River at Kuybyshev. *Kuybyshev.* Even in my mind, I didn't bother to try and pronounce the name at the time. I mean, *Kuybyshev? Pyatigorsk, Kotelnikovo, Kachalinskaya, Buturlinovka, Tsimlanskaya, Ordzhonikidze.* Russian is an absurd language. You take ordinary Nahuatl words like tlapalkolikwee, nakazminkee, ocellotilmatli, xikalcoliuhkwee or ytzkouakoliuhkwee (different kinds of mantas or cloaks) and you see what I mean? Nahuatl just flows off the tongue. And that's with simple things like the names of clothing. But Russian, well . . . nobody can understand it! I was reading my *Official Russian Phrase Book*, Aztek Army issue, on the plane and it put me right to sleep. Right there on the hard bench of the freezing airplane. In my flight jacket with the Mexikan red wolf fur trimmings. I could feel myself nodding off. The wind wailed around the plane, it was bouncing up & down like a truck on ruts in the Road across the Sky, the engines screaming like they were fit to burst, the wind yowling like a banshee, the cold whistling like Whistler's mother thru numerous cracks in the cheaply manufactured sheet metal fusilage, you'd think they might have heaters or something to keep my men and the rest of the Aztek Socialist Imperium's fresh troops and elite forces from freezing our balls off, but no. They did give us jackets and wool socks that smelled like sheep so that was the good part. The bad part was the 25-degrees-below-zero part. My men covered themselves up as best they could and smoked up a storm or talked with the wind drowning out every word, engines ripping away pieces of the conversation into nothingness. After consciousness and conversation had been shredded and dispersed into frozen blasts of wind-tunnel noise, most of the two Jaguar Units packed into the plane just fell out on the cold hard steel benches to sleep. It was one way to keep warm. Korporal Zahuani was looking out thru the window. I was gonna have to keep my eye on "Pirate." He was one suspicious, skeptikal vato. He didn't know yet that I'd singled him out for advancement, that he was a korporal already, but he'd find out at first opportunity. It was all I could do for the moment to read the very small pages of the phrase book, hold them apart with my aching, pallid fingertips: *"How are you, ese? Teotakiltli ixkiltzin?" "I love you: nimitzazotla." "May the sun shine in your face: tlamish Toniatiuh."* I admit, part of my problem with the Russian phrases was figuring out under what circumstances you might use these types of Russianisms: *"All is forgiven: tetlapoplweelo." "They are our people: zanno tehauntin." "He's just like me: yekuel." "Female Spirit of Corn: Kilomen." "It's about time: yeppa."* I was mumbling nonsense like that to keep myself awake when I nodded off. I must have been homesick already, because I dreamed about Beppo. That once sleek ferocious jaguar long since grown lazy, scruffy and grouchy.

It was a good Sign. I knew that, even in the dream.

I don't care if he's old & fucked up. He's my jaguar Spirit.

I dream of whiteness. I don't know if that's a good sign, but I go on dreaming. Whiteness. Blankness. Fogginess. A vague expanse of indefinite ambiguity. Middle distance where everything starts fading away. The airplane is shuddering underneath me, freezing wind whistling thru its sheetmetal seams like someone sucking on his teeth, the temperature too low to drop any further, just yet. The humidity in our breath freezes on the fur-lined hoods of our parkas. This noisy cold tube of airplane, like the hard cold bench under my butt, is there somewhere in the dream. Encased in it I plumb some indefinite distance, a cold blanket of cloudbank or whatever it is, that surrounds me truly, like the gaping, howling, freezing emptiness swirling around the plane itself now, in the dream. Occasionally some shudder jars the plane and drops it, shaking violently as it rises again, engines screeching above the continuous roaring of the wind. Then there was the dream itself, which proved to be strangely portentous. I'll tell you about it later. I was having a good time tho, dreaming that dream. I was feeling warm and comforted by the familiar capacity for dreaming, at home, so to speak, after a long hard trip, after a seasick sea voyage, after irritating cramped quarters of transport and travel, ship deck, truck bed, vehicle bench, take-off, shudders, low cloud cover . . . After the assassination bizness, the bizness of them always trying to kill me, pop music, radio communiques, static interference, everyday conversations and stupid ideas. I slept in peace for a moment, very glad of it too, secretly, in some secret glad part within myself. Communing with that irritable jaguar, with his belly hanging low. With his yellow teeth and acting like he has arthritis.

With his fur flying off patchy as a ragged dandelion head. He was so sleek when I was young. I got older — he got old, older, oldest. That's how it goes with our nahuales. They die before us. Maybe if I'd have been paying attention to my dreams, my jaguar spirit, reading the newspaper and samizdat bulletins, paying attention to subtle whims and secret thots, whatever, I would have had a clue, a better idea, a scope on what was happening, what was about to happen when we hit the ground. Maybe that was what the monkey spirits stole from me when I wasn't looking: an inkling, a hint, something you saw out of the corner of your eye that alerted you to what was about to go down. The things they like to do when you aren't looking, when you're just taking an innocent nap becuz you've just ridden on a rocking steel sea cow of a ship across the Eastern Ocean, stop-over in Gibraltar, a rock the British claim (they can have it), then on to Naples, Napoli the locals called it, the food was good, I had to watch my men in the streets cuz they were getting sick of traveling, sick of being tourists, they didn't want to take snapshots or skribble postcards to their moms — they had tried that already (is this what they'd come halfway around the world for? "No, stupid," I said) — they wanted to kill something, the lokals turned, stared and got out of our way if they had half a notion what wuz good for them as we sauntered the nice little streets in our turquoise feathered kapes, black body paint, skarifikation, tattoos, ear plugs, lip plugs, moseying along with ceremonial grunts, ritual chants, our muskulature flexing itself unbidden with karate reflexes and stretches, tensile ligatures, our warrior vestments clicking along, checking out the Kasbah, quaint architecture, vino and seafood, the dark eyes of the good looking natives of the Italian peninsula, some street kid came up to Amoxhuah and tried to feel some feathers he had tasseling his warrior scalplock, Amoxhuah grinned and tied the boys arms together behind his raggedy butt faster than the child could comprehend, tho he started squawking, squirming & crying out when Amoxhuah tossed him over his shoulder, some women ran out of a shop and gesticulated at us, wagging fingers and tongues at Amoxhuah as he turned with a querulous arched eyebrow, they whined in gibberish, the feminine case as used by Italian women, it was enough like Spanish that I understood they wanted the boy, he was their own, he belonged to their street, etc., Amoxhuah offered them a nice eagle bone flute, he was astonished even shocked when they wouldn't trade, take it for the boy, he offered a bar of Hershey's chokolatl on top of that, sort of contemptuously, becuz what slave child's life was worth a war-

rior's lover's handmade eagle bone flute? And I could tell that we had some local incident brewing, portly squat men of the neighborhood stepped out onto their doorsteps
to stare darkly — arms krossed — the women called to them but they stood staring,
irresolute, faces appeared in windows, I didn't want any extra paperwork to justify
some altercation when we were supposed to be back on the ship, I told Amoxhuah
to untie the boy, put him down, which he did, affekting a disdainful boredom with
the entire affair already, but I could tell that our Scholar, our book-wise worldly student was disturbed, secretly he was confused by the silliness of the trivial incident,
that these woman — he found out (his knowledge of Spanish was, it turned out, even
better than mine, so he was getting the Italian too) — were totally unrelated to the
boy, a street urchin apparently claimed by no one at all, yet they were willing to risk
their necks to interrupt the boy's removal from that world into a whole New World
of Sensation & Aztek Possibility (had he the chance but to complete the trip, but he
was set free so he ran off a distance rubbing the chafed places where his arms had
been tightly bound, he turned and skreeched whippersnapper protests or insults our
way, ridiculous undaunted small scarecrow of a child with shaggy hair hanging over
his big eyes, small patches of scabby eczema at each corner of his open mouth, snot
encrusted under his nose), so Amoxhuah coiled his cordage with a preoccupied air,
wondering, obviously, what kind of place was this, so far from Anahuak, the Aztek
heartland? Weasel and 3 Turkey stepped forward but I stopped them with a glance.
Did these three fat women in worn out clothes and this starving child in rags think
they could mess with us, the leadership cadre of a Jaguar Unit? Nothing short of
amazing, the surface of that moment. We knew something substantial had shifted
below the glossy bubble of perceivable phenomena. It made us wonder where we were.
We sort of woke into the moment, looked at the strange faces and poverty-stricken
clothes of the people knotted in the street, leaning out of windows above us to stare.
Weird barbarian kultures, you never knew what to expect with them. We were far
from home, Anahuak retreating from us as if on the outgoing tide. Plus, the Italian
food was so much better and cheaper in Naples. That was an obvious moment of ini-
tial dissonance, but there were signs and indications throughout the entire voyage,
spektral, subliminal, natural, teknological, that I could have assayed for terms, mean-
ings, korrespondences to our situation, prognostikations, variant potentialities. I don't
know what it was, but I thot of my children, wondered how they were getting along

*at their grandma's house . . . I thot of my kids all the time . . . I supposed we would get some kind of Sign, something in the Air . . . The world is full of signs . . . Stop signs, omens, faded inscriptions on old buildings, indicators, blinking lights, weather reports, routes, configurations, numbers, seabirds flying the wrong way, red sky at morning, dark looks, expressive glances, raised eyebrows, words to the wise, numerology, victimology, cloud formations, prevailing winds, odd noises, circumstances lining up against you, tea leaves, flapping spurts of a bleeding heart, gutteral expletives, secrets revealed, tonalities forming in the air, nodal whiffs forming on the breeze, menstrual cycles of daily life, astrological confections in the opaque heavens remote by entire lifetimes from immediate awareness, little blips in consciousness like spots of glare sinking into the retinae on a scalding summer's day . . . I admit I'm just like anybody else; I'd rather rely on somebody with more on the ball in terms of intelligence to interpret all these signs for me. That's why I particularly resented the fact that it didn't seem like my wife cared whether I lived or died, now that I was in an especially tight situation which I couldn't get a good grasp on. I had always relied on her to tell me What Is To Be Done. Cuz I didn't feel like thinking about all this general Komplexity. But, shit, when they kill the **spirit** of your better half, then you are left to do the dishes yourself and rekonstruct your Life like an Empire State Building out of toothpicks. Tezkatlipoka . . . So I did my best, I thot a few thots all the way thru the best way I could think, then I moped about in a nasty snarling blue funk for the whole trip. Fuck it. We debarked at Istanbul; my men were going crazy by then. I had to give them the teenaged female slave I'd brought along for myself, and even then, after they finished with her (just becuz they'd used up their own damned slaves before they were halfway across the Eastern Ocean), they got into a bit of trouble with our allies, the Turks, resulting in some deaths & hospitalizations on the Turkish side, plus numerous injuries among my men when the A.G. (the Aztek Guard) were called in to escort my men to some barracks alongside the airfield. We stayed over one day till we boarded the transport plane to cross the Black Sea. This lack of discipline would be noted, I knew, when we reached our destination. They'd blame it on me and they'd be right. I hadn't been doing my scientifick duties, been exchanging pleasantries and intelligences with Tezkatlipoka in the guise of Vladimir Lenin, Huitzilopochtli in the semblance of Karl Marx, as back in the kapital, Teknotitlán, literary critik Ramon Mercader was about to take in hand an* *ice axe & split the legendary detektive novelist Leon Trotsky's skull open & splash his brain matter out on the manuscript he was writing about Joe Stalin, fictive criminal mastermind, but I wasn't paying attention to the headlines in the* Teknotitlán Times *either, I wasn't interested in the society pages & the private lives of the celebrities, what did any of that have to do with the lives of those of us on the way to the Front, the unibrow Frida and the 300-pound gordo painter, El Sapo Diego, Tina "the famous beauty" Modotti and the glittering social circles of the city, their gossip, high times and moments of glamor, I had enough to do, to worry about, with my children probably bored to death of the boredom of being dead in spirit, probably storing up resentments to unleash like poison darts at my heart unless I thot of something good, something nice to do for them, some way to bring them back across the borders between worlds, that was probably the only thing they might enjoy for any real length of time, how fickle children are, you know how short their attention spans are, shit what wuz I gonna do, I'd spent a good deal of the trip in the rolling steel cow of a rusty leaking vessel listening to the groaning & creaking of the ship with my head in my hands either figuratively speaking or literally depending on whether I was just thinking & feeling that way or doing it in actuality, entiendes? I had thot the sea crossing would be more wonderful than it turned out to be, cuz the first half was sort of gray, interminable, cold, endless, irritating, rocking, rolling, awful, even when I wasn't throwing up or feeling queasy the whole motion sickness thing gave me a giant headache, maybe that's what fogged up my thinking there. It sure made me irritable, I stabbed one of my men when he stepped into my room to ask me one too many stupid questions (he was trying to get smart with me, he had a map he'd cut out of the newspaper about the Eastern Front, it had arrows representing armies and stuff, he'd taken time to draw little dots of Russian towns on it, he was pointing to them and asking me strategik stuff); I didn't even feel like stabbing him two times, I just whipped out my keen Aztek blade and sliced him once akross the belly good, I allowed him to stumble backward through the cabin door, gasping, out into the corridor, moaning, bleeding, holding himself, where he backed up against the wall, then fell over on his side & he didn't die, he gasped and held himself, made a big puddle of blood that someone was going to have to mop up with a bucket, 3 Turkey finished his errand, came back to my room and found the guy there, ascertained the situation, and carried him to the ship's doctor. At least the kid wasn't stupid, cuz after*

*his guts healed up, he didn't go around telling the men that I didn't know the
answers to the make-up of forces converging on Stalingrad or I would have cut his
tongue out & sent it back to his mother wrapped in a note saying what a disappointment he'd been to me, mid-ocean, on a bad day, in the midst of war, praise be
to Huitzilopochtli. Instead the kid grew up to be a stand-up guy, one of our best,
strongest & brightest, what can I say, in any number of ways he was more of man
than I'll ever be, even tho he was so much younger, just a kid basikally, he was the
kind of kid you'd hope to become yourself, or at least, hope to meet later on in life
when you yourself have blown your chances in middle age, but he shouldn't have
messed with me on a morning when I hadn't had my coffee yet, I nearly screwed him
over permanently by mistake, but instead, he became a hero when he was killed fighting the Nazis during the war. Oh well. If I could remember his name I'd mention
it here. You might know who I'm talking about if I could think of exactly what his
name was. Ah well. There's a lot more like him where he came from. The flower of
the Aztek youth in all their agility & exquisiteness. Fuckin' kidz. Better not mess
with me.* "Keeper of the House of Darkness. Master Zenzontli, sir, wake up."
"What, what the fuck?" "You're mumbling things in your sleep, sir, stupid
things, insensibilities, inanities, platitudes," Amoxhuah was saying to me as I
unbent myself out of a sleep-enforced slouch. He was staring at me; I stared
back and brought him into focus. "Commonplaces, sir, euphemisms, stock
phrases, tripe," Amoxhuah added, "I'm sorry sir, but from what I could catch
they were the kind of empty phraseology that you might hear from your so-
called experts. It was pretty scary." "Who, me?" I grumbled, rubbing my face
with both hands. Half my face was numb with cold. The other half was numb
with something else. I think I had a stroke while I was sleeping, suffered a
seizure of some kind, had drooled on the hood of my parka. But in millisec-
onds I regained my composure as a kool soldier of the Aztek Socialist
Imperium. "I don't mind sounding incoherent," I said, "but wuz it at least creative? Wuz it perky? Did you write any of it down?" "No, sir," Amoxhuah
glanced at me edgily, talking overloud becuz of the roar of the airplane. I
reached into my shirt pocket and he stepped back and put up both hands:
"Don't stab me, sir!" I tossed him a ballpoint pen. "What's wrong with you?"
I growled. He pulled a small notepad out of his back pocket and made ready

to take notes. "Go ahead. Note down anything I said that you can remember. It's important we keep records," I instructed. He nodded, moved off to a bench, sat down, began to write. He filled up several pages and returned it to me, I glanced at it, folded it in half, stuffed it into the side pocket of my parka. Later I read it over, Amoxhuah's note consisting entirely of hyperventilated over-intellectualizing, the mental doodles of my driver and adjutant, the Scholar:

If I had to explain it, [Amoxhuah had written] I'd describe our predikament according to the following notations:

Misterioso

piano: Thelonious Monk
vibes: Milt Jackson
bass: John Simmons
drums: Shadow Wilson

.00 The introduction consists of the first four measures of the tune (2 phrases).

.10 The written melody is being played by the piano, vibes & bass. The melody is heard in the bottom notes of the 'walking sixths' (played louder by Monk).

.44 Vibraphone solo (blues): the piano plays a low note followed immediately by the 7th of the chord; no chords are used as accompaniment.

1.20 Piano solo: dissonant extensions end the phrases, no accompaniment from the vibes.

1.40 Ascending runs ending on dissonant notes.

1:47 Again, ascending runs up to dissonant notes (altho these might sound like mistakes).

1.57 2nd solo chorus by Monk: the obvious dissonant intervals are minor 2nds.

2.04 Large melodic leaps.

2.35 Vibraphone enters with the melody, piano develops accompaniment idea (low note, high note), Monk creates melodic & rhythmik tensions.

2:58 Piano joins vibes with the melody.

3.09 Ending (improvised).

3.13 End.

(Introduction to Jazz History by Donald D. Megill & Richard S. Demory, page 131); that's how I would describe our situation to a T—except it's not that

good; besides it's my conclusion that being Komrade Zenzontli's driver and adjutant sucks, cuz, the first thing I found out wuz not only did the last two D.A.s get slaughtered in assassination attempts on the Komrade but I heard, rumor has it, that they don't really get offered any chance for advancement in their careers, plus the war-bond insurance offered their parents as far as death benefits is a skam, the fund is mostly bankrupt so they give the next of kin a certificate worth 500 dollars redeemable after 25 years or something, I also don't like how the D.A.'s job is to spend their whole life following up every cricket-like notion and unaesthetik koncept of the Master, Komrade Zenzontli, with his supercilious bad moods, violent fits of temper, bad jokes, violent jokes, bad temper, bad clothes & violent farts, tasteless wardrobe koncept and gas attacks (inability to digest long strands of complex proteins, he truly needs Russian <u>yogurt therapy</u> but considers it to be the purest village super-stition) he farts so much his wife left a note on the refrigerator saying to see a dok-tor just the week before we all got sent to Russia becuz of yet another of his outrageously alarming politikal total miskalkulations — which, in any case, did have the benefit of opening up this current position for me, they seemed really pleased when I interviewed for this driver adjutant job; I admit I do make a good impres-sion in person, I do a better interview than my resume alone indicates, they seemed really impressed with my mental alakrities when they posed the questions about what would I do in purely hypothetical cases of assassination attempts or shitfits from dysentery, etc., plus I get a neat new little D.A. badge to wear on my sleeve with the insignia of Ehekatl (Wind), coiled two-headed feathered dragon with feathers made of kool jade, I'm allowed to wear the Master's House of Darkness colors as body paint, which is black, matte black and glossy black, which are kool colors, I like them a lot, we get to wear special warrior lip plugs & earlobe plugs, which make us look really weird, strong, ferocious & that's really kool, too, I guess it's worth it, you know, the uniform, the whole gig, to risk your life for the master's senseless undertakings and superficial insights into what he is always calling pompously, "reality god damn it, this is the fucking real world we're talkin' about here," which anyway I know all about, I read about the war and the front lines in groovy magazines published by the Armed Forces, in the best-selling thrilling memoirs of generals of the armed forces, War they say it's bad, sad & crazy, but hey, so what, it's War, nothing quite like War to get the cold blood boiling, people need something to get the juices flowing, they *flow all over the map like spilled bedpans in a convalescent home staffed by over-worked Filipinos getting minimum wage, pretty kool, all in all, don't you think, especially like when you get to wear kool body paint and headdresses of the elite Jaguar Unit, plus getting sent to famous unusual sites of history called Stalingrad, or whatever. Cuz I heard that this place wuz going down in History. There we were! Well, we're not there yet. We're at some place called Krapsnoskoye, or Pitsnakeoilyaya. We're coming in for a landing. I'm kinda scared. But I'm real glad to be here. Cuz this is like where the Nazis are gonna meet their match. They been screwing up the world. Nobody has to put up with their Nazi Bullshit and let 'em get away with that. Count on us Aztex to fix things up! Lickety-split. Our Russian komrades seem to have been able to stop them at the Volga. It's up to us, the Aztex, the Mixteks, the Yanomamo, Warani and other indigenous allies of the Mexika to come in & prove to the Nazis that they just aren't as tough as they probably like to think! Those motherfuckers! Vandals. Soccer hooligans. I'm sure we're gonna win the honors that will be due to us becuz of our tuffness, our komradely leadership for the Russkies, our natural charisma under fire, & most of all, our sexiness on the field of battle. Which, cuz we're Aztex, Number One (after all) (the flower of our youth, scattered jade poesy of War, our metaphysikal feathered War kostumes, our interdimensional body paint, etc.), we are the epitome. We're gonna kill us some bad Nazis, come home with oodles of slaves to get rich, famous & be somebody! That's why I want to be a doktor. We are somebody! Keep hope alive! That's what the other dudes are talking about anyway, but I am doing it for my country & my party & for my mom. Cuz my mom said it would be a good thing, get a good job, go to medical school, become a doktor, etc. That's, you know, how come I feel so strongly about this deal. It's great to be here. Okay sometimes I have mixed feelings like anybody. Sometimes I feel confused. I don't care. Komrade Zenzontli wants me to write some stuff here. It's true that most of these ideas outlined here are my own paraphrase of things he said in his sleep. Okay. The plane is starting to go down now. I think we're going to land now. Or crash maybe. The ground is coming up mighty fast, the wings are shaking like they are about to fall off. It's impossible to hear anything cuz the noise is so loud. I'm scared I'm about to die. Just don't let me get shot in the throat, drowned & frozen to death. Anything but that. Anyway, hey, what's the chance of something like that happening? I better finish. I think I'm about done.*

6 00 carcasses rime with frost as they rode the conveyor in the chilling
room. Under refrigeration, each splayed, unquartered hog began glazing
over like the tiny window in the steel door. Max instructed me to stamp
each headless hunk on glistening muscle or exposed fat with the steel stamp,
leaving a blue USDA tattoo bleeding, mottled, in fatty tissue. It was like a
big staple gun. I tacked each hog a few times. They've all been cleared, Max
told me, as I peered at him suspiciously. This was the easiest job he'd given
me all week. Why go easy on me now? What was he hiding this time? I did
my job quickly, quietly and efficiently, if you can call singing "La Bamba" at
the top of my lungs till I was screaming it out hoarse as a goat, cabrón,
stamping my feet to ward off the chill, pressing the blue USDA circle deep
into the flesh, hardening as it cooled, an hour or so off the killing floor. I
started to sweat, which made it worse. I was freezing. Maybe that was Max's
hidden plan. Maybe if I got sick, sucking up my own snot here in the chilling room alone with 600 carcasses, a case of walking pneumonia, he'd get
me fired for contaminating the lot, $10,000 worth of meat! "Fuck you
Maxtla!" I screamed to the dead pigs hanging in an automated curtain of
flesh on all sides, "Yo no soy marinero, soy capitán!"

I could've sworn I saw someone watching me out of the corner of my
eye. I was leaning around the side of a carcass and suddenly I stopped doing
what I was doing and stood still, looking up and down the line. No way
somebody could duck out, instantly, like that, disappear behind the racked

hogs into the shadows! I don't think so, anyway. Max must be finally getting to me after all. I walked up the line, along the chilling room wall to
the door, glancing through the small window, expecting to see Max's grinning face pressed against the glass. You could see a bit of the empty corridor through the little window, that's all. Passing a break in the line, I leaned
my head around the other side of the chalky, roseate slabs which seemed to
be vibrating imperceptibly. Nobody was there. When the timer started the
conveyor, I jerked my head back, glancing up and down the line, peering
hard into the shadows, feeling like someone was watching and laughing.
There was nobody but nobody there, and I was so cold my fingers were
stiff and wouldn't bend right, shivering, and my nose was running.

On one level, I was standing on that frozen bit of tarmac with my Jaguar
Unit (plus the somewhat more robust, coordinated & threatening Eagle
Unit of Komrade Maxtla, Keeper of the House of Mist—a man with
grotesquely broad, massively muscled shoulders that made him seem as
wide as some short men were tall) waiting for the Russians, who themselves emerged as five distinct figures trudging toward us in their long coats
amidst the blowing ice crystals. *On one level* the airplane we'd flown in on
crouched above the parallel squads of men like a matched pair of Jaguar
Spirits, *heavily coiled & powerful*, but *on another level* the plane itself was an
empty, thin shell of a jerry-rigged sheet-metal contraption, severely out-
gunned by larger, faster German airships—it creaked and swayed slightly in
the howling wind. *On one level* everything in the material world is a
shadow, a physical shadow but nevertheless merely a shadow, of shifting
realities within the spiritual world. *On another level* our nahuales and our
spirits operate on various interconnected or disjointed swooping planes like
jungle animals moving soundlessly thru the roof canopy of trees insuring
that we are never alone, below, on the ground, in the struggle for existence.
(The Europians had some similar notion regarding this existential correla-
tion they called "angels"—but their pictures of these angels revealed their
conception to be farcical & sentimental, krucially flawed in poetik koncept
with chubby-cheeked saccharine cherubs wielding toy bows & arrows, and

pudgy, pasty Rubenesque full-figured women in flowing robes with pigeon wings attached to their shoulders—certainly pinkish whitebread entities such as those were entirely incapable of performing the necessary Organik maneuvers, machinations and transformations required by the teknospiritual complexities of the modern world.) It was precisely in our scientifikness that we Aztex were able to connect with the most teknocratikally advanced spiritual beings refracted in the multitudinous multivalent wheeling planes of the universe, both inside and outside of Time. And therefore we, the Azteks prevail all across this world and into the next, becuz it's not that we're "the chosen race" or any bullshit like that, it's just that fundamentally—where it counts—we're *better*. More completely developed, trained, tempered, hardened, sharpened. We invented the krucial teknological advances of Ritual Offering of the Heart During Human Sacrifice (a critical improvement over the ancient Toltek rituals involving mere slayings, torture & bloodbath of the kind you might find in the underdeveloped world, such as, say, in gloomy back rooms of stagnant Amerika, for example) plus our other Aztek teknospiritual innovations of which I assure you I shall inform you further. We, privileged citizens of Anahuak, the Aztek Socialist Imperium, are simply more advanced and more fully developed in all fundamental aspekts of the basik human personality as developed historikally over the course of Civilization(s). Plus we look too kool in our tattoos, feathers, lip and ear plugs and sunscreen war paint, so we leave the competition far behind. I mean who would you want on your side, the Amerikans or the Swedes, the Eskimos or the Kwakiutl? Or us? That's what I thot. It's no real contest.) *On one level* I was swaying in the freezing breeze in my clammy boots, *on another level* I was moving thru the rain forests of Anahuak in my heart. *On one level* we were preparing mentally or physically to go into battle with the legions of Nazi forces and fascist allies, the Romanian and Hungarian battalions, and *on another level* we had already won out against them, we didn't even have to worry about conquering the tedious and murderous German hordes, we'd shattered their broken, encircled 6th Army; we always had perservered triumphantly—we always would. We'd destroy our enemies forever and ever, forever and ever and on thru eternity till their defeat crumbled into nothingness inside every jagged ice crystal and snowflake that had blown across the Russian steppe that winter of 1942.

Komrade Captain Preobrazhenski was a man after my own heart. First he saluted, then I saluted, then he smiled and nodded, then I grinned and nodded, then he saluted the Keeper of the House of Mists, Maxtla, who smirked and nodded curtly, too Aztek to salute, presumably. Preobrazhenski (tall, round-faced man with moustache, goatee & eyeglasses) shook my hand, growling in Slavik Nahuatl, "On one level, I'm glad to see you, but on another level, to be frank, this international solidarity puts us in a bind: on one level, it shows up our anarchist inefficiencies on the battlefield—it aids the propaganda of the Black Hand and plays upon their ultranational-ist fantasies of greater Slavik pride; plus—on a whole other level, I tell you this man to man, komrade to komrade—we've heard strange and terrible stories about how the Aztex treat their prisoners, which I am hoping is total bullshit made up by the reactionary multinational fascist propaganda machines. *On one level* it might seem like Russian Social Anarchism under Generalissimo Makhno is being beaten to death in full retreat to the Urals and has showed itself to the world for the fatally flawed social system that it is, but *on another level* this strategic retreat is preparation for defeat of the fascist forces on a world scale. *On one level* Stalingrad is just some pointless industrial burg on an elbow of the Volga River, but *on another level* the fate of the war, the destinies of all nations and all civilization hinges upon our win or loss here. *On one level* the Germans have punished us so badly over the last year that they believe still that we are a stateless people in full rout, an army in name only, an undisciplined rabble of paramilitary partisans and irregular forces that their precision military machine is chewing up & spit-ting out like broken teeth. *On an entirely different level*," Preobrazhenski con-tinued, oblivious to the discomfort of all the men waiting in the biting wind, "*we're already dead*. The situation at Stalingrad is so bad, so intense, with millions of men having died to secure this currently unstable front line, that in some ways Russian Social Anarchism has been defeated, our cause lost somehow by the fact of our own moral confusion, spiritual ruination and heady embrace of Bolshevism's democratic centralism. On that level, any victory here will be so Pyrrhic as to constitute for the world the vindication of some other ideology and social system, which is why, on one level—komrade—I say I am not truly happy to see you here. You Aztek Socialists, I believe you are here to **win or die**." Preobrazhenski's glance was as sharp and dark as obsidian. "Okay!" I said, "All right! Look forward to working with you! This is a great place you got here. Is the weather always like this? Chilly!"

After working all night under fluorescent tubes that cast a cold pallor over everything, giving the whole interior of the meat packing plant a submerged submarine cast after awhile, then you were outside in real sunshine, blinking. The difference was slightly nauseating. The sunlight seemed at once to be fresh and hard and also to have a palpable grit to it, distinct features of reality evidencing a hard, discernible edge. Automobiles moved through the sunlight like insects warming up into motion. When you weren't blinded by the light, objects seem to have a greenish sheen at their edge like some effect of bad cinematography. But even if you put your hand up quickly to shield your eyes, there was a definite glare, pixilated spots refracting off the chrome of parked cars, imprinting sunspots on your field of vision. The cloudy motion of cars in traffic thru all the sudden shine, things happening along your peripheral vision, left an impression of vibrant absence or erasure. In the endless L.A. sunlight, I sensed a force that would sooner or later obliterate us all. "Well, fuck me," I could have sworn 3 Turkey said, but it was Cuzatli. I looked up and down the sidewalk at people walking thru the daylight as if it were nothing.

Nekok Yaotl, Enemy on Both Sides.

Telpochtli, Young Man.

I slipped her message across the table with the tips of my fingers. After leaving work I'd reread the note slipped into my locker. It was written on the back of a green leaflet, the reverse of which announced a housing rights march and rally in Leimert Park. As I approached the sandwich place indicated in the note, Legaspi's Deli, I saw that it was open to the street with its green awning hanging over the sidewalk, and in spite of deliberately thinking about other things (I think someone is on fire) I grew tense—my heart pounded like a rock drummer let loose on his favorite solo, coked to the gills. I stood in the glare of sunshine, glancing into the back of the sandwich place. Two long delicatessen cases full of the usual pasta salads, cheese blocks, rounds, sausages and sandwich makings, big bottles of pigs feet & huge dill pickles perched next to the cash register, flies buzzing around in the coolness of shady middle distance. As my eyes adjusted to the dimness of the interior, I noticed two things at once, the sign saying COFFEE 10 CENTS, and that long drink of water, Nita the union organizer, sitting at a table with her legs crossed, head cocked at an angle, watching me thru her sunglasses, smoking a cigarette. This woman was so beautiful I had to caution myself, *cut that shit out! Stop dreaming about her with your eyes open.* My heart began pounding like a piledriver, like a jackhammer, like the coal-fired engines of an ocean liner. *Nita.* I could feel the white flags snapping in the sea breeze, I could smell the ocean at Santa Monica (thirty miles inland from the beach, I began to feel the sea breeze), I could feel the earth move, the waves arriving off the sea. It took me a second, staring at her, before I could move. *All right.* If she was going to be cool, if she was just going to sit there, lean forward, drink coffee from a paper cup, look up and nod at me, two could play at that game. I dropped into the seat across from her and slid the note across the table ("Meet me at Legaspi's after work. It's important that we talk."). "What's all this secrecy bullshit, Nita? Why have you been keeping me in the dark all this time? You don't know what I've been going thru," I said, leaning forward. She stiffened, as if I'd poked her with my finger, blowing smoke out of the side of her mouth. I'd never seen her do that before! When had she taken up the tobako habit? Kaffeine, too! My goodness, what was next? Tattoos, bellydancing, sex fetishes, gourmet dining, Saturday night bingo? "Give me a darned kiss," I growled, "I thot you were dead! Huitzilopochtli! You don't know what I've been thru in the past few weeks! Nightmares, tooth decay, moral rot, bad ideas, failure of nerve, I thot I was cashiered irredeemably in my soul, Nita, facing lots of criticism on the job and the disdain of social superiors, our entire life—culture—call it what you will!—wiped off the map, a scene of real problems and certain difficulty, I don't have to tell you." "What the hell are you talking about?" Nita frowned. I could tell she actually didn't understand my jabbering. What else was new? Half the time nobody understood what I was talking about, they only put up with me because of my winning personality, my Good Looks, a Degree of Charm. I couldn't see her eyes behind her dark green shades. I leaned closer, brought my voice down a notch. "I've been going nuts. You can't imagine. Between real visions and fake insights, between fake visions and real delusions, I can't tell what time it is, whether the big hand is on the three or the little hand is on the six, or the little hand is on the three or the big hand is on the six. Why didn't you get a message to me?" "I still don't know what you're talking about. They told me you were a hard case, but they didn't say anything about you being flat-out crazy." "So that's the way you're gonna play it," I nodded. I leaned back to scratch my head, "What do you mean, you don't know what I'm talking about. Come here and give me a kiss." "I didn't ask you here for anything like that," Nita said coldly, indicating that she was, indeed, knowledgeable about my various behaviors and furthermore, typical of the woman, she didn't give an owl's hoot in hell whether or not my various peccadilloes, permutations and perpetrations were carried out under extreme hardship or not. She didn't give a Shit what I had been going thru (to be fair, there was no way that I could know what had been happening to her either, of course, though I did want to know). Nita had always acted as if my state of mind was not now, nor had it ever been any of her concern. As usual, she was all Bizness. As always, she had her agenda and she wasn't about to let anything come between her and her Objectives. She didn't give a shit about anything Else. Huitzilipochtli! All she wanted to know was would I hold up my end of the deal or not? As usual, I was somewhat slow on the uptake, not knowing what exactly she wanted now any more than I had at any point in the past. She addressed me coldly, to indicate that she was taking neither excuses nor any funny stuff at this point. When Nita was like this, there was little more to do than try to obey her instructions to the letter and find out what she really wanted afterwards. I did wish that I understood exactly what point in time this was, but I was unclear on that for the moment—at least I hoped it was for the moment, though I would have admitted, if pressed, that this lack of clarity regarding certain linear conventions or color-coded notions as to the timelines of history, chronology, numerology, arithmetic, psychology (& butterfly collecting) were simply beyond me on a Regular Basis. I had only been a C student at best, after all. I owed my success in life to hanging out with sharper minds like this Representative of Teamsters, Boilermakers, Wichita Linemen & Derby Hatted Officers. Now that Nita had reappeared, things were looking up, I was quite certain. I was back in the saddle again! Glancing out into the sunbleached street, I was sure that—meat trucks and traffic whizzing by, a white stepvan pulling up to the curb & a milkman unhooking his dolly from the back—it was December, or thereabouts, 1942, and I—we—happened to be stuck in some godforsaken burg, backwater, some 3rd-class city called Los Angeles, someplace to the north. Kalifornia or some fucking thing, Western civilization, the New World, they called it. Amerika, Golden Gate Bridge, Disneyland, Chinatown, beaches, suntan lotion. Peaches, lettuce. Palm trees, gambling ships anchored offshore beyond the 3-mile line. Locally, I was given to understand, they grew oranges, cantaloupes, made movies & airplanes, welcomed bogus & feeble-minded quasi-religious cults like Aimee Simple McPerson that couldn't get a foot hold in someplace more sensible like Chicago, New York or Teknotitlán. Celebrities like Bugsy Seigel called it home, thanks to friends in the mayor's office. Japs had been carted off to concentration camps out in the desert, which was too bad, cuz I could have used some raw fish and tofu right about that time, wasabi horse radish on my sashimi, tempura and curry over rice, chop chop. I was working up an appetite of one kind or another sitting across the table from that sharp representative of the working classes for the first time in who knows how long. I jumped out of my chair, rushed over to the counter and plopped a dime down on the glass countertop. Damn, I felt agitated and senseless. First time I had seen Nita in weeks, after all my recent troubles at work, and here she was treating me as if she didn't know me! She didn't know what was going thru my head; she didn't know what I was feeling (neither did I, of course, but it was causing me to tremble and shake). I didn't deserve this, it seemed to me, even tho it felt perfectly normal given everything that had been happening lately (it's true, any number of bizarre or uncontrollable emotions, spiritual visions, ideological eruptions burst inside me on a daily basis, so what?). The nice white man behind the counter, with perspiration on his upper lip and temples, his moist skin pink and soft enough to fall off his bones like the pigs feet in the jar next to his head, wiped his hands on his apron and placed a cup of coffee on the counter for me. I licked my lips, nodded and he nodded back, his eyes washed out, bluish and tired. Limp strands of hair swerved toward his concentrated forehead; I heard the sound of fat sizzling, skin popping and cracking as a spitted carcass turned over a bed of coals. Luau, the Hawaiians called it. I sipped the hot coffee, grimacing, as I leaned against the glass case with my elbows on the counter and contemplated the CIO maid from a bit of distance, her black hair permed in curls that spread across the broad shoulders of her lab coat. What was I gonna do now? I had to play it cool. I had to act normal. I had to quell the shaking in my hands and trembling in my knees. I was shaking so badly that I had to set the coffee on the counter, hold myself as if from a sudden chill. I admit, I had been remiss in the way I had lived my life lately, in the way I had conducted myself in both private and public, I was unworthy, I would be the first to admit. I grabbed the paper cup, splashing my fingers as I swilled hot coffee, burning my mouth. Nita glanced casually back toward me. I forced myself to put one foot in front of another, staggering back toward the table. My nerves were screaming, I was experiencing fierce muscle spasms of some kind. *Nita, please give me some sign that everything's going to be okay.* I was worried. Nita seemed upset by something herself. She smoked nervously, pensively staring out at the street; pursing her lips as she blew smoke out the side of her mouth. She snatched up the leaflet on the table before her ("Stop the Bombings of Our Negro Neighbors!"), turned it over, looked at it and tossed it aside. She was frowning as I sat back down at the table. I felt like a man on fire as I looked at her and she considered me impassively from behind those sunglasses that gave me the sudden impulse to reach across the table and rip them off her face. I resisted that impulse, trembling the more for it, trying to get a grip on myself. I sneezed mightily, grabbed a napkin and blew my nose for all it was worth.

I don't know what Nita thot I was doing, leaking snot at the table beside her. I sniffed, slobbered, wiped the fluids off my face with a thin paper napkin crumpled in the palm of my hand. "Sorry, sorry," I apologized. "Bad days at the pork packing plant. Haven't been feeling myself. Been sick. Been under the weather." She rubbed her own forehead as if she was in some tight circumstances herself, stubbed her cigarette butt out and sighed, "Sorry to hear that," in a tone resolutely lacking all sympathy, "My problem is they've been telling me that you're key to an organizing project at the plant. They tell me you're the most influential man among the new guys who've just signed on across the street, especially on the night shift. You could be key. I don't have time to go into how crucial it is to the whole industrial sector of the city at this time. I was really hoping you'd be able to help us." "Us?" I said. She snapped open a small coin purse, removed a card and handed it to me: '*Nita Yahui*, Field Representative, International Brotherhood of Meat Cutters, Packers, Popeyes & 3-Fingered Teamsters, CIO. 2-6345' "Keep it," she said. Then she added, reluctantly, "I don't know tho, maybe you're not up to it." Again, she rubbed her forehead, thinking. "The bosses got new legislation, becuz of the war effort, you know. They're holding even more cards than usual. It ain't gonna be easy. Maybe you have too many other, uh, things on your mind. Like I say, maybe you ain't feeling up to . . ." I held up my hand, suddenly, clenching my muscles against the paroxysms flashing thru me, "Whatever it is, you can count on me. I'm your man." Nita regarded me evenly. "You sure?" she asked, "Lemme warn you, there's forces out there against us who want this to fail in a big way. Trotskyites, anarchists, bosses' lackeys, race baiters, opportunists in our own party, gold brickers, religious fundamentalists, Santería priests, voodoo ekonomists, they're all hoping that the union is broken, that anyone who works with us, and me in particular, gets accused of spurious infractions, placed on ultrahazardous duty, goaded and pushed to the limit of exhaustion so he falls into his meat saw, is sliced to ribbons in the bologna. Then he'll get fired for substandard productivity. You up to that pressure?" I hoped that she didn't see me trembling. "Are you kidding?" I attempted a smile, "I'm your man." Suddenly she sat up bolt upright. "Oh my God!" she cried. I turned and followed her gaze into the street. Some guy was running down the middle of the street, smoke coming out of his hair and clothes; he was on fire. "He's on fire!" Nita blurted. "Yep, I thot there was someone on fire," I nodded. Then I shook my head. "But I don't know that guy, I swear. Never saw him before," I said. "No friend of mine would go around like that. He looks like a loser and a big fuck-up to me." There was a popping sound as if a couple firecrackers had gone off down the street. "Oh no! The police are shooting at him now!" Nita gasped, pushing back her chair. The man on fire grabbed his leg, fell to the street, rolling and tumbling. He dragged himself between two parked cars, struggled to his feet and limped up the steps, fast as a wounded man could go, to an apartment building. We heard sirens. Nita turned to me, her face a mask of concern. I jerked my thumb in the direction of the guy who had just disappeared. "Really, I'm tellin' you. A loser. That guy and me got nothing in common," I assured her. "You got me on your side you don't gotta worry about nothing like that. Count on it. You need to organize the plant. Fine. You got me," I nodded. A cop car screeched to a halt across the street in front of us, red light redundantly flashing. Two cops jumped out, guns in hand, and ran up the walkway to the porch of the apartment building. Nita raised her eyebrows at me. I nodded expectantly, smiling as I held out my hand. My nose was running again.

5

I SNAPPED my fingers. It came to me (*What?* I'm, like, a genius! How do I do it?), I knew exactly what I had to do to ensure enough signatures for the union ratification vote to take place according to rules of law of the National Labor Relations Board as promulgated by President Roosevelt in the year Zippity-doo-dah. Thru strange coincidence, I'd found a job myself at the same locale, Farmer John's Meat Company, along with my so-called friends, 3 Turkey, Ray, Nakatl, Pirate, Weasel, and also a few miscellaneous enemies. How were we to know they hired illegal Mexikans by the truck-load to run the meat processing & packing industry for the entire city, the entire southland region? The whole ekonomy was built upon the backs of our people, so-called illegals. Lucky for us. We just took our feathers off, shoved them in the pockets of our swapmeet jeans, swabbed our garish paint off our war faces into a borrowed used snot rag, tied our hair back like lokos from who knows where in our stolen Mongol motorcycle gang jackets, brandishing our tattoos as we filled out the job applications in hieroglyphik Nahua script, never got our paychecks to no avail, needed a vacation all those years, supported the Social Security System with our taxes & our labor, we did what we could. I noticed a bunch of guys from the Unit sitting around the personnel office at the plant pretending they didn't know each other, glancing warily at each other but too shy to admit none of us could write any English. It didn't matter. Slicing meat was right up our alley. Meat, flesh & blood, guts, menudo, gristle, chicharrones, neck bones, feet, tripe, puddled intestines, brains, carcasses split open & hanging upside down from hooks, strings of blood swaying like a beaded curtain across a doorway, fluids hosed down a steel drain, heads with the eyes removed, or sometimes not, sclerotic in a pile, floppy ears, tails, snouts, skin, yellow blubber, pieces of gray meat cleaned out of the machinery & off the floor—all processed into Farmer John wieners. 100% beef except for the pork. We were right at home. That is to say, I mean, *in the continuum of time* I emerge thru the steam. I push a dolly, a cart. Rubber wheels on a concrete floor. Steam wells up around me. The steam always wells up from the ground like lowland fog. Ferns, broad green elephant ear plants outlined by mist. I trudge thru the ground fog in the rubble of Stalingrad breathing out fog myself. Strapped across my back, a bag, a submachinegun? Chasing Nazi ghosts into the mists of history? I better hustle. I turn the corner of the meat packing plant. Garish fluorescent light glares on the yellow enamel cinderblock hallway and the concrete floor. That always happens. The sound of wind rushing through the canopy hundreds of feet overhead, the stillness of the shadows on the rainforest floor. A window left open, a brown leaf flattened on the floor in front of the urinals. A big steel tub of guts, tubal entrails looping & snaking like white PVC hose thru the pinkish water. I'm forever finding myself sitting on the forklift, staring down at . . . whatever it is . . . a pallet of breakfast sausage. . . . The wind rushing through the canopy, a bird flying, crying as if lost. The wide river delta, an estuary opening out to the sea below the mouth of the river. Sometimes I don't know exactly where I am, which way next. Then, a tapping noise against the sheet-metal door of the walk-in freezer. Someone wants in. Something rattles like a machine gun blocks away in Stalingrad. Burnt out blocks of tenement apartments emerge thru the smoke, empty windows against the pall. It will continue happening. The world goes on & on. "Reality is infinite," says the Farmer John toilet stall door graffiti scratched in at eye level. "Shit is infinite," someone scratched below that. Stalingrad or East Los, our homeland, the sea, our world. It will never stop. I'm thinking that, later, too (or earlier), staring at the lettering on the freezer carton, "Farmer John's Finest Pork Sausage," the logo with the smiling farmer. Wasn't this part of what I glimpsed one day, shuddering out of a nightmare vision, thinking about something else entirely, walking along my garden path, with a splitting headache? But when had that ever happened? I could no longer recall exactly when it began. But I knew that it would never end.

Meat smacking the cement floor.

Water splashing on stones.

Darkness.

Amoxhuah, kneeling in the prow of the vessel, turned to watch the boats following us out across the river, like big black birds gliding across the flickering water. The oars moved soundlessly for the most part, synchronized, flashing. We were nearly across, and Amoxhuah grinned at me, gave me the thumbs up. I nodded and then his neck burst open with a thwack, face falling & neck broke, Amoxhuah took a slow tumble into the water. The sharp crack of a distant rifle came from somewhere. Everybody started rowing faster all of a sudden. They were splashing now & not at all quiet about it. More pops, as guys fell out of the boats behind us. I leaned over the edge of the boat and grabbed at Amoxhuah's cape like a bubble on the water, as the warrior beside me lifted his oar out of my way. The warrior jerked backwards as his head exploded, spewing bone and tissue. He fell back in the stern as I leaned back, pulling at Amoxhuah's cape. It was sodden and heavy as I pulled it hand over hand, then suddenly it was lighter. I had pulled enuf of the sodden cape out of the water to know he'd rolled out of it. The current had sucked him underneath the boat. I'd lost him. I tossed the cape aside and lurched to the stern, gripping the gunnel and leaning over the water, but I could see nothing. The glinting black water did not even seem reflective. It roiled with current but Amoxhuah did not resurface. *Huitzilopochtli sighed, "The electron is as **inexhaustible** as the atom, nature is infinite, but it infinitely **exists**." (Lenin,* Materialism & Empirio-Criticism, *page 314)*

Someone else was hit and bellowed with pain. As soon as the boat scud-
ded into the shallows, we were off and running.

The crack of a rifle drifted off above my head like the snap of a broken
stick. I heard the sniper's rifle snap two more times, a high dry crackling. I
instructed my squad to fan out, secure the beachhead, don't fuck around,
you bastards. The squad saw somebody coming toward us & put him down
with a couple volleys. I ran cursing along the foot of the bluff looking for
a ravine, a tunnel, a trench, a rope, a pipe, footholds scraped out of the dirt.
At the entrance to a ravine, a Russian was lying on his back. He looked
very surprised against the snow. I knelt beside him, but he couldn't speak.
He looked at me, opening his mouth, blood dripping off of his chin.
"Sorry," I said, leaving him, as I sprinted up the well-worn path into the
ravine, fortified with timbers on both sides. My heart was thumping, my
saliva tasted like blood, the long heavy Mauser swung around in front of my
legs and banged against my thighs. I shrugged it off, let it clatter to the
ground and sprinted up the pathway, jumping the foul-smelling sewage
running in a ditch in the bottom, trickling out of yawning dark tunnels
angling off into the hillside. I sprinted up the switchbacks of frozen mud
reinforced with scraps of wood, past small lean-to shelters where a couple
of exhausted Russian soldiers barely noticed me as I went rushing by. Then
over the top: I scrambled on hands and knees over the rise to scan the
uneven terrain of riverfront bluffs. I couldn't see much of anything. Wispy
clouds of black smoke drifted out of Stalingrad over the Volga, the pall in
the air catching like hair at the back of my throat. The moon had dropped
low, its last light flickered on the stony ground in white patches like
windswept snow. Ravines or gullies looked like holes of shadow where the
blackness of night shone thru the punished, torn earthworks. I guesstimated
the necessary trajectory of the shots, then ran off on a ragged semicircle
counter-clockwise. Some Russian from a position behind me fired a burst
from his machine gun my way, I heard the rounds buzz by like bees making my ears turn red in the chilly weather, but I couldn't see the lay of the
ground, I tripped and fell headlong into a hole. Rolling and sliding down

the scrabbly slope, I fetched up against a body. Or most of a body. Some dead guy was busy stinking up his hole, he had his arms at his sides, he wasn't keeping anything to himself, his soul alone on a barque traveling the water routes and jungle estuaries leading thru the past, into the underworld. I scrambled up out of the hole, left him to his night's business. I repeated an Aztek catechism to myself, in the voice of Huitzilopochtli, "*. . . for every materialist, the laws of thot have not merely a subjective significance; in other words, the laws of thot reflect the forms of actual existence of objects, fully resemble, & do not differ from, these forms.*" (*Lenin,* Materialism & Empirio-Criticism, *page 438*). I reached a high point where the splintered remains of a blackened and blasted shed swayed jaggedly in the billowing smoke. I krouched below it amid bits of wooden debris and peered thru the visible air. The dark breeze blew vagaries of chill thru my damp feathered kape. Against a partially revealed slope of snowbank below, I thought I saw a figure detach from one black shape, attach itself to another. It amounted to the flicker of a shadow in the blowing smoke. It might have just been the movement of my eye, some effect of blurred vision. It might have been nothing. *Ketzalkoatl was murmuring, "In its mystified form, the dialectik became the fashion in Germany, becuz it seemed to transfigure and to glorify the existing state of things. In its rational form it is a scandal and abomination to bourgeoisdom and its doctrinaire professors, becuz it includes in its comprehension and affirmative recognition of the existing state of things, at the same time also, the recognition of the negation of that state, of its inevitable breaking up; becuz it regards every historically developed social form as in fluid movement, & therefore takes into account its transient nature not less than its momentary existence; becuz it lets nothing impose upon it . . ."* (*Marx,* Capital, *Volume 1, page 20*). The railway had run along the river, thru the factory district, the warehouses that were piles of brick and tangled rubble now. I thot the sniper would transect between the smashed warehouses along the line of the tracks, keeping the hulking ruins between himself and the river. He could have fled south, past the train station, across the boulevards south of Red Square (in front of the train station, concrete children held hands and danced around a concrete crocodile as the buildings of the square burned day and night), but he didn't (I was glad), or he could have dropped into the Tsaritsa ravine and taken it back into his own lines (but maybe that was too risky, some sentry in his own lines might've fired on him, or the terrain was too rough, maybe), instead the sniper was heading due west—the most direct route thru the empty expanse of railyard switching lanes—when I spotted him. He jogged casually, carrying the long rifle like a fishing pole. If he spotted me, he'd veer off in some other direction, disappear into the tunnels, sewers and cellars of the ruined city. I sprinted back in a wide arc so I was out somewhere in front of him. I moved from object to object, from blasted foundation to pile of debris to blackened twisted wreckage. I lay on my belly beneath the wheel carriage of a burnt-out boxcar to study his figure at a distance. He was still too far off to see his face. He wore a soft cap and carried a long rifle almost as tall as he was. He glanced back over his shoulder every now and then. As he approached, I moved back out of sight. I crouched behind the big steel wheels, listening for him. I expected him to alter his route soon; he wouldn't run straight into the city, he'd look for more cover. Two burnt-out boxcars provided some cover from any pursuit from the direction of the river. I stayed out of sight behind one of them; I was unarmed becuz I had thrown away the stupid Mauser. I looked about and found a heavy length of pipe, bent and rusty with a solid knob of extruded rust at one end. Then I crouched till his footfalls announced his arrival. His footsteps pattered, regular; I listened to them, I sung them inside me, the rhythm of each successive crunch in the snow. Quickly, my footsteps fell in place exactly within his own, moving at the exact same pace, so when I appeared from around the boxcar crouched low he must've thot it was some animal flushed out of a hole, a shadow, he was so surprised, his eyes widened, his light eyelashes fluttered, his mouth made a little O, he was a tough little man with close shaven hair graying at the temples, steel gray eyes that seemed not to be able to fix upon me as he lifted the long rifle with its large sniperscope, I stepped directly into his path as he came up short, startled, but out of breath (I must have appeared before him as suddenly as a reflection in a mirror); I locked my gaze on his. I looked deep into his cold gray eyes as I raised my left hand, palm-forward, fingers open. He jumped back a step, shifted the rifle, inserted his hand into the trigger guard and raised the barrel toward my face. I leaped forward over the barrel and brought the rusty pipe down hard onto his square little head, knocking aside that prim felt cap from his brow with a blow that dropped him like a sack of potatoes. He wasn't done yet. He groaned angrily and tried to turn over. I bent over and hit the back of his skull, hard.

He was light weight, the sniper. I trotted back to the river with him over my shoulder, his long rifle in one hand. Thru the blowing smoke, I felt as protective of him as a child as he slept. That was the main difference between our allies and ourselves. The Russians went about rabidly slaughtering Nazis every chance they could. They were suicidal in their urgency to rid Mother Russia of the hated invaders. We Azteks wanted our opponents alive. We didn't get such prime specimens every day. These Germans were kultured, cultivated, highly educated, terrifikally civilized and philosophized, they had a reputation for great efficiency, an obvious talent for scientifik teknology, evidenced fine athletic ability and a tremendous sense of graphic design, I could go on & on, we Azteks had simply never encountered better stock for our purposes. The little man's head bouncing against my back gave me a thrill of happiness as I threaded my way thru the partial cover of the shattered railyard. He was to be the first of hundreds and thousands, if I had my way.

Once, I had to duck Russian fire as I entered Russian lines, accidently dropping the little sniper against a pile of bricks. He groaned softly without regaining consciousness, blood crusting about his nostril and the corner of his mouth. I looked at him fondly, straightening his collar with the cute Nazi insignia.

As I expected, the guys back at the front were mighty pissed off and discontented. Maxtla, Keeper of the House of Mist and the Russian liaison officer Preobranzhenski had deployed our men along a series of fortified trenchworks along the bluff, not far from the blasted shed that was the high point; it would have been a good lookout position to direct attacks on the railyard had it not been open and exposed to enemy fire, mortars especially. It was supposed to be a temporary position. We weren't supposed to have to hold it for any length of time. We were supposed to go on the offensive soon. Preobranzhenski later said it was astonishing that I crossed that slope without being blasted by mortar fire, especially on a moonlit night such as this. I told him that I had a reputation for being lucky; I didn't bother to go into purported cloaking abilities lent to the tutored Aztek warrior by spirit forces such as the Olmek jaguar of our dreams. I had no time. I could see disgruntlement clouding the faces of my men. They looked doubtful and worried when I dropped the little sniper at their feet. A sergeant, it turned out. He didn't look like much, sprawled senseless on the ground. (He did not look like the cusp of Teutonik civilization, Klassic Meso-europian Kulture of the 20th Century, but I was thrilled with expectation, myself. I knelt and rifled his pockets, relishing the little artifacts of the Reich, the little insignias and trifles, a couple scraps of identification in Deutsche, little gold cross on a chain around his neck, exotic personal effects such as small tool kit with nostril hair tweezers, etc., *Swiss wristwatch*, etc.) I could hear the Azteks grumbling soundlessly—Nahuatl makes a loud grumbling in small minds—about the four men we'd just lost cross-ing the Volga. We had not even entered Stalingrad and we'd suffered losses already. It was about to become a cloudy, freezing morning and the men were feeling sorry for themselves. Such a thing, especially with me in kom-mand of the first squad (we only lost four men! only one badly wounded!) boded ill, was a bad omen, gave them a bad taste in their mouths, the ingrates. They stared, sullen. My attitude was, GET OVER IT! So I ges-tured at the figure on the ground and stood, gesticulating as I pronounced a speech to cheer them up. I don't recall exactly what I said.

I nodded to Nita and I told her exactly what I thot, deleting 98%, leav-ing out the parts about weird stuff happening inside the slaughterhouse on a daily basis, like the time after hosing down the kill floor with Nakatl, 3Turkey & Ray (with the air-conditioned air blown in at a chilly 50 degrees, the water from the high-pressure hoses condensed in the air as mist, rising from the pools on the concrete floor as if it was hot steam), I could've sworn I saw animal tracks leading to the knife rack across the floor then out a side door—they looked like tiny human footprints or *monkey* tracks across the floor. Things I couldn't account for or explain (plus why did I have to think about them if everybody else just takes all these circumstances, facts of life, and unusual feelings for granted). Basically I said, "You communists have this industrial sector organizing drive, I'm sure I'll hear all about for hours in some meeting in a musty room somewhere, meanwhile let me assure you I have the plant sewed up as far as the petition drive goes, as far as a union ratification vote goes we'll mobilize a majority of these irritable feisty proletarians to do some good on their own behalf, on behalf of the City of Vernon, and on behalf of their moms." I don't know if I was supposed to add, "on behalf of world revolution, on behalf of democratik centralism" but she got my drift anyway, she nodded peremptorily, blew smoke jagged from the side of her mouth and gave me the hint of a fake smile; pleased by this, I wadded up a mess of sopping paper napkins and put them in my pocket. "You'll find that there will be significant benefits to our backing," she went on, the breeze blowing hair across her cheek, which I thought was particularly charming in a windswept outdoorsy way, the same breeze whipping the cigarette smoke out of her mouth, adroitly as you please. "What kind of timeline are we looking at on this ratification vote procedure activity thing, if I may ask?" I asked. "You may," Nita said, "We're looking at between January 7 and 26th, which gives us at least, oh I'd say a couple weeks. Why, is that an issue?" "No, no," I said, "I'm used to working with either a slim margin or none. I'm good to go." "Good. I'll get you the petition materials right away," she said, staring at my hands apprehensively as we simultaneously rose from our seats and I stuck my hand out to her. She pinched my finger with her thumb and forefinger and gave it a little shake. "I'll be in touch soon," she said, taking a step back. "Yes," I said.

So it was I started sneaking around the different buildings, the kill house and smokehouse, the warehouse and the stock pens, at all hours, on both shifts I was in the plant, disseminating cards, CIO leaflets, signing everybody up on NLRB petitions. You know when I get into something like that I can approach almost anybody and talk to all kinds of people I might not otherwise have anything to do with. I'm sure I used it as a pretext to chat up the pert front office secretaries; I'm sure it was getting back to Max, Handler and Auerbach and whoever else just exactly what it was I was doing. But it didn't matter to me, what were they going to do to me they hadn't tried already? Besides, time was short and if it all worked out, the vote would be scheduled before they had a chance to do anything. Sure, Max started acting even stranger than ever, as if I'd personally turned his baby sister loose on the worst relationship she ever experienced, then she went & committed suicide in a lonely room, how can you argue with someone with a snappy attitude like that? *Besides freezing my ass off, I got the same headache I get all the time. I didn't know what this headache was from, but it was having some disturbing effekts, like I was stamping my feet against the concrete floor, my teeth aching and my breath coming out in feathery plumes, I was shivering badly and screaming out made-up verses to my personal version of "La Bamba" ("Para bailar la bamba, you be jammin' en la samba! You'll get yer ass up in a jamba! P-p-p-p-p-pa' bailar la bamba!" etc.) and tacking the blue USDA label on hundreds of flank cuts, babyback ribs, crown and rump roasts, tenderloin cutlets and loin chops along a line of tons of hanging pork, below which I shivered and sneezed, sweating and frozen at the same time I wuz singing and stamping in some kind of desperation, trying to figure out some way to get thru all this, some way to endure whatever this is (this headache, this moment, this Life), and get away—in my mind I am leaning my forehead against the freezing cinderblocks of the corridor wall outside, causing the sweat to freeze against my skin, burning as it cools, frosting up my eyebrows & my whiskers, dreaming ahead to when I was finished with this shitty job, done, taking a breather, breathing hard and trying to soak a little warmth back into my bones. In my mind somehow I am already done with this job. In my mind I am somewhere else. Other worlds exist.* I skipped over to the tiny window in the chilling room, and peeked out. Corridor, vague thru the frost. I tossed the stamp up on a slab of pork and scooted out the door, ran headlong, clattering down the steel stairs, stopping short at the door in the bottom of the stairwell. I eased it open, peeking out across the yard, illuminated in wide swaths by spotlights and in other areas shrouded in pitch black shadows darker even than the night sky overhead, its stars erased by the pall of street lamps and vague fumes or striations. I adjusted my long white labcoat and wiped the snot on my sleeve and ducked out the door, making nonchalantly for the nearest shadow. I made my way thru the pens, some full of stoats, some with a couple downers — the pigs who came in too sick or injured to walk, broken legs or busted spines, crushed in transit by steel doors — or massive hogs, leaning unsteadily in their own blood or waste, or lying in it, squealing weakly at intervals. I made my way to the far side, signing up a couple of the maintenance workers, guys who hauled the downers to the rendering dock, cleaned out the dirty pens and threw dry straw on the floor of empties. Then I followed the chute from the pen area to the kill floor, pushing my way past the pigs down the ramp onto the floor, hitting the emergency shut-off switch to make my point. The men turned with careful deliberation, razor-sharp knives & serrated saws at the ready, steam wafting about them as if emitted from their own hearts. "You know why I'm here!" I called out when they turned around to see who had shut them down. Blood ran from their black aprons, it dripped from their goggles down the sides of their mouths and from their chins. They were getting used to the pause, catching their breath, laying off for the moment, even as something itched inside them to get back to work. "I been standing toe to toe with the foreman and management for you," I said. "I been taking double shifts so you wouldn't have to. You know that's how it's been. That's why you're gonna sign this petition to vote the union in here. And if the union don't get voted in here, you won't have to worry about it, or me, either." So they all signed. Maybe 3 Turkey or Pirate had been talking to them, too. But I knew they'd all heard, and some had no doubt seen Max's tricks, plus the other thievery against the working man that was always going on. It was enuf. The clipboard was smudged and bloody when it came back to me but I waved it over my head, said, "I thank you, gentlemen!" and flipped the kill switch back on. I rushed out of there, running back across the yard, taking the steel steps three at a time, trying to control my breathing as I dashed down the corridor back into the chill room, which was, apart from the pork having conveyed farther up the line unstamped, silently the same. I glanced around for any sign that Max may have been by, checking up, and was immediately hit by a sneezing fit, all the warmth accumulated in a few minutes in the night outside vanishing from my lab coat as fast as if I had zipped it open and flapped it back and forth to rid myself of heat. Wiping my nose on my sleeve (clipboard hidden under one arm under the white coat), I hit the last unstamped hog with my shoulder like a tackle at football practice, and the metal stamp fell with a clatter onto the concrete floor. I was furiously stamping dozens and dozens of hogs, trying to catch up to where the line had left me behind, when I felt a funny unease like an itch, and since I'd worked my way back by the steel door with its little window, I stepped over and peered thru it. Max glared at me from the other side of the frosted glass, malevolent eyes widening darkly as I brought my face to within an inch or two of my side of it. For a heartbeat, my face reflected over his like a photographic double exposure. Then his face vanished from the little window, and by the time I opened the steel door and peered outside, he'd sauntered down to the bend in the corridor and turned the corner.

Later, which is to say earlier, toward morning I mean, as I was hurrying thru the refrigerated rooms of the warehouse, the barrels of pork intestine on pallets waiting to be loaded on trucks to be taken to the sausage factories, I rushed past the big steel tubs on wheels that were used to carry out the meat byproducts off the disassembly line for sorting, and I thought I saw something that I immediately dismissed because it had to be wrong. At the time I was too rushed, too exhausted and too busy, heedless, to care about it, especially since I figured it was just some mistake on my part, just some trick of the light as I pushed one of the tubs back into line with a bang against the wall, the distortion of bad fluorescent lighting on a pool of bloody water rippling in the stainless steel tub full of intestinal tubing and meat scraps. I went and got the signatures of the warehouse workers, except for one who was hiding from me (at least that's what I thought, *pinche chicken — you can't get away from me that easy* —intending to return later for him), and hurried back to my post via another route, to avoid getting caught out of my area. But it came back to me later when I woke up at home, late in the day with the sun hot against the curtains and the air stuffy and dry in the room. I thought to myself, *you know that ain't right. It can't be. It looked like a face, a human face—eyeless mask of a skinned face floating underwater, terrible white bloodless skin wrinkled by the pink bloody water as the water moved, but it had to have been a pig's head, maybe a small pig's head. Maybe just a bit of torn pig skin that looked like a face, something one of the guys made out of a scrap of pig skin. Stupid. Why see the eyeless thing floating in bloody pink light when I wake up?*

Kapitan Preobrazhenski escorted Komrade Maxtla and myself into a dugout in the earthworks where we were provided a nice hot cup of coffee. I burnt my mouth gulping it out of the tin cup, I didn't know I was so thirsty. Preobrazhenski unfolded a map on a rickety card table to brief us on current enemy lines, positions, artillery range and capability, air-cover situation (not in Russian favor), etc., while I nodded thotfully and wondered how long it would be before I'd be able to taste things with my scalded tongue. As soon as Preobrazhenski was called to the field phone to report on our arrival, arranging respectfully for our remaining Aztek dead on the bank of the Volga to be removed to the airfield, etc., ("maybe the other bodies will surface in the river before spring & we can recover them," etc.), Komrade Maxtla leaned over and nudged me with his knee, locking me in his baleful stare. He muttered gruffly, "That was pretty amazing, how you could fuck up a simple maneuver like getting your men across the river. I never saw anything like it. Your moves should be studied in the akademy to originate a Science of Oppositology so that everybody could learn how to do the exact Opposite of you. The rumor is that you're such a total fuck-up, you're a Law of Nature. Tezkatlipoka must be whispering over your shoulder, making sure you turn left every time you're supposed to turn right." "Fuck you, Maxtla. Your mom is so ugly the winos run away when she comes out on the front porch to give them a quarter. Three-legged dogs run around neighborhood yards crying and pissing on themselves to get out of her way. Get your salamander breath out of my face.

Besides, Tezkatlipoka doesn't whisper, he talks in the voice of Lenin or Marx, tho sometimes it's not him, it's somebody else. Sometimes I don't know who it is. Sometimes there's other voices, too, Bessie Smith, Oscar Zeta Acosta, Blind Willie McTell, some long-dead Olmek were-jaguar; it's hard to tell. There's a whole lot of talking going on." "Is there, now? Well, how you like them marbles? I heard you were one sick puppy, and now I've had a chance to check you out up close, I'd say you're a walking advertisement for forced sterilization of the retarded. I guess this close to breakfast time I'm lucky the snow plastered your hair down over those gnarly scabs and scars on your forehead. It just looks like you never comb your hair, that's all. Can't those voices ever get you to do the right thing once in awhile? Just every now and then, for a change of pace?" "You're laughing now but you won't be laughing later." "What?" "What've they got for breakfast here at Stalingrad? Coffee grounds mixed with mudpuddle water? Asbestos fibers, silica dust and steel slivers, in blood sausage/chorizo?" "Look, Zenzontli, forget about breakfast. You are a Party member, full-fledged Aztek warrior (tho there's some rumor about Japanese infiltration of your bloodlines someplace, it's none of my business, I don't care, as long as you don't sit by me at official functions or anywhere we might be seen together in public), all I wanna say is, you're a good guy. Deep down. Basically you're all right, it's probably not your fault you're a few cards short of a full deck, just maybe on a long shot chance. Maybe you just weren't cut out for this line of work. You go around thinking it was you who all the time saved the Aztek empire from the Spanish invaders, when simple arthmetic would convince any normal person that it was your great-great-grandfather who came up with the theory that the Spanish in the year Reed 1 were not gods from the East, they were not Ketzalkoatl and his homies in metal shirts with guns, but were heinous invaders with stunted imaginations who deserved to be terminated both sexually and socially with *main force*, with every possible resource, with *extreme prejudice*! Their Manifest Destiny was to be tendered to Aztek sacred knives. Your household and your family deserves great perks for coming up with that idea and saving the Aztek people from stupefying consumerism, saffron in their paella and kissing the Pope's ring every time he swishes thru town. Your clan saved Anahuak and all native kultures from foreign overlords, a bunch of saints wearing dresses and insufferable Gothik kitsch, total intolerable exploitation of our indigenous natural and spiritual resources, selling off our intellectual kapital such as the the tomato to the Italians so they could invent the pizza pie and Pasta Night down on the corner, selling off the ear of maize to the Anglos so they could invent Iowa, selling off the tortilla to the Koreans so they could run shitty Taco Bells throughout Southern California, exporting the chile peppers across the world so everyone else could fire up their lovelife and their home fires and compete with sexy Aztek socialism on a world scale, you know all this, sure, your predecessors came up with this theory, we all had to learn about it in first grade, how the Spanish wanted to sell off the chokolatl bean to the Swiss and English for pennies, for centavos, leaving us nothing, nada, sitting on the curb in D.F. in our chonis sniffing glue, starving, slaves in silver and gold mines, dying of their syphilis and measles, TB and whatnot literally *by the millions*, our standard of living could've really bottomed out, but luckily your family saved our ass. *Fine*, I say. But brother, I'm here to tell you you been living in a fucking dream all this time thinking that it was you who done it, it was the ancestor of your grandpa, man! Get real! The whole reason they sent you here to Stalingrad is so that you could get killed off in a *good way*, a way that befits a scion of a beloved old family like yours, so that they don't have to use other methods of assassination that many have been itching, *just itching* I tell you, to try out at the earliest possible convenience." "That would explain a few things. But you didn't explain what's for breakfast. I been up all night, chasing down snipers from the Wermacht, I been fighting the Nazis and attacking Stalingrad and shit, I only caught one, but I need a nap, I'm suddenly real thirsty and I'd like huevos rancheros, please, a side of chorizo, and a glass of iced tea! Do me a favor Maxtla, hurry up with that order, cuz, you know what? I am tired. I am tired of your blah blah blah." "I'm trying to help you out Zenzontli. I'm here to inform you that there are two ways out of this jam, alive or dead." "*You don't bring me my breakfast in two minutes flat, you won't get a tip from me, Maxtla*. And I don't want none of that grease-packed pork fat Carmelita chorizo either. Save that shit for the enlisted men. You know, you do have a point, tho." "What's that?" the grim Maxtla suddenly brightened. "See!" I exclaimed, "If you don't know, how can I keep track of your aimless babbling? Make yourself useful, go into town and raid some Nazi food stores for some fucking food why don't you?" "Like I said, Zenzontli. Two options. These are the only two choices you have left. Listen carefully now, before the Russian gets back. The first is, if you want to live, you lead your unit on a suicide mission into the Red Oktobr Traktor Factory where your unit will be wiped out to the last man; you just make the last man standing be yourself, and you'll make it out of here alive, we'll evacuate you — with certain requisite injuries, self-inflicted or not — quietly to an elite convalescent hospital on the shores of Lake Texkoko where you can put your feet up, ask for a glass of water, look at the lake all day as you flip thru magazines. There are big things happening in the future of our Party which you can choose to be a part of. Take it or leave it. Or, maybe you're the type to prefer Death with Honor (our files contain psychological profiles which peg you as a highly unstable personality, a danger to all involved, risky commodity, someone whose survival may not be in the best interests of the state), for reasons of your own you may prefer a heroic death, KIA, killed in action in the taking of the Red Oktobr Plant (something that you'll have to devise in the end one way or another, *how you secure and hold the tractor plant is your problem either way*), in which case your men who have served you faithfully up till this point, however many survive that is, may be rotated to the rear in Italy or some other theater with a cheap floorshow, beachfront real estate, investment potential. Your men can remember you well as they sojourn in the countryside among the living with comely Latin honeys, wine, cheese & salami, instead of having their spirits shattered like fragments of ice crystal blown across the Russian steppe this December — it's your choice. Make your decision. People more important than you and me are attending to the details, as you decide." "People more important than me and you could get us some fucking service at this place, if they really gave a shit. If you're not gonna be forthcoming with the huevos rancheros I'm going outside, I think, so I can throw up these coffee grounds attacking my stomach lining like incendiary anarchists. Thanks for the big advice, Maxtla." I got up to leave, my stomach lurching like a cat in a bag. "This is your last chance, Zenzontli. You're lucky they kept you on the line this long. I wouldn't take too long to decide, tho. There's a time element," he said, "they may not choose to wait." Preobrazenhski watched as I set my cup down and headed for the door (snow melting darkly beneath the blanket hung across the opening). "The time element is not the hassle," I replied, "it's the bullshit element that's the hassle." As I pushed thru the flap of dank blanket and outside into the sudden zero chill dark, Maxtla called after me, "You may call it bullshit, but it's life or death for millions." "That's why it's bullshit," I muttered, gripping my midsection, staggering along the emankment and leaning against it as I puked out a sloshing spray of coffee. I heaved; it splashed on the frosty banked earth and glistened in the bad light. There wasn't much to it. My stomach clenched repeatedly after the fluid was gone. I was trembling when the footsteps halted behind me. I turned slowly; 3Turkey looked worried. Fierce cold pinched his big dark face. His skin waxy and gray, his stare was fixed like he was holding himself together with muscular tension. "Bad news?" 3Turkey asked. "Bad water," I sighed raggedly. I pushed grit out between my teeth with my tongue, hawked and spit. "Maxwell House. Good to the last gob. 3Turkeyvulture, man, do me a favor and go down the line—tell the squad leaders things are looking up; tell the men to try to get a little rest," I said, "Tomorrow we attack the Red Oktobr Traktor Factory."

Sometimes when I got home Xiuh was asleep on the couch, wine glass upright or spilled on the rug, TV going, "Hi, I'm Cal Worthington & this is my dog Spot"—used car salesman millionaire buffoon in cowboy hat with a chimpanzee on a leash. I might fall asleep rubbing her feet like two cats. If I woke her up, she'd be irritable, grumbling, "Leave me alone!"—take herself off to the bathroom, then to bed. Usually she didn't wake up, occasionally mumbling regretful things to herself in her sleep that I didn't catch.

6

SECOND shift, 2 or 3 A.M. one night, swabbing down a long, dark corridor, second floor of the smokehouse (the air even more acrid, tainted) when I noticed a dark spot—a rat, I thought, but not moving, a low spot along the floor where it met the wall, I thought, *not moving*—a dead rat. I stopped mopping, leaned the mop against the wall and walked down near the end where the corridor turned the corner and leaned over to look at the rodent, I figured, but it was a piece of meat, a flattened organ of some kind, purplish shade of dark blood, dropped neatly into the angle of the floor & the wall. I didn't know what a piece of meat might be doing on the second floor of the smokehouse; it looked as if it had grown there. I threw it in the trashcan of the nearby restroom and swabbed down the length of hallway so it was shiny & silent, left the bucket and mop in the restroom and ran off to collect signatures.

I turned the corner, rushed thru the doorway and then I felt the concussion before I heard or saw the blast, the wall & ceiling vanished from the stairwell—a red sky exposed like the inside of an eyelid; finally it had happened, it seemed—the world had blown up. Whatever it was we'd been waiting for. The rest of the building was gone—completely shattered in an instant, shorn and blown away; I stood on the landing (that much was left for the most part), all along the horizon the ruins of the city smoldered under a smoke-filled dark sky contoured with occasional bursts of high explosives lighting up the columns of black smoke, drifting pall, the atmosphere lit from underneath by the fires of destruction. The shockwave thundered overhead, roiling the air with crackling vibrations, filling it with ozone and pulverized mortar. I had to cough, peering over the edge of the wall down at the smashed landscape, trying to make sense out of the orange light glowing inside burnt-out buildings, endless piles of rubble, roiling clouds of smoke, etc. *The longitudinal & latitudinal geometry of the walls still standing indicate the intersection of four main avenues into a square, which my men attempted to cross — as the most direct route — like bozos. There are piles, mounds and parts of structures reduced to rubble everywhere, which provide cover from ground fire, but not from the machine-gun nest which they should have realized was in one of the upper stories overlooking the open ground. Now, what is to be done? Explosions and screams point to the necessity for speed at all costs. The pounding of the heart and coursing of adrenaline point to the risk of movement. The clatter of another machine gun off to the left points to the need to evade crossfire. The chilly breeze points to the deepening of the winter, 1942. Growling of my stomach points to no breakfast & Maxtla being an asshole. Sweat on your palms points to difficult agglutinization of thot. Patches of blue appearing once or twice thru smoke and haze point to awe and wonder under most impraktikal situations. Shimmering waves of light around objects point to the laughter of Tezkatlipoka. The aura of death emanating from beneath the earth points to portals of the Dark House. The brittleness of your fingertips points to mortality. The curling of your toes under repeated concussion points to tail twitches of ancestral cats and monkeys. Your own forgetfulness points to something that communist organizer Nita Yahui warned you about, but whatever it was, you just can't recall. Variations in tonalities of machine-gun fire point to crossfire from at least two directions. Two directions point to at least two squads of Germans. All the racket points to considerable disagreement. The deportment of the Aztek dead points to a German machine gun placed off to the left, at ground level. The general terrain points to the likelihood that the machine gunners anchoring the base of the L-shaped ambush are firing from a basement they have fortified. Experience points to the fact that soldiers like a route back to their own lines where possible, so likely some rear entrances exist to their positions, probably under cover.* Now for a closer look: Puffs of dust at impact point to trajectory. Billowing haze and smoke point to wind direction. Windows point to number of stories. Numbers of stories point to stairwell access.

Facades point to rear areas. Lack of birds points to high explosives. Usage of terrain points to psychology. Ideology points to reliance on historical method. Tactics and action point to results. Lack of visible sky points to limited visibility. Frequency of shelling points to chronology. Screams of the targeted point to margins of event. Unevenness of the landscape points to possibility. I pointed to my right eyebrow. It had to be me.

I let the destruction of my men distract the Germans for a moment. That was all I needed. I took out both German machine-gun nests, the hard one first. There was a sewer opening or basement down on the square where my men were pinned down, but how to get to it? The Germans pulled their heavy machine gun on a tripod back down into their hole once they'd fired off a volley. They were covered from above by the nest in the third floor of a gutted apartment building. The most difficult thing was to detach all my Aztek finery, my jewelry and lip plug (leaving the unsightly lip hole thru which the hardened warrior occasionally drools when his plug happens to be removed, that's why we hate to take them out), ceremoniously remove my feathers as I set up a sort of shrine to all my doo-dads and important paraphenalia, symbolik feathers & such, the lack of which was going to sorely hamper me for the next half an hour; I tossed a dead German sergeant's overcoat about my shoulders and tied it off. I needed something to cover my damned long hair, but I didn't really have anything, then what do you know, glancing around as I tied it up, there was a German steel-pot helmet looking like a larger sturdier version of a little plastic California motorcyclist's helmet, lying bucket-up on the ground, so I grabbed it and cinched it about my head. Of course I had thrown away my Mauser, useless thing anyway, so I tucked my heavy steel-flanged Aztek war club underneath the gray German overcoat (all right, I admit it, it *was a little* warmer than my feathered cape) and I circled around to the base of the apartment building. They had to have somebody guarding the stairwell. I took my big sharp knife out, drew a nice fast slash across my forehead and waited for the blood to pour down my face. Then I put my left hand over my face like I'd been wounded in the eyes but actually I was peeking thru my fingers as I took the stairs, three at a time. Under my breath, I was whistling, "Lili Marlene," "Mack the Knife," "The Alabama Song," "Horst Wessel Bubba," Beethoven's Fifth & any other German melody I could think of, to give myself the appropriate aura. As your own jaguar familiar or totem can inform you if you care to ask, *the proper energy, vibe, coloration & rhythm overall is all-important for creating the necessary impression.* It's important to kare about how you look. So take kare of yourself. I tried to evoke thru gestures and posture under that cloak, with its small evidence of blood spattering, camouflaging concepts, a possible Teutonik racial memory or collective konsciousness. Briefly, I placed a mental picture of der Führer on the fly-specked wall in the back office of my mind, attempted to rouse some resentment against Jews, Turks or homoseXuals, and least likely of the lot, I attempted to develop a hankering for a cuisine that consisted of bland, fatty foods such as sausage, pastry or cabbage. At each landing as I ascended the stairs, I made a pretense of stumbling at the penultimate step, going down on one knee, one hand over my dark bloody face, groaning, dripping a little blood here and there, smudging it around so that I looked a complete mess (this, mind you, on top of the black and yellow war paint I had so carefully applied previously), so that when the sentry at the third floor landing saw me stumble into view, fall heavily to the steps and struggle to rise, he at first stepped back, startled, hesitating, but then he called out to his mates, who didn't hear him becuz of all the firing and shelling, he alone hurried down the steps to lift me by my arm. Luckily he didn't study me too closely as he pulled me up the stairs, calling, again to his mates. I put up no resistance, I took the next couple steps without any help from him, he was surprised, he smelled something fishy as he turned, scowling, I took my bloody hand from my face grinning at him—"Ach! Was ist nicht eine klein Wunderbar?" he was about to cry out as he reached for his submachine gun against the wall. This compounded his error, his guard down, his hands out from the center of his body as he gaped at me, unable to recognize anything that he was seeing except the German helmet and overcoat, so I kicked him directly in the face. It spun him about, slamming him against the brick wall. I stepped in with an elbow to the back of his neck,

which slammed his face into the wall again. I grabbed the back of his coat
and tossed him off the side of the building, the remnants of a metal railing
not detaining his headlong fall, his arms spread wide. He went to earth
soundlessly, and I turned to snatch his submachine gun before going back
downstairs. I knew he was still alive, probably. "Don't you die on us, Aryan
Brother. We want you for later," I thot, leaping downstairs three at time,
submachine gun strapped over my shoulder. It was like the old slave trade
days, finding the sentry insensate below, broken up on a pile of rubble, broken limbs and internal injuries, dragging him under cover below the stairs,
hogtying him with his own belt. Then, as if I were him, with his own gun,
I hunched over and scurried along a trench toward the rear of the basement
that had been converted into a pillbox. The Germans had obligingly connected their breastworks to fortify their advance, so I followed their escape
route to the back door of the basement, under the eyes of the machine
gunners on the third floor, who either assumed some preconception in
error if they saw me or ignored the movement taking place in their own
lines. That was the perfect interstitial nexus to move thru, where they could
not recognize me, for the moment, hidden in plain sight. Like walking
under cloud shadows, stepping between raindrops. But life's variants, vari-
ables, tangents, interrelations, circumstances, conditions, modes, tonalities,
are of course subject to immediate change, are changing, in fact. So it just
didn't work when I approached the entrance to the sub-basement from
which the German machine gun had cut off the line of retreat for my men.
Some tall thin Nazi kid in his big Wermacht helmet with binoculars
around his neck stepped out as if to light a cigarette or take the air, so
immediately I placed my left hand over my face and did the staggering,
shuffling and moaning act, but he's a kid with a bad attitude, *fucking Nazi*,
alienated young fascist twerp, too tall for his own good, gawky motherfucker, he doesn't go for it! He doesn't give a shit if I'm a German soldier
with a face wound, he's suspicious by nature, he didn't care about anybody
but himself, he didn't attempt to light a cigarette, calling something back
thru the doorway to his komrades, he turned to re-enter the little bunker
they've made in the sub-basement, he forced me to shoot him! He forced

me! I didn't want to! I figured, who knows what condition this machine pistol is in, probably the amateur mistreats it, never cleans or oils it, it'll probably misfire and jam after two shots, who knows how much ammo's left in the clip, I didn't even know how to work the mechanism, where the safety was, I doubted if it had one, but—anyway, those raw misgivings flashed thru my mind as I brought the muzzle up and blasted the boy back into the bunker. I *squeezed* (not *pulled,* not *jerked*) the trigger and what do ya know, a burst from the gun stitched the back of his coat and he fell forward into the dark cellar. Then the shit hit the fan. I hit the ground, threw myself down several steps onto my stomach as the bullets zipped and zinged around me (somebody was firing on me from above), the residents of the sub-basement began shooting small arms at me thru a knee-high vent covered by wooden slats which readily disintegrated. Bullets pocked the brick wall above my head, others pelted it from above, popping and ricocheting around me, snarling like angry bees. I shoved the submachine gun around the doorframe and emptied the clip in a low semicircle. Boy, did they scream. They brought the heavy machine gun around, opening up on the doorway as I shoved myself back, pressing my face against the cement walkway littered with cracked masonry, cornices, chips. Wagner on a V-1 rocket, three of the Four Horsemen of the Apocalypse and all their leftover horsepower, sheet lightning on the North Sea, the fat lady in a Viking hat and masterworks of German philosophers poured thru that doorway, shattering the brick wall opposite, smashing apart the vent, shredding the machine gun and the dead kid as well. Hopelessly, futilely, I placed the barrel of my Tokarev pistol over the edge of the vent and pulled the trigger a few times. They stopped firing. A stick grenade clanked out, but before it could bounce twice, I swung bodily around and kicked it back inside with an all-pro Aztek football move, *win or die*. I didn't play varsity Aztek football in high school for nothing! They shot me thru my left calf as the grenade went off. Then the Germans in there finally shut up. Someone was still firing from above. I unstrapped the Nazi helmet, undid my beautiful hair and shook it loose, hopefully I could find a mirror soon, fix up my smeared war paint. I leaped thru the doorway, swinging my flanged club.

My left calf stung. (You know how it feels when someone hits you with a baseball bat.) One or two swings of my mighty klub krushed the kraniums of the German soldiers trying to kill me. "THEY ARE ALL DEAD IN HERE GOD DAMN IT!" I yelled out the portal the Germans had been using for the machine gun, having pulled a few cinder blocks out so I could see across the open ground to where my Jaguar Unit crouched, ducking the mortar shells (still falling, intermittently, closer to their stairwell), "I'm ankle deep in blood in here; I'm *not* wearing my favorite feathers and jewelry and I had to take my lip plug out so my lip hangs loose like a Saint Bernard's, and I don't appreciate this shit! You see all these dead people? I'm docking all of you two captives each for every dead fascist I count that we're not able to take back to Anahuak with us! Now stop jerking off in that hole and get your asses over here right this minute!" They scurried across the open ground, a few got dismembered, quartered or transmogrified by mortar blasts, a couple of jokers got drilled—*'filled full of lead!'*—by the machine gunners on the third floor of the building, but the rest of the squad dove thru the hole I had enlarged in the sub-basement window. They were chastened, humiliated, they crawled thru the hole with their feathers between their legs, just your average teens, the acting squad leader had been one of the first killed, having walked them into the ambush; it wasn't their fault, they didn't understand why I was being so mean to them, yelling at them, some had ferocious wounds, probably fatal, others would be traumatized or mutilated for life. Ah, everything's hard, there were only seven or eight of the squad left, depending on if the worst-wounded guy didn't die right this minute, he only had one eye left, I looked him in his *one eye* after they dragged his sorry ass thru the hole, I told him, "Soldier, what's your name, G.I.?" "Tlazatzontli, sir." "We'll call you Popeye from now on, won't we?" "Yes, sir." "Don't you die on us, Popeye. I'm warning you. I have agents on the other side who will search you out. They will find you in the underworld. They will make Death a living hell. You understand?" "Yes, sir." Then he fainted. I couldn't waste any more time on him. He wasn't listening to a thing. Serve him right if he missed out on the good parts. I could see the rest of those boys needed a talking to. They had the look of terror in their eyes, shell-shock surfacing against the pupil like jaguar spots, they blinked, unseeing, like albino rabbits in full sun, they cringed as the artillery continued to pound the former city square, they clutched their semi-useless Mausers for dear life, their faces were pale but dark, their faces were pale *and* dark, they were real Azteks under that sun-tan, they had to get their shit together, they had to come out of the sub-basement swinging, they had to come out fighting, and so I had to give one of my better speeches. I had to land combinations like Julio Cesar Chávez, Roberto Durán & Oscar de la Hoya combined, with no sweat. I tied off the flesh wound in my calf in their sight to indicate that I had shed some blood just like most of them *and I wasn't complaining, was I?* "Wake that man up there, I have something kool to say," I ordered the warrior cradling the head of his one-eyed komrade in his lap. "We have to run thru this trench out back and knock out that machine gun on the third floor. I'd do it myself, but that's your job! They're waiting for you, don't think they aren't. They saw me come in here and they've figured out what's happened to their fellow fascist storm troopers and they aren't gonna be happy about it. Even now they're gonna be repositioning themselves, fortifying that stair-well as best they can, to keep us from killing them. Of course, we don't want to kill them! *We don't have one god damn captive yet to show for all of our troubles in this whole fucking war!* We want them *alive!* But, just look at your-selves. Do you think you can just go out there and grab some Nazis in your condition? I doubt it! From the looks of you, you've all suffered some ter-rible defeats! Your ideology has failed you, you're full of existential anguish, the kind that makes you want to masturbate and cut off your own penis at the same time, mutilate yourself with the jagged edge of a tincan lid, the kind of hopeless anguish that makes you want to fling your bloody sawed-off member into the black skies into the glowering face of Tezkatlipoka. Believe me, I know that feeling myself, you didn't invent it. You're feeling like a political prisoner in some Third World country, Turkey or Iran or Indonesia or Afghanistan or Brazil or the Kalifornia Youth Authority, the big guys have been holding you down and they've been giving you AIDS and other diseases, it's not your fault, you're sore, and you just don't feel like your old self. But everything's looking up! I'm here to tell you, my komrades, that Tezkatlipoka, Black Tezkatlipoka, Night and the Wind, is on our side! For once. I assure you. I am a scientifik socialist, I know all about these things, I never make a mistake, hardly ever. You may have seen me make one once, but that wuz the only one. Nahuales, your doubles, totems, spirits and familiars are watching over you. They are moving thru the tree canopy of our homeland, they are moving across the wild terrain, they are flitting across the chaparral like long shadows of a desert twilight, a multitude underground in the darkness of their burrows, across the land and sea, up in the skies. Totems, familiars, nahuales are lending you strength, vibes and *chismes*. Your physical bodies have suffered grievous wounds, and probably you will die today, so what? You didn't have shit to start with; we recruited you off the streets of the kapital, we made you into warriors. The ones who survive will be rich. If we ever get out of here alive. And we will. Or, we might. That's certain. Some of you could, or would, or did already in fact, depending on which wheel of the calendar of synchronous time you checked out on. So what's happening here should be news to no one. Probably you've all gone thru similar experiences in multiple past lives. So don't feel worried or fucked up. Worse things have happened to you, worse things will. None of you are even married yet, are you? I am going to skip the scientifik results and findings. I am going to skip the metaphysical efforts of the nahuales engaged on your behalf on parallel planes and alternate realities, in the ocean currents, high mountain slopes or dry wooded hills. I am going to skip the convergences of algebraic factors of the dilemmas of existence, let's cut straight to the chase. You must learn all these dialectiks, modes and details if you are to survive, but let's take one step at a time. First, we gotta get rid of that machine-gun nest. How are we gonna make it thru the trench, up the stairs under fire the entire time, take out the nest, take some live captives so we'll have something to show the folks back home when and if we ever get there? Some of you are never gonna get home, so what, that's a whole other story. You can get your kicks on Route 66! The thing is, how do we take out the Nazis? How do we win? How do we prevail in our attempts to try hard? Listen hard and listen well.

Everything I'm gonna tell you is True and it will all work in our fight against Nazism, corporate greed, golf shoes, environmental degradation, putrid aesthetiks or moral obfuskation. Aztek Secret Intelligence (ASÍ) has uncovered this numerology thru our revolutionary hallucinations, and I am revealing it here on the Home Shopping Channel only becuz we are in a life or death situation, we are stuck here in a tight spot between Point A & Point B, between a rock and an erased place. Remember, the following numbers are not to be used for evil purposes. *SMOKING CRACK, ROCK OR FREEBASING? Do you want to stop? Acupuncture & yoga relaxation techniques. Call now! 1-800-810-5551. SEXY YOUNG GIRLS EXPLORE THEIR SEXUALITY IN THEIR OWN HOME VIDEOS. Only $19.95 + $3.95 S&H. Media Vision Films 18375 Ventura Blvd., #173 Tarzana CA 91356 (818) 420-9843. CASH FOR YOUR CAR WHILE YOU DRIVE IT! Lease not a loan (888) 678-6866. LARGER BREASTS! 100% Natural Safe & Affordable alternative to surgery! Fast & Guaranteed Results! Toll Free 1-877-6-BREAST. PET BEHAVIOR PROBLEMS? Solved! Call for psychic counseling LISA (310) 391-7762. SAFE SEX GET PAID! MEN! 18-45 yr $1,000/wk cash! L.A. area (310) 281-8227 www.safesexgetpaid.com. 8 HOURS TOTAL DETOX Methadone & Laam, Vicodin, Percodan, Percocet, Loracet, Loratab, and all Opiates HEROIN No conscious suffering No physical craving 1-800-423-2482 www.opiates.com. NEVER FORGET AGAIN We will remind you for life (213) 368-6646. PENIS ENLARGEMENT FDA-Approved vacuum pump/surgical enlargement Gain 1-3" Permanent & Safe Enhance Erection Dr. Joel Kaplan (619) 574-PUMP. BANKRUPTCY! Protect your assets, wipe out credit card debt, stop foreclosures, repossessions, garnishments, harassing creditors, fruit fly infestation, Republicans. Free consultation. Call Atty. Jerry Bregman, Bregman & Associates (310) 312-8085.* Some of you look doubtful. I assure you, I have called all of these numbers, I have tried all these treatments, I know for a fact that they all work. Don't I look great? Our spies captured these secret tactics from decoded German documents and Aztek intelligence has tried all of these techniques out on prisoners of war before we tried them out on ourselves to insure complete safety and reliability OR YOUR MONEY BACK. OK boys, that's my speech, now go out and take that machine-gun nest! Any questions? I have copies of all those phone numbers here on these crib sheets I'll pass around, just take one." With their chanklas making a sucking noise in the coagulating blood awash on the floor of the sub-basement, those boys went out of there, spilling over themselves into the chill sunshine like lions. *Like tigers.*

Or, perhaps they killed us all.

Prove you are alive. Prove it.

Was that noise the chirp of a bird or a piece of steel slicing thru my spine?

Perspiration dripped off my brow, begrimed with the dust of a flattened city, into my eyes. It stung. My skin was caked with cement dust, powdered mortar, flecks of brick and cinderblock, ashes. Everyone was developing a gray film on their skin as we ventured further into the ghost city. We'd taken out the 3rd-floor nest and I decided to give my boys a short break. I sent a runner back to the spot where I'd left my proud Aztek plumage, my important precision jewelry items, my golden lip plug, ivory ear plugs, condoms, First Aid Kit, mezcal, morphine, mescaline & tobako, extra magazines for light reading in transit centers, waiting rooms or field hospitals of the war, plus the souvenirs I was collecting of Stalingrad. "This is a life and death mission, I'm warning you, you're gonna get it both ways, coming & going," I warned the shaken but determined kid I'd selected to retrieve my stuff: "Bring back all my gear intact. Fail at this and not only do you face a horrible death, but we leave your lead-ass spirit behind in Stalingrad forever. Even when they change the name to Volgograd and life goes on, the Russians rebuild the city, modernize everything with parks built atop the mass graves and no one remembers the devastation long after the war, the lovers stroll arm and arm over the sleeping bones of forgotten millions, you — you sorry motherfucker — will always wander the ruins of the city once called Stalingrad among the dead, the German artillery still rolling on the horizon beyond the smoking ruins like thunder." The warrior nodded briskly as if he understood instantly and believed everything; he flew downstairs, a jaguar-skin cape tossed thru the air. I told another warrior with a bloody, shattered arm. "Report to 3Turkey and Corporal Zahuani our position and circumstances. Outline our losses and tell them we have no captives worth anything. Tell them we have secured this location and will rendezvous with them at Point B. Get the medic to look at your arm and do a little dance. Tell him to suck out the evil spirits with his fingers like a Filipino curandero." I was suddenly very tired as he left. The wounded warrior fled soundlessly downstairs, we heard him slip and fall on the midfloor landing below, where the broken bone in his gunshot arm caused him to screech like wildcats mating, he cried out—several komrades laughed—we heard him curse and then hurry on.

I wished to recite a poem before we went over to the attack. This was the traditional Aztek thing to do. "Scattering jade," some called it. Some called it less positive things. "Fuck poetry," one unbeliever grumbled. These recalcitrants were considered to be marginal characters, no-brainers, unpatriotik, the most unlucky of the unlucky. Against the background tympany and thrumming of explosions and firefights, with the susurration of ice against the shore of the slushy Volga, I raised myself up above the men and intoned:

"I have met them at close of day
coming with vivid faces
from counter or desk among gray
ticky tacky houses.
I have passed with a nod of the head
or polite meaningless words,
& listened to their ultraleftist drivel
about annihilating the bourgeoisie,
& thot before I had done
of a jive-ass old-time story
to remind us on the corner
of our big ideas & dreams back when:

all changed, changed utterly:
a terrible beauty is born.

That woman's days were spent
in ignorant goodwill,
her nights tussling in the sheets
till her voice got shrill.
What voice more sweet than hers
when, young & beautiful
she told everybody what to do?
This man had reported big news
till the deputy sheriff shot him
in the head in the Silver Dollar Bar,
this other his helper & friend
organized the movement in a big way;
he might have won fame in the end
so daring & sweet his thot,
but he ended up just a crackhead.
This other man I dreamed
a drunken, vainglorious lout.
He did do the most chickenshit things
to everyone close to me,
yet I remember him in my song,
he too has resigned his part
in the casual comedy;
he too has been changed in his turn,
transformed utterly:
a terrible beauty is born.

Hearts with one purpose alone
through summer & winter seem . . .
Through summer & winter, ah mmmm,
seem, through something & something, uh

something, something, something.

Too long a sacrifice
can make a stone of the heart,
Azteks don't like that.
We been lifting weights
to make our biceps punch like pineapples,
so when with our enemies we rapple,
we shall twist their heads like farm workers
grab the lechuga. What is it
but Night & the Wind?
No, no, not Huitzilopochtli,
was it Tezkatlipoka after all?
Those Nazis are out there having
a good time, a good time for all.
We know their dream; enough
to know they dreamed & are dead;
meanwhile we want to take them home
& show them our Pyramid heights.
I write it out in a verse —
Tlalok of the House of Mist
Huitzilopochtli of the House of Jaguars
Tezkatlipoka of the House of Darkness
Koatlikway of the House of Razors
now & in time to be,
whenever we happen to show up,
it's changed, changed utterly:
a ragged glory is born."
"Thank you very much," I nodded, as our troops sniffed, hiccupped, coughed, frowned and clapped softly, as if bewildered by their own conflictive emotions or lack of the same. "I wrote that myself, last night, standing on the ramparts facing into the subzero chill while you men all had a snooze," I went on, breath coming out foggy in the air, the men staring

blackly at my mouth as if next from it might issue forth some antipersonnel mine that would blast them to ribbons, "I call that poem, *Stalingrad, 1942*. I wrote it here on the battlefront for our moms and dads. I wrote it for the probation officers of our youth, for the public defenders, for the pro bono attorneys who promised to do right by us whether they did anything really or not or just wrote it off on their taxes." They were looking at me with their red eyes. I always like to give a peppy talk like that. It pumps them up. I leaned against the wall and closed my eyes. *It felt good to close my burning eyes. . . . I found myself in the House of Darkness. . . . Thousands of frosty white carcasses — decapitated torsos — hung on hooks, swaying gently as they proceeded along a vast overhead conveyor, creaking slightly. . . . I thought these carcasses must be solid and cold as stone, stiff hundreds of pounds each, and I turned to peer up the line, trying to distinguish an end to it, but the shifting, swaying bodies emerged endlessly out of the darkness, swung into sight, blocking my view — I stepped back, looked up and down the line but could see no end; it doubled back and ascended above me and you could hear the rumble of artillery as if at some great distance, like some beast bellowing from afar as it searched you out.* The only way to escape the enemy shelling was to close with the German lines, so that they could not be sure they wouldn't target their own men. Was that not ever the way in life? Outmaneuver your enemies by closing with them, joining your movements to theirs? (Check the oven gauges on honey baked hams.) Hide in their own shadows, emerge from their peripheral vision so they never had a clear image of you? They never had a clear shot, if you did it right, their last image was your face. They never knew what hit them, you'd appear as some flicker of movement out of the corner of their eye. They would think, "What? Aztek warriors in Stalingrad! How can that be?" By then it's too late! Man, by then it's way too late for them. Sometimes something in existence appears too strange, corny, absurd or outrageous to exist — that's when you gotta watch out cuz you might get killed right there. That's how it is. That's why these Germans don't have a chance here in Stalingrad. Cuz they're just going along, doing their job as they see it, not expecting the unexpected, then some Aztek warriors jump out at them! Then they're fucked, right? Cuz who has the element of surprise? The

Germans, who think they're over here clearing out some lebensraum from lesser Slavik races so they can erect fortress cities across the steppes, built on a plan of Teutonik efficiency, the local population cleared out except for slave labor camps? Or us—your Aztek special forces warriors—who are sneaky, tough, hardened, intelligent, good looking, all around nice guys, studded with all type of metaphysikal dekorations, war paint, spiritual jewelry studs sticking out of our faces, stern, determined brows, quetzal feathers and plumes of rare vanishing species of the rainforests? No contest, right? Now you know why the Germans had to lose World War 2. They didn't stand a chance. Cuz they didn't have an **open mind**—that's the whole reason in a nutshell right there—cuz fascism is this old Baroque mechanistik mode of thinking, too narrow-minded and short-sighted in nightmarish vision even if it does produce in a limited number of cases interesting color coordinations and design graphiks based on German Expressionism or the muted or flat matte color schemes of **Modernism**. Certainly there was a hard-edged aesthetik concept & color scheme to their ideology that was a definite real threat to the entire globe, that's why their regime had to be destroyed. It's a pity that the Nazis didn't use their evil powers to do good! It's a pity that early explorers and labor contractors such as myself had to destroy much of the Europian civilizations that we came into contact with, but in those days we kind of didn't know any better. It's one of the great sadnesses of my life that unknowingly I participated in the total destruction of kool ancient civilizations of the Caucasians. Nowadays tourists visit the **ruins** of ancient sites such as Berlin, Dresden, Stuttgart or Kologne (where primitive forerunners of modern day cologne was first invented, that's a fact most people are not aware of, even when we Azteks get things we take for granted like **fragrances** from ancient civilizations); people nowadays wonder, "Whatever happened to German civilization? Did they just disappear or did they go away? Were they good looking or were they goofy like polka music? How could a people who built stirring monuments like kathedrals, autobahns, stadiums, printing presses and draft beer just vanish as a civilization? Were they sad when they left or did they just get the hell out like they were told?" The modern day tourist who walks among the ruins of the ancient civilization of the Aryans finds himself filled with questions. "Who were these people? How did they live? What were their weird beliefs? What strange **religions** or goofy nonsense caused them to build all this stuff? Why did they plan and execute this massive system of freeways on such an immense scale when the safest, cleanest and most efficient system would have been **mass transit**, pedestrian walkways and canals like ours?" Actually, the Germans, more so than other Europian tribes, had developed a crude subway and rail transit system, canals and waterways (not on the scale of Teknotitlán, but still remarkable for their level of primitive civilization at the time); they even had rudimentary bike paths and a surprisingly good system of hiking trails. All these things pointed to their scientifik achievements. But then their whole civilization just collapsed. Okay, to be fair, it had some help. We ended up sacrificing on a wholesale scale all of their armies, brigades, battlions and corps, Wermacht, Luftwaffe, Waffen SS and a lot of their civilian population on our pyramidz, cutting their hearts out and offering them up to our so-called "gods" (primitive Third World kultures around the globe view our scientifik theories thru the barbarous superstitions of their primitive ancient religions, calling our complex conceptualizations "gods"). In fact, too much breeding stock of various Europian kultures were sacrificed, according to modern critics of older ways of doing bizness. We Azteks must admit that if we had paid more attention to Europian concepts such as "ekology"—natural organic beliefs which come from primitive people who live closer to the Earth (Tlazayotl—Eater of Filth)—we could have been more conservation-minded and we could have—as Moctezuma 4 did later—regulated licensing & bureacratization of the global slave supply along with the industries related to sacrifice and torture of captives. Many of our contemporary problems with shortages, pollution, slave population decline (due to decimation of breeding stock) could have been avoided. People got too enthusiastic and carried away with all the bloodshed in olden days. I admit to being a party to it myself. We Aztex also gotta admit that we have things to learn from the peoples whose hearts we're cutting out. We have to control our own science, teknology and power when we subjugate primitive kultures and cut their hearts out in the most cost-efficient, legal manner possible. That's all there is to it. I know this is not a popular position. I know the New Ekonomic Policy of free market socialism is all the rage these days and that I am in the minority on this. But it was just another thot that came to me while I was holding my aching head, squatting against a wall there in Stalingrad, when massive German 88s, the largest shells they had, landed on the floor above us and blew the top off the building.

I sauntered to the restroom to retrieve my mop & bucket (tin bucket on wheels). The bucket full of gray water had not been moved, the mop leaning against the wall anchored by its thick wad of dirty braid partially enfolded. But I had to go bad by then and I pissed like a horse, standing before the row of urinals seemingly for minutes. As I zipped and turned on my heel, flicking off the light switch by the door, the filthy opaque wire-reinforced glass of the long high window threw dappled shadows and splotches of light across the wall above the urinals. Maybe I dropped something—there was a dark spot of something back by the urinals that I paused to examine; it turned out was only a leaf of some kind.

Y OU know, you are lucky you are reading this Codex instead of some other horseshit Propaganda like those written by Nazis, urbane closet fascists, the Black Hand, Christian fundamentalists, Brown Shirts, wankers, weed-whackers, Victimologists, apologists, tobacconists, Sinologists, herpetologists, hack screenwriters, boxing promoters, after-hours bouncers, market analysts, teknocrats, middle managers, desk jockeys, Democrats, Republicrips, Nixon aides, patty-cake players, Cabinet ministers, Scandal mongers, White House reporters, Cokie Roberts, Norman Schwartzkopf, Bebe Rebozo, the Warren Commission, Dean Martin, Frank Sinatra, Sammy Davis, Jr., and all the other world-famous intellects and analysts of our time. Instead of their *lies*, falsehoods, half-truths and self-deceptions, you are receiving the unannointed Truth and the unalloyed facts of <u>someone who was there</u>. Let me repeat. *Someone who was there.* That's why everything that I say is completely objective and everything happened exactly like I say. Becuz . . . I can't remember exactly why . . . but I'm sure it's true . . . probably becuz I suspect that everything happened just like the way that I think it did happen, probably . . .

Other reasons may come to me and I shall relay them to you as I proceed with the *True History of the Konquest of Europa: a Treatise on the Heathen Superstitions That Live Today Among the Gringos Native to This Europa, 1942*. I, Zenzontli, Keeper of the House of Darkness, subconscious citizen of the most happening city of Teknotitlán of the People's Republik of Anahuak of the Aztek Socialist Imperium, who just happened to be one of the first discoverers and konquerors of Europa and its Eastern and Mediterranean provinces, not to mention Spain (where we discovered Cork Trees and the women wore black every day), Italy (pasta), Turkey (our allies), Egypt (cotton, etc.), Morrocco (thanks a lot), France (?), Swizzleland (pocket knives, watches, banks: all things you can manipulate with your hand in someone's pocket), all that lies across that Sea of Troubles, myself, Native of the very noble distinguished kalpulli of the Eastside, son of its former Clan Elder, Mazacoatl 2 ("Antlered Caterpillar"), who was in his youth called "Dreamer" or "Chato" or "Chino" (may his soul fly thru the trees like a quetzal), I swear that this is the truth, the whole truth and nothing but. *Once, long ago during a more peaceful period in my life as I was strolling out of the garden I heard Omotli, the old gardener talking to someone at a side gate. Always curious about matters of security, unlocked gates and all such things that don't concern me, I closed the chokolatl-colored human-skin journal within which I had been scribbling dribbles of poetry & epiphanies, sauntered out of the ferns, elephant ear & shapeless topiary, as Omotli stepped back, the pretty little Spanish starveling withdrawing a slim hand from underneath his loin wrap as they both turned to me with the familiar trepidation. Omotli mumbled that he was just about to call 3 Turkey because he'd heard a scratching at the gate (if 3 Turkey learned that Omotli had opened the gate on his own, the old gardener would probably be used for target practice that very same afternoon), Omotli muttered something sheepishly unintelligible & I allowed him to shamefacedly pick up his shears & slink away. I studied the girl, who, accepting her discovery, searched my face with a glance that was proud & defiant. But finding no sympathy, only a little curiosity — perhaps the typical reaction under these circumstances — her face fell, she looked at the ground. She trembled slightly as I circled her, checking her out up & down. She was, indeed, a pretty little thing. Her dirty limp brown hair hung about a long slim neck; she had a small, well-*

shaped head . . . more edge to her bone structure than would have been natural had she been eating well, the fragile elasticity of her softness remained . . . her hunger itself was enticing . . . My silence alarmed her. With a supplicatory gesture to denote that she meant business, she held open her ragged shirt, exposing one small, famished breast. Normally I don't go in for dry-humping the starving, if I can get away with it, tho I carry a little vial of linament with me at all times. I leaned forward, as if to study this breast, which brought my face in proximity to her own. I sniffed . . . (She could not know that this was a life-or-death test I had performed on slaves before: do they think enough of themselves to maintain a system of hygiene even under the rigors of captivity? Such professional standards make me successful in my line of business.) My face inches from hers, I met her desperate gaze with mine, allowed the wild darkness in her eyes to veer from the dead-on steadiness of my own fixed stare. I wrinkled my nose, savoring the human fragrance of sweat, warmth, unwashed hair. She smelled all right for someone who was probably ill with malnutrition, with parasites of various sorts possibly, whose teeth were perhaps loose from lack of food. This one smelled a bit smoky, warm & alive, just slightly ammoniac. She must have some luck to have survived hidden in the parks, gardens & forest scattered throughout Teknotitlán, she must have some familiar spirit, an ocelotl perhaps, looking after her. Resourceful girl! Maybe this chika was part Aztek, who knows. I'd have to feed, clean & try her out. I put one hand on the back of her neck & led her, describing to her all the while how nice it was, what a nice day it was that she had arrived at my door, surrendering her to the caretaker of my slave pens. It seemed to me, on thinking back on all that, that her skin was among those I'd noticed amid the desiccated corpses abandoned in the moldy cages behind the garden overgrown with jungle. During the war, apparently, some of my leftover slaves had been forgotten. Somebody was gonna pay for that! It seemed to me that one thing I'd noticed glinting on the concrete floor of the slave pen stained with bodily fluids was that slave's favorite anklet chain around a tibia in its torn sheath of blackened skin. But it was no use getting too nostalgik.

8

1492, Christopher Columbus sailed the ocean blue, a brand New World I know about & so do you. You probably are reading this in the future, way far ahead in a distant Future of some unknown Space Age year like April 10, 1968 in Memphis Tennessee, you know all this already. All this is like ancient history to you. You're probably used to taking rocket ship vacations to Mars & Cancun, probably you get all the nutrition you need from a little white pill every day and the only reason you need to eat solid food is to keep your digestive trakt limber, so your asshole doesn't shrivel up & close off completely—human beings of the future might swell up like shit balloons & pop—in the Future you probably have no idea what war & disease is like except you have read about diseases in books and books themselves are probably obsolete, nobody reads, they get all their info plugged into their brains on a Wire, probably in your World of the future they have discovered amazing stuff like DNA fingerprints, penicillin pencils, free jazz & fusion, 8-track tapes, San Fernando porno-Valley, I can't even imagine all the kool stuff they could discover in the Future, like maybe they will figure out how to take fucked up people & replace them with exact duplicates of people who happen to be kool, maybe they will invent organ transplants so people can get vital organs from prisoners executed in places like China & Indonesia or imported from some dude driving up to a shed on a ranchito outside of Juarez to deliver an ice chest duct-taped closed for the exchange, all this for probably like the equivalent in today's money of $150, who knows, I mean probably in *your world* poverty & hunger has disappeared so everybody will be getting fat, everybody will be growing a lard ass fast as they can, they will dress in spaceman clothes like Miles Davis at the end, they will have spaced-out Looks on their faces from ESP or mental telepathy or potato chips, human heads will be swelling up with Big Brains, complex ideas they will get from Science & teknology cuz of the Internet, your hats won't fit becuz human heads will increase daily. You will be having mental sex, thinking about it, eye-gasms. You probably use lots of eyewash, mouthwash, brainwash. What will they have invented in your Life Time? I can't even begin to imagine. Probably they'll invent a machine that will cross a man with a fly, a monster with a fly's head and scissor-like mandibles for hands to wander around scaring people in darkened suburbs of black & white loneliness, and a fly who gets stuck with Vincent Price's face gets trapped in a deadly spiderweb in a rose garden outside Luther Burbank's house in Santa Rosa, California, screaming in a tiny voice nobody can hear, but that's just a wild guess on my part. I don't know where an idea like that could come from. Tokyo could be destroyed by UFOs, chupacabras, Godzilla, a craving for ramen noodles. Anything could be possible in the future. That's why I know it comes as no surprise to you anything involved in this History I am about to relate. Cuz in a certain sense, tho all these events are gonna happen for me in the future, for you it's all in the Past.

It occurs to me that reality gets complicated, time spirals in & out of hidden histories we barely heard about so we don't even remember where we heard it, worlds collide, *The Day When Time Stood Still*, war leaders say somebody must die, NOTICE TO ALL PERSONS OF JAPANESE ANCESTRY, somebody attacked, fuck it, civil rights are suspended, cities on fire, National Guard tracers fired from machine guns into buildings in Watts, you might want to live some kind of quiet life working at a slaughterhouse in Los Angeles, go home to sleep in your stucco bungalow in El Sereno in East L.A., you might suddenly find out something completely different. That's why the Council of Tlatoani of the Party of Aztek Socialism determined we must Defend & protect our way of life thru War, our standard of living (War), our freedom of religion (War) (1000 hearts per day mini-mum), plus links to a thousand other worlds where Aztex & First World peoples faced extermination at the hands of ravenging hordes of Europians released like virulent strains of smallpox bursting from massive pustules. On some worlds, foreigners showed up wanting to buy Manhattan with glass beads, driving taxis. On some worlds, motherfuckers spread smallpox across continents with blankets & infected clothing. On some worlds, they achieved the same effekt with alcohol, crack cokaine & household glue. On some worlds, they went from door to door with pamphlets, or stood on the street corner spouting pure lunacy. On some worlds, they used Hotchkiss & Gatling guns, napalm & spent plutonium & left people piled in ditches, in infinite variations, mix & match, with Europian Imperialism aimed like an obsidian dagger at the Heart of Aztek Socialism. That's why when the kool old geezers on the Central Committee said we have to intervene in the Europian wars, we have to defeat fascism, Hitler won't take no for an answer, *we got a thousand worlds to do something about,* we're not gonna kol-onize Europe per se, except psychologikally, spiritually, economikally, ergonomikally, contextually, poetikally, aesthetikally, & most importantly, football-wise, that's why I said yes. Of course I said no to the war at first, but then I said yes. I said **No** it seemed to me pretty clearly at first I was saying No a few times and then I was forced to say **yes** later.

"So what? Who gives a shit?" I'd tell myself, "Snap out of it."

I was in the garden. The humidity exuded by plantlife, the pungency of the breathing earth, softly enveloping shadows of immense trees. Small clicks & whirrings of insects. The day buoyed like a fulvent chinampa by greenery, birdsong, sunshine of the broadest-spectrum radiation in cool mysterious common air. The moment trembles with its own ripeness. One has the sense in the Aztek kapital, where waterways like arteries course through the metropolis, that this city is a living organism integrated with the heart of the world, this city that is the heart of the world. As it is, so it must be. "Everything that exists has had some reason for being," that schoolbook principle of Aztek science propounded by Tezozomok 4 that we're made to repeat at an early age till we can no longer hear ourselves saying it, "Those reasons, that being, must be found in order to change our existence. So, all you gotta do is do what I say." But why go about looking for reasons, change, secrets? Isn't Existence & Being strange & wonderful enuf as it is, without reflektion, that smoking mirror? Certainly that must be the purpose of gardens like these, to lose our sense of the linearity and direction of avenues, the hectic bustle of the shops and markets, the squabbling of neighbors and hectoring gossip of the kalpulli, the headlines & pronouncements of the Aztek State in the city's main plazas, the heights of the twin-towered Pyramid of Tlalok & Huitzilopochtli, the Yopiko Temple, Tlatelolko in the smoggy distance, etc. In a garden in the city such as this we feel we're away from the city itself, even if we are deeper inside it; we feel away from ourselves even if we're allowed deeper inside ourselves, we're getting farther away to go deeper within (typical metaphysical bullshit, Tezkatlipoka's little tricks of reality). I'd love to chat with my gardener about the sakred sciences of gardening but it was my bad luck, my memo had already gone thru, so his hapless head was grinning at me from atop the wall, poked on a pike, skin already blackened & cracking in the tropical afternoon. He was a great guy, that gardener—what was his name again, oh yes, Omotli—(memories of previous conversations with him rushed back to mind—I recall the real sense of his humanity, Omotli's distinctive gentleness and generosity, his ability to make things grow, allow plantlife to flourish, vegetative wisdom of the years he had spent attending to, studying & creating the sacred space of living garden where I now wandered)—and, as often happened in the garden, I started feeling lucky. Blessed. Glad to be alive. Happy to be a human being, stand-up Aztek citizen, father figure, Keeper of the House of Darkness, one-time big shot warrior respected among the peers who knew a thing or two, etc. All of that at once. Feeling all right with myself. I knew I had the gardener to thank for a certain peace of mind I'd been able to retain across all the troubled years precisely becuz he had so devoted his life to overseeing the intricate and organic living organism of my garden, the pulsing heart of my quarters and living compound, something that connected it and me to the living heart of the world, its jungle vastnesses (Mayan redoubts of the Yukatan, pharmaceutical rainforest storehouses of immense richness, red klay roads akross the Peten), Amazonian rainforests (Lungs of the Earth), flyways and byways of the migratory birdlife stopping over on their circulations from Tierra del Fuego to Alayeska and back again (making their forlorn birdcalls, kurlews, bitterns, terns, petrels, kites, hummingbirds—maybe not the hummingbirds—kestrels, sparrow hawks, killdeer, loony owls—owls, whom the Algonkin & other North Amerikan tribes ascertain as a sign of death; we Aztex ascertain *death* to be a sign of Death . . . & War, Murder, extrajudicial executions, *desaparecidos,* flaying captives alive, putting their skulls atop huge vermin-infested tzompantli skull racks downtown, eating of their flesh, wanton killing of poor people whenever the military gets in a randy mood, brutalization of passersby or unfortunate eye-witnesses to excess, devastating friendly fire on our own troops or their families or whole villages, you might think things along these lines were omens of Death or signs of DEATH . . . but we Aztex . . . ascertain in them . . . signs of *Life!* . . .). And in the pulsing heart of our kapital . . . the life of the world confluent & conjoined with our infinitesimal tiny lives as individuals under the immense mirror of the sky . . . Colored by wisps of cirrus clouds . . . high winds of the stratosphere unrevealed to those below . . . Auroras . . . Those vast skyways . . . The breezes & winds of the world from the Sahara to Indian Ocean, farts from Madagascar & sea lion snorts from Kalifornia, swampy methane susurrations from Okefenokee, flutelike Kiowa burps from Texas, shit-fragrant ripples from the Hindustan subcontinent, choppy & petulant bursts of air from Northern Europe, greasy smoke from Nazi ovens (they could no longer be allowed to exTerminate each other, dense Europians!) (chilly & cold where we were slaughtering them, according to weather reports—those Europians—they were slaughtering themselves, the Russians were giving them a Slavik bear hug—we were gonna have to promulgate some new policy, some new Politix if we didn't want the poor savage Europian races to go extinct on their Peninsula jutting off of the kontinent of Asia! At this rate our main source of sacrificial captives could go extinct!), all these gaseous air currents floated tenderly thru the airs & breezes of the kapital, & so as well thru my little, big, tall, vine-hung, deep, enfolding, blue-green, shady, ornate foliage of my peaceful garden. All this my gardener had overseen for most of his life. He'd served me & my family for a generation with true humility, creative genius, scientifik holiness, teknocratic awe & wonder. Shit! Where was I gonna ever get a replacement for Omotli? See, the hardships of office, the trials & tribulations of being a VIP? You can't imagine. It's really tuff. One day (probably soon, when the memo got carried out, unless I weakened, unless I allowed myself to stupidly slacken in my core duties as Aztek citizen) Omotli's grizzled skull would perch lopsided, jaw-unhinged, in vines atop the compound wall & we'd be munching some blackened shishkabob of meat strips from his stringy calves on the back patio & saying how this meat really wasn't very good at all & it would come to me, staring into the dense screen of flourishing jungle, & it would strike me then, I knew, what an irreplaceable guy my gardener had been all these years! Oh well. That's just the way it was! That's just the way it goes! That's just how things are *(sigh). Just gotta be nice to people while they're around. Just gotta be good to people while you have them. Ya gotta let people know how you feel about them while you can. Just gotta treat people right before you kill them.* These were just some of the scientifik principles or laws governing all human relations and interactions outside of the House of Darkness (luckily inside the House of Darkness that crap was not allowed, not even spoken of!). Feeling a strange weakness in my knees, as if age or mortality and all that bullshit was suddenly creeping into my system, I picked my way along a trail under the treetops far overhead. A luxuriant monarch butterfly bobbled across the path. A hidden waterway gurgled underneath the underbrush. Black water with dust & leaves on it flowed out of the subcutaneous earth. Some lizard in a hurry or fat rat or grinning opossum or venomous slithering copperhead scurried thru crackling dry leaves nearby. Oh Maria this wingéd world. My footsteps were a little hesitant, something that seemed particularly stupid to me—did I need to start walking like an old man all of a sudden?—but it occurred to me that these sensations, weakness, inability to perceive depth perception, itching of flaky dandruff, inability to burp on command, unfulfilled wish fulfillment quotas, whimsical death wish or deep hatred & loathing of my brother & in fact all clergy the whole world over, all of these sensations were perhaps preludes to my falling into a trance state, another vision, either world-shaking & prophetik or merely cheap in an off-hand way. If I didn't watch my step—I had the sudden vertiginous sensation—I might fall between footfalls, between worlds, and I would plunge straight through the fabrik of existence into weird awful unknowable worlds, bizarre unfathomable unknown existences, for example, I might end up a meat cutter at Farmer John Meat Packing Plant. But it was easy to shake off that idea, after all, I hoped not, I wuz a big Aztek warrior wuz I not? Surely such a strange fate could never happen to me. Still, the passing sensation, like the glimmering of an idea, gave me pause. I paused on the path to recollect my wits & collect my thoughts, fart, sniff, scratch my left forearm with my right hand, my right forearm with my left hand, scratch here & there about my body & my person, maybe it was ticks, mites, biting ants . . . Was I about to go into another epileptic transmutation of the spirit from one plane to another? I took three deep breaths. Nothing happened. I slapped a mosquito attempting to suck juice out of my forehead & my fingers came away bloody. Perhaps this was all a vision, all an altered state of consciousness? I slapped another mosquito against my cheek. Okay. Perhaps not. It was all too real. That's when I knew Tezkatlipoka was making fun of me.

"Snap out of it," I told myself. Unless it was Tezkatlipoka speaking. You can't be sure. The only thing I could be certain of was that it wasn't my wife—she was back somewhere in the past. But I did snap out of my moody mood when the ground began to vibrate. It was like the prelude to an earthquake, but more gradual. The ground reflected a thunder rolling out of the sky. The roar in the sky deepening, growing louder as if rising out of the ground. The thunder came across the sky from hundreds of points, thousands. As if the moon was about to erupt from the belly of the earth & be born, a new planet in new skies, as if something immense was being born of the power of the Aztek people and their nation, the Aztek Socialist Imperium. The air vibrated with power. I looked up, & thru the spaces between the trees, thru the tattered clouds, you could see the regular formations now passing overhead, unending Aztek Air Force bombers, bomber after bomber without any accompanying fighter squadrons, B-29 Flying Fortresses in squadron after squadron in their hundreds & thousands. They covered the sky like flocks of giant steel-green birds. The earth resonated with the rumbling of their engines, in their thousands upon thousands. The air was purged of all sound but the cumulative succession of their thundering engines as the bombers passed over the kapital on their way to bases in the Yukatan & the Karibean, on their way to Italy & North Afrika. These were indeed the engines promulgating the birth of a New World, Kinto Sol, the International Socialist Order with a perky Aztek twist. It made me want to stand up & salute. So I did. I raised my fist up to the sky in the traditional salutation. "Power to the people."

Thank you Tezkatlipoka. Thank you for letting me see this day.

You have allowed me to see it. I thank you.

9

TAKE 36 divisions, One Million Men, two thousand aircraft, fifteen hundred guns, *one million* bombs and point them on a line along the Volga River and tell them to kill One Million Russians on the other side. Bog them down fighting around a city of 150,000, Stalingrad, tractor factory belle of the Volga. Focus one fifth of the German infantry, a third of all fascist tanks, one Italian and two Rumanian armies on the taking of this single industrial city. *Six hundred* heavy German bombers attempt to wipe the city off the map on August 23, 1942, reducing it to rubble, killing 40,000 men, women, children, joggers, pencil pushers, liberals, blow-hards, clowns, professors, Einsteins, bueyes, hueros, fruitcakes, punks, ballerinas. That's a lot of citizenry turned into hamburger meat of a summer's day. Stalingrad that day became a "cauldron," as the Nazis called it, for thirty miles along the river. Russians retreated into the city center; civilians evacuated east across the river. September 13, the Nazi forces succeed in penetrating the town. The citizenry had dug flimsy trenchworks, anarchist militia committees defended their town with defensive perimeters; the Nazi forces tossed them aside like a shredded peasant bodice. General Rodimtsev's 13th Guards Division (once 10,000 strong) was *sacrificed* during the next couple of days (something we Aztex know something about), holding the center of town against tank attacks. 70,000 Stuka and Messerschmidt sorties over Stalingrad, unopposed except by sporadic anti-airkraft fire, made all ground travel hazardous. Anarchosyndikalist General Chuykov, who'd been appointed Kommander of the 62nd Army

September 12th (responsible for the defense of the city) spent the following day moving his kommand post from Mamay Hill in the center of town, down into the Tsaritza ravine, into a large dugout shelter near the river between two railway stations. "We turned the town into a burning Hell," smirked some smarmy Nazi air kapitán. Workers in factories fought off tanks. Russian soldiers and snipers lying in wait in the rubble watched Nazis arriving by the truckload, jumping drunkenly onto the pavement, playing harmonicas, bellowing and dancing. They shot them. The Nazis kept coming, they were following orders, couldn't think of anything else better to do. Mass slaughter was taking place on both sides, hundreds of thousands of men blown to bits, shot dead all over the place. What a waste. Tremendous noise & racket. Walls crashing down, mounds of blasted brick and mortar piling up, shell fragments whistling thru the air, smoke roiling furiously into the lowering sky from petroleum tanks, rolling thunder of bombardment, chattering snare drums of small arms fire. The generals on both sides tried to put some order into their mass catastrophe, but without real success and without any substantial Modern aesthetik guidelines. In our Aztek view, that was their main flaw, the whole reason why the war was not progressing. All this death and destruction without any poetik or aesthetik point to it meant that Tezkatlipoka, Huitzilopochtli, and the universal forces they represent would never really take any notice, nothing would come of it, it was all hurly burly, helter skelter, heebie jeebies and chimichangas with a gnashing of teeth that could never amount to anything—not where it counted on the teknospiritual plane, or in any existential scheme of things. But try to tell that to Europians. They just didn't get it. They just wanted to fight it out like little kids, to weep, cry, sob, wail and hold to some vague notion of War, the German Fatherland or Mother Russia, waiting for him or her to wipe their bloody noses without any mature dispassionate display of Teknospiritual Koncepts. The Germans, it must be said, did have a highly developed aesthetik sensibility about how to conduct their war—which accounted for their early success—becuz they chose the koolest immaculate uniforms of gray wool, Sam Brown belts with snap-on attachments or accoutrements and flared helmets like industrial samurais and stylistik master strokes like zippy emblems such as swastikas (we assume they took them from the Navajos, cuz Navajos swear they invented the swastikas first by staring at the sun for a long time without sunglasses), which did a lot for their cause, having all those great authentik items and perks of office, and they had kool designs like the iron cross, Death's Head insignia, double lightning bolts for the SS, etc., all that good stuff, *plus the proper attitude (a certain pride in business undertakings, giving it 100%),* which led to enormous successes penetrating new markets all across the world, from North Afrika to Paris, Amsterdam, Kiev, Smolensk, Prague, etc. *But they were about to meet their match with the Azteks on the scene!* Anyhow, that was how Teknotitlán HQ had explained the situation—our jobs as Aztek envoys and advisors was to instruct the Russians on the finer points of Aztek warfare so that they could win this dang war. Sorry Europians were making a mess of the whole bloodbath, with their heavy-handed efforts in deep need of Aztek sensitivities. They were dying for it. Millions of men were dying for it in the day-to-day. By September 24 the Germans controlled the Stalingrad city center; on Sept. 27 the fascists went on the offensive against the industrial zone. Mamay Hill, the highest point in the city, changed hands several times, with the Nazis losing 1,500 men and fifty tanks, leaving 500 corpses on the hill on Sept. 28th alone. Such a big pile of corpses—and for what? Not in the least artfully arranged. All those hearts rotting on the ground! Stupid, imebecilic, ignorant, unscientifik. Plain clueless, we could've told 'em. There was simply no point. What a disaster. By mid-Oktober, the Germans had advanced with heavy hand-to-hand fighting, just about destroying Chuykov's 62nd Army. The plan was—the reason we'd been invited in as advisors to save the situation, what we were told wuz: salvage the war effort, win the war for the forces of Freedom and Terrorism—we must save Chuykov's butt in Stalingrad and hold the city. Then the Russian armies of the Southwest and Don Fronts under Rokossovsky and Vatutin would attack from the south at the same time as Yeremenko from the Stalingrad front would attack from the north and they'd encircle Von Paulus's 6th army and just maybe catch other big Nazi armies under Hoth and Von Mainstein in the trap, too. Sometime in

1943, if it all worked out, we'd win the war, and we'd go home like Big Stars (they'd told us). If it didn't work out we'd probably get our heads blown off and our hearts would rot on the ground on the smashed up streets of Stalingrad for Nothing. Our lost souls would flit thru the trees on windy nights back in our homeland like dried birdshit encrusted on some nervous parakeet's ass. We set off in a convoy of trucks from Krapsnoskoye on Oktober 31, the Day of the Dead (in the dark, to evade detection and strafing by German planes) . . . the transport transmissions gnashing, the engines growling, the wind was freezing, every man was left alone with his own thoughts . . . Stalingrad was raging somewhere out there in the cold black Night (so much for the good news, we knew that much for sure, what was the bad news? What we didn't know was probably worse.) . . . *Second shift, anyway, like it or not, Max was nowhere to be seen. Second shift, the foreman was Bob Handler, a guy who though he seemed initially colder & meaner than Max himself, at least he came off as indifferent or impartial. Bob could care less about the details of your particular crew assignment or work detail, as long as you got the job done without problems. His major concern was not to be made to look like a fool before his superiors, who were, of course, his father and his uncles, the owners. They expected him to know the bizness inside & out (building on his management degree from the University of California, Davis), and he did in fact show appreciation for anything that made his shifts run more efficiently, more productive, accident-free. He took an active interest learning the operations of the plant. Handler knew that in the long run he'd reap all the benefits of his labor, real or perceived, while Max, well— Max would just remain a foreman for a long, long time. So, unlike Max, Bob would listen to his workers, attentive to their needs & moods, and he would leave them alone if they did their jobs well. While Max attempted to demonstrate somehow that he wuz the most outstanding foreman that ever lived, Bob planned bigger things for his future than living out of the dusty foreman's office. Bob let everyone else attend to petty details. That meant that although Max could put me and the rest of the crew on double shifts, he couldn't ride us all night. The harder Max pushed us during the day shift, the more during the night shift we moved pallets from one side of the warehouse to the other, or the longer we took washing out the vats that nite, or took throwing "downers" into the truck to the rendering plant, before cleaning out the pens*

& putting new straw on the cement. Bob Handler knew he had the reputation among the old-timers at the plant of being a candy-ass (he was about 30, though he could pass for 25) in the Handler family, so he wuz surprised and somewhat grateful when the books always showed that the night shift wuz usually even more productive than the day shift. Bob didn't know how that happened, but he had his suspicions. No matter what heroic measures Max had undertaken to make it otherwise, the day shift usually, one way or another, left nearly completed some crucial inventory that later showed up on the night shift's books. Max couldn't understand it. He attempted to prowl the entire plant, to watch all operations all the time, but the plant slaughtered six thousand pigs a day, making them into hams, honey-baked and smoked, franks, wieners & Polish sausages, bacon & bacon bits, intestines packed into blue plastic barrels for the overseas Asian market, bones shipped out to grind up into animal feed, etc. Max would never be able to supervize each and every operation, although, on paper, that wuz his job. Somehow Max, who had started at the plant as a regular line worker with old-timers who remembered him from those days, was never gonna get the breaks that were coming to Bob Handler, no matter what he did, and it wuz a bitter taste in his mouth too, you could see it in his face some mornings when he came into the plant. He'd try to wash out that taste with taco truck coffee, standing by the picnic tables, watching trucks coming in the front gate, dawn breaking over the eastern edge of the city with a sharp brittle glare.

Meanwhile, how about assigning them the dirtiest job late at night when they were filthy tired already from working two shifts back-to-back, then wait till they vacated the rooftop, pushing the dolly inside the freight elevator. Come out of the stairwell with heavy plastic buckets filled with disposal gunk, remove the housing from the filter stacks to liberally pour that reeking slop down onto the newly cleaned filters. Replace the housing and cowling and get rid of those dirty buckets, maybe take the stairs down to the yard — ah, hell no, why bother bullshitting around?—just go about your bizness. Your hands are clean. They've been wiped; the rag is gone. Those clowns must be done downstairs by now, anyway, if they know what's good for them. What a surprise to step into the big freight elevator, wrapped up behind your own cloudbank of thoughts and regrets, thinking you're alone poking at the G button, descending into the darkness of some universal night. (Even as Union Pacific loco-

motives cross the Mojave, cattle cars coupled in long trains all night, carrying thousands upon thousands of hogs this way.) Tho as the the elevator starts its descent it's clear that you are not alone; someone else is standing just behind you in the shadows at the back. You probably noticed him standing there except you were busy with your own preoccupations. Fuck it, anyway, what difference could it make, who would ever dare fuck with you?

Once, cleaning out the filter unit on the roof of the smokehouse, I swear I saw an animal scurry over the edge of the roof; it must have been a raccoon or a possum but it's four stories down to the yard and when I went to the edge of the roof the flat planes of blank walls and the asphalt yard were empty under spotlamps and nothing was moving. I was looking across the corrugated tin rooftops of the holding pens when 3Turkey came out of the elevator and said, "Hey, you didn't eat my fucking burrito did you? I could swear I left it right here. My stomach is grumbling, vato."

10

SOMETIMES working all night next to some dude like Zahuani you had to listen to his bullshit, like it or not, you got another version of his life story: "If I searched the city of night with my eyes closed, if I walked under the hanging leaves, in the roadless interior of the darkened heart, would the jaguar call, or would there only be Night and the Wind? Whose world is this anyway? The Fifth Sun or the Sixth? Dark Night and the Wind . . . As you know, we got split up. We could not maintain contact. I stepped on a crack, broke my mother's back. Five, six, I picked up sticks. Nine, ten, I rolled back down the hill again. Things were touch & go there at the beginning. I went downtown to the bus station to scout out the territory. Went across the street, got myself a hat. Borodino, nothing too expensive. Something with a feather in the band, so I blended with the locals. S.O.P. Ate hot fried chicken at a chicken stand. Dripped grease down my wrist. Sucked chicken juice off my fingertips looking at winos tilt down the street like there's a hurricane wind. Gave me an idea. I followed some nobodies down to the back of deserted buildings. I slashed some losers over there on skid row, I killed them where they lay in the dark shadows of the big buildings, just to make myself feel at home, reciting ceremonial prayers while the dying men shook involuntarily in spreading pools of blood, sighing out the little death rattle. Made use of a giant carving knife, an ice pick, broken windowpane wrapped in a rag, a piece of wrought iron fence sharpened to a point on the cement, plus my fingernails. The *L.A. Times* started going on about this "Skidrow Slasher," talking about "mutilated victims," which was insulting, frankly, think about it, considering the religious quality of my work, the Surgical Accuracy, the removal of specific glands & bodily organs of special significance at particular points in time, palpitating them in my hands while the Victim went into shock & shook, attempted to speak beneath my touch, licking my fingers clean when I finished. You know how it goes—sooner or later you have to get a real job. I had already moved over to the Eastside. It was natural, with my skills as a meatcutter & knife-thrower, I went to work for Farmer John in the City of Vernon. Packing, working the saw, chopping with that cleaver, grinding pork. Watch that lapse of attention at a fateful moment, I must say. These are the Modern Days, too much machinery. Lost the tip of my finger in the breakfast sausage. It shipped citywide in the early AM. Got off shift at 8:15, tied off my finger with a leather boot lace, grabbed my windbreaker, my bus transfer, a pay stub, my baseball cap & a chickenshit grin, bumped into the glass door on the way out. Just didn't feel like my old self. Traipsed across to the Blue Hen Diner kitty corner across the street, dodging traffic like a bullfighter doing a wily impersonation of a windmill on a shaky day. Ordered the breakfast special, three eggs over easy in bacon grease, huevos rancheros with apple sauce & habanero salsa, a short stack with fat glob of margarine melting on the side, coffee, black, thank you, more ice water please, change for a dollar, too, please, I punched Lyle Lovett & Freddy Fender on the jukebox, looking up daring anybody to say anything, my finger throbbed & hurt like hell, felt like it was ejaculating sparks & fire like a Roman Candle, I looked up & saw some kind of situation going down. Suffered two gunshot wounds subsequently in a failed robbery at the greasy spoon. Lost the tip of my tongue bitten off in the fisticuffs. Scalded my throat on too much hot coffee. Coughed & spit & strained my esophagus when they started shooting. Slipped on a wet spot on the diner steps, broke my glottal stop on a slippery dipthong derived from middle English. Two guys were robbing the place. They were wearing white T-shirts & white aprons & chef hats. I think they were former cooks. I think they didn't like the food. I think they shot the waitress by mistake. I think she was a friend of theirs. I think she was the true love of the shorter of the men. I think he was from Las Vegas & she was from Bakersfield. I think he lost his soul-mate right then & there on the linoleum floor. She dropped like a sack of Cal Rose rice. He dropped to one knee. Somebody screamed. Maybe it was me. The shit-for-brains had shot me by mistake too. Beside the stools along the counter, with a clatter of ceramic dishes. I think the other guy mourned silently for his partner as he licked his finger & counted out the greenbacks. I think they were collecting their back pay. I think they were planning a fast getaway to an island paradise, bargain prices, $275 one way. I think they had it all planned to a T. Except for the part where I looked down at my stomach & saw the blood gushing out between my fingers, had a salty taste & a stinging where a bullet had removed my upper lip. I came up out of the booth & slapped the shorter guy, bent over the wait-ress as if he really cared. I slapped him silly. He was about to get furious, his dignity had been sorely offended, he looked up at me with world weary bloodshot eyes as I shoved a water glass into his face. It popped against his cheekbone, causing him to jerk his head backward, leaking vitreous from one ruined eye. He turned to run; his partner saw me coming, got off a couple shots in my direction, cracked the front window & broke the waterfall in a Hamm's beer sign; they were both out the door before you could dial 911, report a double homicide, heart attack, carjacking, no park-ing, no luck, conjunctivitis, wrong number, sky is falling, order an expresso. I think I heard the LAPD gun those two men down as they stood at a wall with their hands behind their heads. But I couldn't really wait around, I just didn't have the time, I had a bus to catch if I was gonna watch my favorite TV show, *Combat* with Vic Morrow. I used to like to put my feet up after work, my feet were killing me, athlete's foot & tendonitis, ingrown toenails & kosmological emptiness resulting in restless itching feet that wanted to wander down that open highway. Best thing to do, prop them up on a kitchen chair pulled off the dinette set, pop the tab on that XX beer & unfold the paper tentlike over my head. Then I wake up in the morning still in the chair, on the wrong side of the bed. It's only insomnia, many must have it."

After cutting the throats of 1800 hogs, spraying the concrete floor with high-pressure hoses, rolling two stainless steel tubs of pig heads to the corridor outside the disassembly line, doing a second shift on the clean-up crew with Zahuani, 3Turkey, Nakatl, Ray, and Weasel, swabbing buildings & corridors and grinders, sweeping out floors & wiping down carts & stainless steel tubs on rubber wheels, all the while we had to listen to Ray's bullshit about the CIA crack cocaine conspiracy, endless horseshit about CIA assassinations and JFK and MLK and Iran-Contra & black helicopters, anthrax & the Twin Towers—it wuz all planned in advance: "Big Bad Baldy John Negroponte, cuckolder of military underlings, crapshooter with the bones of men, penile moustache, testicular grin, testosterone 24-valve roadster, bullet-proof alibi, huh John? Ain't that right, *John?* Rape, torture, murder U.S. nuns *and* Catholik Workers, *John,* son of a gun, what will you do for an encore?" Ray would sigh to himself, retelling the old story to which he had memorized the ending long ago, resigned himself (sighing), continuing, anyway, heedless: "Patrick White, U.S. Ambassador running around trying to find out all about what happened *at El Mozote!* While Big Bad Bald John was sitting in Washington D.C. like a buzzard up a tree, tinkling, tickling his nose hairs with bourbon on the rocks, well John, have the contras throw another wiener on the barbecue, kill another guerrilla in a pit why dontcha, pour gasoline on the bodies, stick a *needle* in *my eye,* for Chrissakes, cross my Maidenform bra, hope to *die, shoot* the rector of the university, his *housekeeper* her whole family and some Jesuits on the *lawn* face down on the asphalt, mum's the word, I *heard.* Fuckface John and all the CIA Langley tea parties! *Shshshshsh.*" Ray would lift a finger to his lips. I'd be shaking my head: "Ray, you got to snap out of that conspiracy pipe dream! Stop spouting that bullshit! No one believes it! No one ever will! Consider the source! The CIA is nothing, amounts to nothing more than a cartel of inside traders on the East Asia drug market! Cut that shit out, Ray, you're losing all credibility, lemme tell ya, as someone with a lot of low credibility, I can speak from experience!" I couldn't see him very well since the other guys were probably spraying him with water hoses in order to get him to shut up or tossing empty plastic buckets at his head but it seemed to me that Ray shook his head as if he couldn't believe what he was hearing, peering sideways at me with ill-concealed disappointment. He'd huff, *"Elliot Abrams'* Camel Cigarette white papers on *the Marlboro Man!* Like *R.J. Reynolds* saying *Nikotine* is not *Addiktive!* Like cokaine grows *out of* in a *hole* in the ground! Like a cop *needs* a donut shop! Like *George Bush* was out of the Loop *My Ass!* You could pull George Bush out of *your ass*—he'd come up clutching *White Papers* & Raul Salinas de Gotari's Swiss account numbers with *his teeth!"* Ray would get more and more insistent if you didn't forestall him in some way, so I'd try to warn him off. *"Shut up, Ray, shut the fuck up!* You gotta stop repeating that lokura or else they won't let you into college! Huitzilopochtli, Ray, try to get a grip on your feeble broken glass mind! We got to get this whole room done & be out of here in a jiffy or we are gonna be shucked like an elote on the corner of 6th and Union by some Salvadoreño." Ray winced, frowning at me, his feelings hurt. "G-7, the Cuban Anti-Communist League *and* the downing of commercial airbuses in international waters off Venezuela," Ray'd pout. I'd throw up both hands. "All right, all right, Ray. Fine. Whatever you say, okay? Just wheel those tubs back to the kill floor lickety split, would ya? This place has to be ready when the next shift rolls in."

Later, when I was finishing up the night in the chill room, I seemed to be hearing things in my mind, which reminded me of Ray, which could lead you to think that we've all been working this job too long, the horrendous loud bizness on the killing floor is getting to each of us in one way or another, but I thot I was hearing sonic echoes from the past, echoes of strange experiences that will never occur again. I could've sworn I heard a slamming jackhammer pinging against solid steel, a high-caliber machine gun fired just outside of the door of the chill room, so I hung the FDA clipboard beside the door and peeked out. The dim corridor was empty and silent.

Max caught me crossing the yard, CIO petition hidden in my armpit, and I thought he was going to ask me what I was doing, keeping to the shadows, what was the rush, where wuz I going? Instead—"What the hell wuz that banging at the end of your shift this morning?" he asked, "What the hell was all that racket in there?" "I don't know, Max, I didn't hear nothing when I was in the chill room. It was all quiet far as I could tell. What did it sound like to you?" I asked. "It sounded like somebody was ripping apart the steel door to the chill room with a jackhammer or shooting a god damn machine gun at it, one or the other." "I didn't see anything wrong with the door, did you?" I asked. He didn't answer me. He was looking off across the yard, with all the bitterness cinched up in his dark face, toward the black shadows of night, the streetlamps of the avenue beyond and the sky beginning to lighten over the rooftops. Soon it would change colors, filling with flames of live flesh, orange as a bird of paradise, white spumes of clouds and streaks of blue fanning in all directions. Pretty day, about time for me to go to sleep. But Max said, "I don't know what you think you're up to, but you take Ray up on the roof of the smokehouse with a dolly, and the two of you clean out the filter stacks." "All right," I said, thinking, *that's one of the dirtiest, stinkingest, filthiest, nastiest jobs in this whole place, Max. When you get done with that you are covered in tarry sooty black grime that stinks of blood, burnt meat and death. It gets in your hair & the pores of your skin, coats the insides of your ears, under your fingernails, and makes your food taste funny all day. You can't hardly wash off that stench even with industrial cleanser, you got black crescents under your fingernails for days. How long you been saving that one up for us?* And I hurried off in the dark to find Ray, presumably, but actually with the clipboard under my arm to go sign up that chickenshit holdout warehouseman on the loading docks who I felt was trying to avoid me. I had almost everybody signed up on the petitions, even three secretaries in the main office.

Returning veteranos of the Eastern Front tell a story they overheard from some Germans who died before they could return to the Nazi Fatherlandia. The hapless genocidal Nazis were struggling thru a furious blizzard someplace on the Stalingrad front, lost in a white-out of howling snow. They pressed on in some direktion they hoped was westerly, homeward, every now & then fearing they were trudging, exhausted in a big circle to their deaths (which they were). Occasionally toward the end, they thot they saw, thru the blowing drifts and snow, a big cat circling them like the approach of nightfall.

Also, Europian writer Ernst Hemingway tells of the mummified remains of a leopard found above 11,000 feet on the peak of Kilimanjaro. No one during his time could account for how it got there or what it must have been thinking. "Am I lost?" or, "I don't want to go home," or what. I mean, nobody knew, it was either mysterious or really hard to imagine or find out about. Now Aztek scientists have solved the mystery. Aztek scientists, following the socialist direktives of the Komission to Investigate Why Do Children Eat Dirt has discovered that the eggs of the parasitikal pointed flatworm Chavalensis Mugrosis which infects the flesh or open wounds of animals living or dead by detaching its mouthpiece from the anuses of certain carrion birds which feed upon carcasses that leopards hang in the acacia trees they use as perches can infect the great cats themselves, where eggs embedded in the meat are ingested in the bloodstream, traveling to leopard brains. When the eggs of the Chavalensis Mugrosis worms hatch in the leopard's brain, it causes pounding headaches, blurred eyesight/partial blindness & epileptik bad dreams (hey, what do ya know!), *causing the leopard to believe that even as it wanders at high altitudes, dying of starvation, to the tip top of Kilimanjaro, it believes it is doing just great. These disturbing scientifik discoveries by Aztek akademicians suggest that far from being the formerly thought fool-proof Guardians of the Night, that even the great Spirit Cats who are our protectors or shadow nahuales in the World of the Night can get brain damage and suffer idiotikally, enduring useless pointless deaths while under hydrophobik delusions that everything is just peachy. How could this happen, you may ask yourself. Who really knows? Teams of Aztek researchers, administrators and soccer moms with the Komission on Why Do Children Eat Dirt continue their investigations.*

"Kool," I reply sarcastically to my own self. El Loko Crazy Ray, bedraggled hair falling in his eyes, hearing me muttering to myself, replies with his own asides, "A. T. & T. *und* the Trilateral Komission. Billy Carter [*he ejects an extremely loud burp*] beer! Screen Actors Guild and the Mob [*he farts tenderly, a large party balloon slowly losing air*]. Nancy Ronald motherfucking Reagan's astrologist, the General Electrik Defense Kontract Hour. Lee Harvey Barnswallow [*burp*]. All I ask for is copulation just once with that C.I.A. hole in Jack Kennedy's skull. Is that too much to ask, I ask you?" "Why ask why?" I ask El Loko Crazy Ray. He farts. "Hey! Loko! If I left the thinking up to you, we'd be in some deep (if you don't mind my saying so) *shit.* You are lucky you found me, Ray. I think I just about got this whole thing figgered out." Ray grins to himself shyly, his dreadlocks swinging in his face as he sways back and forth, full of pride in his Juana's Bakery t-shirt printed with the half-dressed woman revolutionary in a sombrero, wild breasts popping out behind a criss-crossed bullet-filled bandolier, rifle in hand. Luckily, I have one kool dude like Ray to help me out in my time of troubles. Luckily, I am pretty sharp on the uptake in a tight situation. Luckily, I got a lot on the ball when it comes to running with the tuff losers. Luckily, my Timex takes a licking and keeps on ticking. Luckily, whoever was wearing it would know what time it was. Luckily, I had worn socks that match when I left home this morning. Luckily, the shredded remnants of aforementioned stockings are wadded about my ankles in a stiff blood-stained business. Luckily, *even as a child I could laugh so hard Koka Kola came out of my nose. But wait. Now that I'm older, I have mastered my breathing and balance thru Aztek martial arts, I have my driver's license and my Sierra Klub membership kard, I have a veritable panoply — sort of Cinemascope, full Teknicolor — of situation-appropriate smirks, leers, snide tilts of the head, varied arches of either eyebrow or both at the same time, a way I have of fluttering my eyelashes so that the typical dull gaze some people* **think** *they see becomes attenuated as if by actual flicker of impulsive energy or interest. In short, I have what is called among politicians* **charisma,** *among used car dealers it is called* **the touch,** *among high-strung real estate agents on the coast it is known as* **savvy,** *Long Range Patrol vets (LRPs) have termed it* **the 100-yard stare,** *among cab drivers on the graveyard shift they may talk of* **night horrors,** *short order cooks with grease-spattered faces they call what I got* **the second wind,** *among twelve-year-old boys socking each other in the nerve endings it may be called* **the Charlie Horse,** *and amidst the dismayed silence of a García Lorca being put against the wall, just before* *burping reports of the carbines, you may hear it called the* **duende**, *something Hispanik like that. Rolled up into a ball, such qualities may smack of a certain crackle in the air when I walk into the room, like the air certainly crackles during a period of asbestos removal. When you add to this a compensity for X-Ray vision, my goodness, not to mention ragged, filthy clothing slept in for weeks, a violently odiferous right-hand man, fake delusions of grandeur supplied by the dominant kulture, toss in the random railroad noise, the unforgiving pounding inside my head, insignifikant dust motes floating thru the overbearing sunbeams from the Toltek sun, idiot goldfish swimming thru a warm bowl of memories, add all that together, boy, what have you got? I surely don't know. Ask Ray. Ray's got an answer for everything. Unfortunately it's the same answer, we heard it all before.*

Me and Ray got the heavy duty dolly, works on hydraulics of some sort, gliding the length of long concrete corridors with four-hundred-pound payloads with just a push of one hand. I rolled it into the freight elevator of the smokehouse with Ray shutting the wooden gate behind us; the open-faced elevator so capacious that its blackened & eroded, scarred plywood walls leaned away from me into the distance when I thumbed the button for the roof and stepped back, resting a hand on the handle of the dolly, Ray leaning back against the wall as if exhausted, looking for all the world like a Mexican Ray Milland in a dirty T-shirt, *The Man with the X-Ray Eyes* (and no sense) staring hypnotized at the floors passing by with their wooden gates. Roof level, the steel door opened outwards.

꒭꒭꒭

*S*MOKE.

A face in the mind.

Mist in the trees. A heron's reflection skimming the water.

"Get out of my way, Ray, I'm going first. Just follow me." I am down on
my hands and knees, climbing up the big slippery stone steps of the pyramid, the sharp granite edges dangerously slick with blood, my hands are
filthy with it, boy those Nazis sure gush out blood by the cubik gallon, it
smells like steel, sweetish steel, their salty blood lemme taste some of it, I
suck the tip of my finger, yep that's regular type O-positive blood all right,
what do ya know tastes just like Spanish blood or Aztek blood for that matter when you come down to it in spite of all that sauerkraut, wiener-
schnitzel & beer, it still tastes like human blood and tears, going up this
mother of a long, long, long stairway, so steep I got to look almost straight
up to see, I can't see the top, lucky my X-Ray Vision seems to be cutting
out, I am getting my normal eyesight back, *it's about time*, lemme tell ya, the
hell with X-Ray Vision, I won't miss it, the afternoon reeks of smoke, sweet
charred flesh, sickish whiffs wafting in the shifting breeze, the stone face of
the Great Pyramid glows bright orange in the long rays of late afternoon
sun, multihued plumes of smoke roil up around us, Ray climbs side by side

with me, he's a good guy when you come right down to it, my wife is always putting down my friends telling me they are Dickheads, Psychos, Losers, Alcoholiks, Retards, Womanizers, small animals weren't safe around them, you wouldn't want to leave your children in their care, so what? All of that could be perfectly true, but they are my friends, not hers, sure Ray had his faults, he can't look anyone in the face, he refuses to meet your gaze, mocoso, smells like roadkill, he has been driven off the deep end by over-work years ago in some other lifetime, in short, he is a regular guy, far as I can tell, he might've been a head case or a derelict in some people's eyes, but *they were gonna kill us all in the end anyway, they were gonna do it with relish*—sweet relish, pickled habanero relish, obsidian blades and a charcoal brazier—they weren't gonna make it easy on us, either, making me climb on my hands and knees up the 999 steps of the Great Pyramid in the exakt center of Teknotitlán, in the center of the Great Plaza, shrieks and screams of agony heard high above us, oh stop your screaming, *all right I am coming! I know I'm late!* "Hold on a second Ray, Ray wait! Sit down for a second, lemme catch my breath! You know, if they wanted to make it easy on us they would have made these pyramidz a little smaller. That's one of the benefits of getting sakrificed out in the country. They got these little pyra-midz that don't take more than five minutes to climb up, just our luck we get assigned to the Great Pyramid of Teknotitlán, *mamasota* of them all. Sit down a second, relax, if you get too tired you might slip in all this blood and fall down to the bottom of the steps, break your neck. Look out, they're throwing down another body. You don't want to fall down like that when you're alive! It'd hurt like hell! Worse than that, it might just leave you smashed up and paralyzed! Oh, watch out, there goes another one! Boy some of those Nazis look ugly naked, it's just *my opinion,* but really, if they wanted *good looking* sakrifices they would stick to indigenous peoples of Anahuak, not go for the Europians, no offense Ray." I have pissed Ray off, I sense, with that casual remark. His lips press together sullenly, his jaw set in a hard line as he scans the swirling masses of people in the crowd below. I immediately change my tone of voice, "Some Europians, Ray, just *some Europians,* these big German guys are built like walruses or sea elephants,

Ray. Where were your ancestors from? England? Wales? Scotland, something like that? Those *indigenous tribes of Europians*, they're *okay*. But, the Teutons—well, for example take a look at the next guy they toss down. There, that guy! Did you see him? Did he or did he not look like a fat cow? I don't think it's a prejudice, that it's racist in any way if I say that the Northern Europians just don't make for *good* human sakrifices. In *human rites*, especially in human sakrifices, *aesthetiks* are of prime importance. If the aesthetiks are off, and here's where I think our so-called leaders are making a big, BIG mistake, then the whole ritual simply won't work. It won't *funktion*. Teknology is a very *exakt* science. It's got to *look good* or otherwise Huizilopochtli, Tezkatlipoka, Coyoxaukee, Tlazayotl, or whoever won't even notice; the whole bloody affair won't *accrue* the same economik benefit as you would get from a *fine, graceful, beautiful* sakrifice. Look at all these fat Germans they are killing today. They're just going for *quantity*, on the hoof, numbers, by the pound! The whole *aesthetik aspekt* is being overlooked. They are making a *big* mistake." I reached over to clap Ray on a shoulder. "At least they got you and me Ray. We'll leave better looking corpses than these fat-ass racists. Listen to them scream, bloody Huitzilopochtli! You'd think it was a bunch of women being sakrificed if you didn't see them climbing the pyramid then flying down to the bottom, head first, chest gashed wide open, dead as a doornail, except fat, white as a carcass hung up in the kooling room. Just my luck, to get sakrificed with a bunch of Pillsbury Dough Boys. You know what Ray, maybe I know some of these witch doktors up at the top, probably if they got the main guys working today, they're a bunch of my brother's friends. I'm gonna tell them, too, that all this white meat is *no good*. Sure, one white guy gives you enuf meat to feed half the neighborhood, but it has *no taste*. I don't know if you ever noticed that Ray, but the average Europian—*don't give me that sullen look, Ray, I'm not talking about **you**, now, you know that*—they got so much meat on them, they are like a Samoan, or a grizzly bear or something, they get dry when the long muscles of the limbs are skewered and broiled over coals. Have you ever had wild boar? It's like that. With the Europian, he needs *basting*. He needs some kind of sauce. Steamed, maybe, with soy sauce and scallions, like the Chinese would do it, that would work. Otherwise . . . *just too dry. Tasteless, really.*" Ray doesn't like my line of conversation at all, I can tell, becuz all of a sudden he turns around and commences climbing. I can tell by the furious, determined and intent way he takes each step that I have pissed him off. "Aw, Ray," I call after him, "I didn't mean it! Never mind what I said. Slow up, Ray, I can't keep up. Come on, Ray. I was just kidding. Ray! *I like the way Europians taste! Different* doesn't always mean *bad.* Aw shit, Ray." But Ray is having none of it. He is climbing fast and furious like a fast furious madman. He doesn't even notice till it's too late, the tumbling immense naked bloated Nazi rolling and sliding his way. Herman Goering! I'd recognize that fat motherfucker anywhere! It was the Luftwaffe general all right, right wing celebrities didn't come any bigger than that except at Republikan fundraisers in Texas! Glad to meet you today, Herman, *on the day you die,* spewing blood from your gaping chest and mouth, sightless eyes half open, wobbly blubbery buttocks cushioning you somewhat as you slip and slide, butting heads with the steps on your way to that whopping heap o' bodies down below. 400-pound Herman Goering rolling down the steps of the Great Pyramid dead, naked, spewing blood from the vacant chest cavity where his heart used to be, that's something you don't see every day. (Which may have been why Ray wasn't on the lookout.) Ray was so intent, climbing hand over hand up the steep dangerous blood-soaked steps, mad at whatever I'd been saying, he didn't even hear me when I yelled out a warning, "Ray! Look out, man!" Boom! Imagine being hit by the distended feet of a 400-pound Nazi man-o'-war half way up the Great Pyramid! I expected Ray to fall to his doom, blitzkrieged backward by those bloated pale flipperlike feet of the tumbling corpse of the air force general. As 400 pounds of dead white Nazi on the hoof slipped, slided, swung about, bouncing down the steep steps with legs splayed, exposing a surprised little sea anemone, the tiny gray-pink genitalia in a scrofulous nest of pubik hair before the vast gut of the corpse rotated, the stiff calves slammed into Ray's midsection at the waist: Ray spun about, shocked, clawing the air futilely, finding no handhold — Ray hung in the air, teetered for a moment, then toppled over, toward the base of the pyramid hundreds of feet below. I was already scooting, sliding straight across the narrow step on a sticky film of blood, screeching, "Ray! I'm coming for you Ray! I got ya!" I reached out as Ray dropped past me, made a desperate grab at him, leaning back against the steps to anchor myself as best I could. As luck had it, the only part of Ray I latched onto as he fell headlong was his thick rat's nest of nasty dreadlocks. I grabbed that mat with my Grip of Steel and gave a mighty jerk on his head—Ray shrieked, yowling in agony as his body swung against the fulcrum of my grip, neck twisting crazily as his feet swing around beneath him, his body drubbed, battered by the steps—then I lost him. His hair ripped out in my grasp, and I was left holding a shank of greasy hair. It was like holding a rotten rope, stiff with packed dirt, the hair of a corpse left in the desert, I tossed it aside, spitting in disgust, wiping my hand on my clothes. Lucky for Ray, this was enuf to break his fall, it stopped his downward momentum; he slid to a halt on the steps a few yards below. *I didn't tell Ray that I'd told him so, didn't I say those Nazis were too fat?* I leaned back on the slimy, sticky stone wiping his awful grease off my hand, while Ray groaned, lifting himself up on one elbow to rub the patch of scalp where a big bunch of hair had been torn out, and I said, "Sorry about the hair, Ray. I was trying for the jacket. You gotta watch out for falling Nazis, Ray. They're falling faster and thicker all the time. It's coming down like cats and dogs. Look, there goes another one now, watch out. I tell you what, Ray, first one to the top buys the cerveza."

Vertikal space.

Sun stone.

*Of course I scrambled up to the top of the Great Pyramid before Ray. I couldn't let myself, Aztek warrior, War Hero, kool dude, etc., be beat out by loko Ray Milland, CIA reject, conspiracy theorist, motorcycle rider, hi-fi buff, collector of high end stereophonix. It wasn't in my genes. I had figured worse came to worse **when I got to the top** I'd just speak to whoever was in charge and everything would all be worked out in a jiffy. We'd arrange some prestidigitation, a bait and switch, jerry-rig*

a Filipino witch doktor movida, where the guy produces a goat liver atop the vik-
tim's skin which he has cleverly indented with his own bloody fingertips, etc., but no,
they understood that I wuz Chikatl's brother, they understood that, <u>neverthe-</u>
<u>less</u>, *they were <u>under strict orders</u> to make sure I did not weasel out of this Sakrificial*
Act. I knew I had met some of those high priests, kardiologists and surgeons before
at various get togethers, ikebana exhibits, tea ceremonies, Central Kommittee
Meetings of one kind or another, but I could tell that they weren't gonna cut me a
break by the way they stared <u>at my chest</u> with their eyes glazed over, downcast, blood-
smeared faces dripping with strings of coagulating blood, grim, they looked tired of
their jobs, I wanted to tell them they needed a break, you been on the job too long,
but I thot they might take it the wrong way, they instructed their assistants to scrub
me down; a wonderful new warrior suit was brought to me. Even tho my sore feet
kept me from standing properly erekt, I was able to put on the fine fashion drapery
with their help. As I dressed, I kept talking, running out my spiel, suggesting that
there might be other ways to resolve this situation than Violence, Bloodshed, Publik
Spectakle, etc., but they were having none of it. My sense was that behind their
masks of frozen glumness and the screen of matted, blood-thickened hair hanging in
front of their faces, they were thinking exaktly the opposite; they were thinking that
it's exactly what was needed when confronted with Implakable Forces of the
Universe, Subatomik Partikles, Existential Anxieties, Class War, the Vicissitude of
History, plus the Unknown, plus Other Hard Questions, in short, all kinda horse-
shit which you may guess is relatively old hat inside the House of Darkness. I could
see that in a situation where they were confronted with the complikated weirdness of
reality, they probably felt exaktly what wuz Necessary wuz **violence**, *bloodshed,*
publik spectakle, human sakrifice, ritual invokations of "gods" (aesthetikally desig-
nated conceptualizations representing universal laws & principles) which, **at best**,
were heedless of human suffering and possibly irritated or annoyed by all the atten-
dant hoopla and whining. Blood and skreams of agony lubrikate the steel wheels of
progress. Teknicolor blood & screams of agony decorate occasions of state. In short, I
could suddenly see, there at the top of the great pyramid as I was being tethered
about my waist and tied to the Stone of Tizok (which is covered with petroglyphs
advertising Tizok, saying what a great tlatoani he wuz, all that crap, everyone knows
he was no good as a politician, Tricky Dick Tizok, Generalissimo Mustachio, he had

to be poisoned by the council of tlatoanis cuz he didn't care to leave, but we're still using his Stone for ritual purposes becuz, well, it weighs 20 tons, & if you carried that thing up to the top of a pyramid as high as a mountain, would you want to carry it back down to the bottom again just becuz the inscription was spelled wrong, *just becuz sponsors had pulled out of the ad campaign?)* **anyway** *I could suddenly see that in spite of all the ingenious scientifik calculations on the part of experts, professors & akademicians such as my wife, in spite of the strange or flat-out obtuse bloodthirsty spiritual explorations by internal explorers and inner-space discoverers such as my brother & Ixquintli the Clan Elder, and our kalpulli chief before him (and even in some smaller way, myself), these guys at the top were fucking everything up!* Their fuck-ups were suddenly clear to me as they were strapping me to the Stone of Tizok. *They were just going about the duties of ruling the known universe by* **rote** *& they weren't really paying attention to* details. *They were attending to the economik health of the State & of the entire land & its Many Races of people while they were being fooled, entranced, deluded or confused by their own Existential Stupidness and Korruption. That's what I decided when one of their assistants placed the stick in my hand, my Weapon of Last Defense, a piñata stick decorated with white pigeon feathers. I knew what came next. Sure enuf, Maxtla, Eagle Warrior, Kommander & Keeper of the House of Mist, showed up with six front-line shock troops; they were fully arrayed in their grandest finery, ketzal feather headdresses, handwoven kevlar mantas, war paint masking their ugly faces, big steel-flanged war klubs, kombat chanklas, swollen tattoos, clean white T-shirts, big knives. They were looking forward to debilitating me in a serious way. They were so eager they did not dare to even smile for fear of breaking out into raucous laughter atop the holy site of the Great Pyramid. They were itching to start. I didn't feel too good, a hollow nausea spreading out of my gut, my knees weak, the deep ache of fear descending into the bones of my hands and legs. My mouth went dry, I worked it, trying to think of something to say. Usually you are thinking there must be something you can say or do to make everything OK, but that's stupid. My wife had stopped paying attention about ten years previous, my mother-in-law, probably the most important person in my life whether I knew it or not, had stopped taking my calls, my so-called friends were dead or gone, these guys were going to take me one on one until I was too injured to fight anymore, so what was there to say? I leaned* *back against the Stone of Tizok, to which I had been firmly attached, easing my sore feet, anyway, while I prepared a major speech which would denounce the current failed leadership <u>and</u> their deluded policies of the state, the tlatoanis on the Central Kommittee whose opportunist polices were leading to Environmental Degradation on a Planetwide Skale, Spiritual Pollution of Key Populations, Aesthetik Destruktion of Our Way Of Life, I prepped my <u>Mind</u> to start deklaiming the evils of the Elite especially that chump the Minister of Labor Xalatokli (Sandy Alluvial Soil) & his klique of Neoliberal Ekonomists. I swear I was about to marshal all Necessary Fakts, Figures or Rhetorikal Flourishes in order to speechify in such a way before the Great Crowd in the Central Plaza below that everyone's hearts would be ripped out, they would gape in astonishment, their thinking would be Revolutionized in that very instant, they'd titter with half-assed satori & enlightenment, they'd be struck breathless, they'd go, "This vato is one kool dude!" But when I opened my mouth to talk, all I could manage was a squawk like a crow, my throat was so dry I started to cough, I held up my hand & said, "Wait a minute," but the head priest with his face painted black and gray said, "Shut up & fight," and then the fight was on.*

The first guy they sent to fight me was Big & Ugly. Some vatos their skulls look too big for their eyes, their eyes sink deeply into their skulls, their eyes look out like weasel eyes from little weasel holes, desperate, dim, fierce and beady under a thick Neanderthal brow. "Is that a hairy helmet or is that whole thing your head? I'm gonna kill ya," I said, smirking. Big Ugly didn't appear to hear me; he shifted his ten-pound steel-flanged klub in his right hand & stepped in, slicing the air diagonally with the weapon. I attempted to scurry around the other side of the Tizok Stone, to put it between me and Big Ugly, but I was tied off, I was stuck. I moved a few steps laterally then jerked taut at the end of the rope, I stepped inside his swing and jabbed the piñata stick in Big Ugly's face, which caused him a moment's hesitation. He blinked, and I screeched like a papagayo. Big Ugly was about to break my bones. He shifted the klub in his hand again, stepped in, I leaned back, my back pressed against the stone. He pulled his arm back for a bone-crushing swing as I shrieked like two women rolling around in a catfight, I kicked him direktly in his gut, sinking the ball of my foot in, even tho my feet did hurt and still do, causing him to exhale, sending him staggering backwards, out of breath. "Fuck this," I whined, striking my light little piñata stick against the Tizok Stone as hard as I could, once, twice, till the end snapped off, like I wanted, giving me a jagged spike. I stepped laterally, weaving back and forth as much as the tether would allow, testing my freedom of movement and pointing the jagged tip of the stick at him, asking Big Ugly, "You ugly fuck, you ever see the Ali/Foreman fight in Zaire? You ever see the Rope-a-Dope? That's what I'm gonna do to you. When you get tired of hitting me with that big klub, I'm gonna stick this piece of wood in your eye till it pushes out the back of your bone head." Big Ugly snorted derisively as he swung the klub with amazing LAPD agility at my head, all I had time to do was give a frisky *yip!* like a coyote pup, leap sideways to the end of my rope, lose my balance, the klub striking my left shoulder, breaking the collarbone, it snapped like a hot pretzel, my left arm went useless, I leaned to that side, bringing my right arm up as Big Ugly stepped into the motion of his arc, I thrust the pointed stick into his neck below his ear, angling up, *hard as I could!* Talk about Satisfaktion, when that went in! Just behind his jaw, which opened wide, but which produced no sound that could be heard above the roar of the appreciative crowd. Big Ugly turned away & I jumped for the klub, but the klub spun out of his fingertips, clanking like a crowbar as it bounced away on the pyramid stone, disappearing over the Edge. Big Ugly staggered a couple steps, then went down on one knee, reaching up to pull the stick out of his neck. Then he yelled or groaned like it really *hurt all that much*. Wasn't he a Huitzilopochtli izquintli-eating warrior supposed to be able to withstand *stoikally* all manner of physikal insult? Instead what was the matter with him that his komrades were helping him to his feet so that he could stagger away? Rope-a-Dope motherfucker! Kontender Number Two stepped up watchfully, a tall skinny kid with all sorts of Asian tattoos like a Yakuza, dragons fulminating in Hiroshige klouds on both shoulderblades, Zapotek calaveras with horns grinning down his arms, pointed teeth dripping blood at his wrists, "Estrada Kourts Rifa, c/s," enscribed on his pechos, three dots between his thumb & pointer, "XIII Siempre" tattooed akross the back of his neck, blue jailhouse tear drops from the korner of one eye signifying he had killed at least one man every year since he was 12, Virgin of Guadalupe emblazoned with skroll ("Brown Pride") on his stomach, and just like the last guy, this homie seemed to have no sense of humor. Yakuza Vato waved a big machete like a konduktor's baton in easy figure eights & that worried me, right there. Cuz my pointy stick had gotten away, stuck in the side of Big Ugly's neck. It lay bloody on the stones far out of reach. I looked around hopefully but nobody stepped forward to lend me another piñata stick right at this time. *All right, mano a mano, you fucking Door Man, you bouncer from a Disko Klub.* My feet burned, my shoulder screamed, I felt like a spider half stepped on, parts of me stuck to the floor. Yakuza Vato skirted me in a semi-circle, sizing me up, easily dipping the point of his shiny machete in my direktion. I attempted to stand straight, as if my left arm was fully funktional. Yakuza Vato saw thru this pose, however, when he feinted, thrusting at my chest, I stepped to the right, shielding my left side. He'd been watching; Yak Vato knew the Signs. Nevertheless, I knew he wasn't going for a fatal thrust to the torso, or a mortal chop at my head or neck. Etiquette demanded that he strike another disabling blow at one of my limbs. He was only here to maim me. Yakuza Vato, proud warrior, which limb would he pick? I studied his eyes, hard to read as he squinted in the late afternoon glare. His eyes definitely lingered, I thot, on my knees. It came to me that Yak Vato was a proud man—he wanted to hamstring both legs at the same time! Then I'd be down & immobile—Maxtla, Keeper of the House of Mist was surely next and the big kommander could finish me at leisure with flourishes for the crowd, instant replays for the TV audience. I sensed this in a split second, as immediately Yakuza Vato swung the machete in a high arc down at my left shoulder, expekting me to fall back against the stone, no doubt, exposing my lower body & legs for a backhand blow, instead I stepped forward to sweep his ankle nearest me, kicking it inside; he tripped over his own foot coming into the swing, softening the blow, which sunk into my upper arm—caused me a great deal of sudden shocking pain, a great deal of Distress indeed as you might imagine when a machete chops right into your bicep. Surprised but not undone, like a good warrior Yakuza Vato stumbled but followed thru along his own line of attack, going past me, dancing around the Stone of Tizok for another try. Yakuza Vato with his tightly gripped, flashing machete reminded me of a skorpion. If I hadn't tripped him up his blow would have cut to the bone, possibly breaking my arm. As it was, the already useless arm hung loose, bleeding profusely; I felt like that side was on fire. Yakuza Vato took a deep breath or two, studying me respektfully as he sized up the next attack. This wuz the part I hated. Machete wuz gonna slice me and dice me. Yakuza Vato wasn't a big lunkhead like the last guy. He was careful to do me some damage with every move. I guessed I had one more chance at most before I became Yak Vato's sliced salami. I crouched and he made his move, coming in along the same line as before, same steps, same mistake. This time my right forward sweep was so hard my foot knocked his feet completely out from under him, both his arms flew up, his machete spun up into the sunlight & Yakuza Vato crashed on his back on the stones, the machete clattering as it came down. I wanted the weapon but there was no time to find out if my tether was long enuf, so I went for Yak Vato himself, rolling out of the impakt of his fall without any hesitation, getting his feet under him. I grabbed his shirt, kicked his feet out from under him *again*; pulled him down for the Third Time. His feathers askew, Yak Vato's dark eyes widened in alarm, both hands flew up before his face, on guard, I dropped to one knee to drive my elbow straight down into his center, just below the middle of his breastbone, cartilage inside him making a distinkt snap, I leapt back at the same time as I delivered a hard backhand to his face; I wuz back on my feet, on guard, as he rolled over, rising hunched, guarding his middle with both arms, his face pale, eyes fixed as he hunched over, something broken inside him, as he retreated. I threw myself toward the machete but the cord around my waist wasn't long enough; I threw myself against it, threw myself headlong toward the machete on the ground; jerking taut, the cord cinched at my waist, pulling me down. I fell on my injured side in a glaze of heat, kicking my legs furiously, blind, I contacted the machete with my *toes*. Straining against the limit of the line, frantik someone might move the machete before I reached it, I dragged it back to me with my foot. I rose, triumphant, the weapon in my one good hand, the world dancing in *the last gold light of the afternoon* as the crowd roared approval. I had a real weapon now! This wuz my chance. Kontender Number Three stepped forward smartly, *bow & arrows in hand*. It was Maxtla, Keeper of the House of Mist.

Tied to the Tizok Stone, I did a little dance back and forth, swift evasive maneuvering, busting out my secret moves, drawing on every aspekt of my Secret Shaolin Martial Arts training, sweat stinging my eyes as I gripped the machete as a protektive shield and Komrade Maxtla, Keeper of the House of Mist stepped up and casually let fly *arrow after arrow*. I *almost* deflekted the first arrow, its razor sharp steel quadriflange hunting head pinging off the machete blade as it slid straight up the length of my left forearm, ripping the furrowed skin the whole way, burrowing the length of my forearm to bury its point deep inside my elbow. Yowie! Huitzililo-fucking-pochtli! I never felt anything like that before! Did that hurt or what? *I almost deflekted that one!* Aktually the sensation of that first arrow ripping thru my forearm, burying its point inside my elbow joint reminded me of the time when I wuz eight years old watching my mom cry, asking her why wuz her nose bleeding ("Dad hit her in the face, stupid!" my sister said) I turned to make sure we were together as we departed that life forever, *then the next arrow struck me*. I had just finished a Michael Jackson-type Shirley Temple dance move, which I figured would fake Maxtla out entirely, so he'd either have to miss me completely or strike some vital organ and put me out of my misery *first thing*. But he must've anticipated it, high on the inside, since the arrow embedded itself thru both buttocks in the high part of my ass even as I prepared a *Smirk of Viktory*. The smirk shapeshifted instantly into an astonished yowl of banshee excruciation. "Fuck a Duck! Fuck the Famous Golden Peking Duck Your Mama Rode Into Town On!" I howled. Oxygenated sunflares from outer space blasted my spinal column. I wuz all of a sudden in a Supernova of Hurt. "Yukio Mishima & His Homo Fantasies of Saint Fucking Sebastian!" I gasped. I possibly pissed myself a little there. The second arrow *reminded me* of the time when I thot I was kool at a new skool, the new kid, looking for a brand new start, so I flirted with this cute girl in Art Klass, she flirted with me, I waited for her after skool but she had ditched me, I saw her leaving on the back of some guy's motorcycle, yeh, that sekond arrow *hurt my feelings a lot!* I gritted my teeth & threw the machete at Maxtla, Keeper of the House of Mist. I could no longer see him very well. He was just a shadow to me inside the blood red *last light of afternoon.* It seems he stepped to the side without any exertion, the machete clanked, spinning away into space over the crowd, which was having *the experience of a lifetime!* Ask anyone who wuz there that day, they will tell you it wuz the best thing they'd ever seen! The crowd was roaring. Whoever got hit by the machete when it landed below added his or her own personal blood sakrifice to the whole ritual. They loved it. They'd have the skar of a lifetime, proving *they too were there!* The third arrow struck my right thigh dead center above the knee so I went down. I wuz skreaming you can bet yer ass, or *what*-Huitzilo-fucking-pochtli-*ever*, falling on the arrow, driving it further thru the other side of my leg. One side of my mind wuz annotating the Principles of Thermodynamiks as Propounded by Doktor Tepapakwiltikan in his research of 1905, whilst I was simultaneously whistling "Motherfucking Dixie" like I wuz fit to be fried in the electrik chair! I wuz beside myself. (Convulsing with extra screams.) I busily commenced trying to do a one-handed push up, arrows sticking out of my body. I *used* to be good at that sort of thing. But I couldn't seem to catch my breath. *That last arrow reminded me of the time when I walked the streets day after day in 1930, week after week, looking for work, I wuz 15 years old, half-starved & they all told me they would kall me, none of 'em ever did & the rest of that year I kouldn't even get a full-time job washing dishes scraping the bottoms of peanut butter jars for my dinner. Somebody or something wuz kicking my ass that whole year down all the back alleys of the entire city.* I struggled to sitting position with my back against the Tizok Stone, *when the fourth arrow went thru my right shoulder.* After that I just lost count. I lost all patience! What the hell! I couldn't keep up, not if Maxtla wuz gonna keep shooting arrows *that fast.* You know, when you fill out insurance klaims &

police reports on these types of events, they are always asking you to rekall every detail, but I'm sorry, at that point, I could no longer keep _kount._ *The fourth arrow did happen to remind me of . . . the fuck if I know, I dunno, what? . . . standing in the unemployment line? No, maybe more like the look on the woman's face in the cubikle in the back of the employment office, looking at her contact information, writing out the numbers on skratchpaper for you, handing it to you to get you out of her office, with that look on her face . . . The fourth arrow reminded me of the sound a baby's head makes when it falls out of a high chair onto the floor becuz the mom is busy doing housework, distrakted by something else . . . That fourth arrow reminded me of ice crystals in the wind biting into your face as you finally stand at an old mass grave, long since cemented over, on a sunny winter day . . . it's taken you a long time to arrive at the gravesite . . . the 4th arrow reminded me of the anonymity of death into which they drive whole peoples . . . the fourth arrow hurt, it reminded me of the dark kitchen, the squalor of love . . . the 4th . . . it reminded me not to be afraid, death is like this . . . the 4th quadriflange arrowhead angled thru my shoulder, stopped by the Tizok Stone at my back, as I fell forward this arrow reminded me that my pain is so deep that I ache now without any explanation, my pain is so deep it never had a cause nor does it lack a cause now . . . If they had slashed my throat all the way thru my pain would still be the same . . . no matter what happens . . . I almost dodged all those arrows . . . that sorry bastard just got in one lucky shot, if it wasn't for that . . .*

OK, then they carried me to the chakmool, laid me out on it, opened me up & cut out my heart.

Except that never happened. Let me make that clear, I would never let that happen. That might have happened on some alternate reality when I wuzn't looking, some fucking Other World when they didn't let me get my two cents in. But it didn't happen this time. *Cuz I didn't let it happen.* I had to make my move sooner, at some previous point in History so that could never occur.

112

ASIER said than done, that's what they say. Swim like a motherfucker, I might add, when rising tides bear all boats ceaselessly back to the past. Swim like a son of a bitch, paddle harder. It has its occupational hazards, this gig, Keeper of the House of Darkness for the Party of Aztek Socialism. I could live without it but I need the cash. I got my debts, hobbies, pet projects, broken-down cars, child support payments, old folks in convalescent homes, black holes to throw money down. I've tried numerous other jobs in my time. As a teenager, I was assistant to a Tlatelolko pochteka during the summers; he traveled about Mesoamerika trading slaves, drugs, armaments, clothing, ball players, the typical pochteka mule runs. It was interesting for a kid, of course; I got to see a lot of country—jungle miasmas, lowlands ruled by Tlalok, black wastes of volcanic desert in the Mexikan night, mountainous cordillera, coastal undulations, estuarine lowlands, sumps, sloughs, rises, bluffs, nitrate mines, deserts of Sipan, Tarahumaran Barranka del Cobre, Mayan highlands. . . . We traveled the rivers of the continent in little flatbottom canoes and small motorized launches, navigating bilious networks of waterways that serve as main commercial routes in the bottom country. I became proficient in sleeping while swimming, in collecting rainwater in my bottom lip while paddling furiously, in locating my center of balance in a watery world lacking much definition in terms of either horizon or solid ground. I could bathe without light & right a canoe in my dreams, paddle fiercely while lighting a small fire in the prow of the boat to ward off the malarial zancudos, mosquitoes, pinche deer flies, insidious clouds of gnats, biting black flies, killer flying leeches. . . . I could ward off the half-intentional blow of Xal's (my boss) club while securing the cargo without a look or a thought. . . . We traveled as much in the dark as in the light. . . . We traveled as much in the underworld of our spirits as we did above ground. . . . This man taught me much even tho he was spiritually bankrupt & a kommercial lightweight of no account, just in the stoic attitude he took toward existence. His name was Xalatoktli (Sandy Alluvial Soil) so I called him Sandy or Al. Or maybe I called him Xal. Or maybe I called him sir or he would hit me upside the head out of habit & leave me alone & flat broke holding the bag & waiting for him on the waterfront of some river burg 2,500 miles and five months from home with some nasty jungle rot crawling up my leg toward my privates, itching without a clue. That's more or less what did happen but I'm sure Xal had his reasons. Cuz the life of a pochteka is one without dignity anyway, it's not like he had the intellekt or penetrating idealism of the priest caste or the disciplined intensity of the warrior or the civil servitude of a kommunity leader or malcontent activist or the drug-induced stupitude & caffeine-accelerated heartbeat of goofy-assed artists living in a fantasy world. No, Xal, he had the responsibilities of somebody who has to live in the real world and make money hand over fist or otherwise what is the purpose in life? Cuz I mean, yeah. So what if Xal told me to wait for him for a couple of hours while he went into town & made another deal & he left me on the waterfront in the Mesoamerikan lowlands in some town like Bluefields populated by displaced Afrikanate tribes milling about like nobody's business? So I was sitting on some burlap sacks of fishmeal or rotten cornmeal or whatever it was, stinky stuff—it helped keep the passersby at bay (I couldn't smell it myself cuz of how I smelled), till someone told me to beat it, they were gonna load this on a barge going up the Uxumacinta. So I did what any abandoned abused exploited ignored whiny teenager typically does when left to his own youthful resources in such a situation (having been exploited as apprentice all summer for only the promise of pay): I moved off to the wall of some cannery or warehouse or whatever and cast dark sullen glances at people who were sizing me up for imminent or indifferent threat of some kind. "Fuck you, you fuckers," I was undoubtedly thinking in my heart of hearts, "don't give me those shitty looks, glances, sneers, funny faces, rolling of eyes & curious eye-brow wrinkles you backwoods fruit-eating no-account round-shouldered down-river coastal-cousin-humping Sasquatches I got your number you ain't got nuthin on me shit I ain't like you in no way I don't have nuthin to do with you or your kind I am about to leave this burg in my dust right now just any second now in a minute or 2! Now, where is Xal, where could that man be? I KNOW he will be by here before I can say *spit*. Spit . . ." Ah well, so it turned out that I had worked for Xal all summer helping him tie slaves down in the bottom of the boat where they could not escape into the swamp to their certain deaths or mate with the crocodiles to produce little golden-haired half-breed children in the methane-tainted hillocks rising above the pestilential floodwaters, with their tiny forlorn plots of squash, platanos and maniok that gave you a stomach ache just to think of having to live their pitiful lives stuck out in the sticks that way in the utter darkness of misery snakes poverty & shit (literal shit, I'm talking major malarial black-green diarrhea with parasitik worms, *not* metaphorical poetic shit of some mental type, not existential "shit"—we're talking stomach cramping shits from *birth!* from *day one!* real shits up the cloaca & spurting out, leaping out of the lower intestine!) so it was all to the good, all for the better as Xal was fond of explaining to me, that me and him crept into these clearings in the jungles off the coasts of the pretty waist of Ms. Mesoamerika with nothing more than clubs made of big pieces of ironwood or something very heavy and my minor league martial arts training when we emerged from the under-brush to beat the adults senseless if they tried to stop us from stealing their children. Didn't they know there was a severe labor shortage in the bur-geoning Aztek economy and inflation was on the rise? Didn't they know if they invested in the stock market they'd make a better return on their sav-ings than if they put their money in T-bonds or gold certificates? Didn't they know they should move to the suburbs? Didn't they know we were saving their children from a lifetime of boredom back there in the shitholes of muddy brown water & too many leaves to imagine (the exact number of those rainforest leaves it turned out was the ever-changing combination to the doorway to several alternate realities but you know it's so hard to guess I did get it right one time {23,901,7782,880,633 x K to the 435th power; believe me you don't even want to know how I got it} but the only thing that happened was that I was instantly sitting back at the picnik tables in the sunstricken yard of the Farmer John's Packing Plant where the semis and two-ton delivery trucks pulled through the gates—I got a glimpse of overwhelming fearful realities for just a millisecond, then I fled in terror immediately back to some sort of reality that I was faintly used to, at least I thought it was the right reality, that's right, yeah?) plus, in the bargain, while doing these disadvantaged children the actual service of bringing them to the kapital where they could see the sites, the Big Chicharron, starting with their debut on the platforms of the Eastern Slave Market where they could breathe free of their much worse bonds of misery & ignorance & enjoy the better benefits of our kulture, civilization, ethos, values, tattoos, parking lots, and on top of all that they could feed us, serve us, maybe get sacrificed with great pomp & ceremony upside of some really terrific looking Pyramid (as the tourist guides call 'em), with their hearts finally doing *someone else some good for a change, someone other than themselves*—**yeah**—*they can learn to think of someone besides themselves for a change! They don't have to be so god damned self-centered, the ignorant no-account little imps & swamp spirits & rainforest dwellers, they too can contribute to the betterment of the world & the enlightening of civilization and the growth of the gross domestic product on a globalized scale.* **Yeah.** That's what Xal used to say & that's what I said too. Leastways till he left me in that no-name rotten fish's head of a river town on the Uxumacinta. I was miffed. I was put out. I was somewhat internally disconsolate. After all our weeks & months together, with me having to eat whatever Xal left over of the food he made me cook for him, & having to keep clubbing the little slave children, toddlers or whomever we tossed into the bottom of the boat so Xal could get some god damned sleep, there he left me, up the creek without a paddle, scratching my thigh with its red raw scaly fungus infection that looked sort of like a frightening case of psoriasis on an old man's yellowish skull, I sat there scratching it listlessly till it bled a little & I achieved some measure of relief & there was a little blood underneath my fingernails that I might notice later, pick at, taste to see what dried blood caked under your fingernails might taste like after it's had some time to age . . . "Xal, Xal, Xal (Sandy Alluvial Soil) how could you do this to me I thought you were my friend, I thot you treated me so callously and you wouldn't give me food just cuz you were having a bad day that happened to stretch into weeks and months & I went from thinking you always had a headache and were in a bad mood to thinking you were a giant headache & I'd like to club you as hard as I could across your meaty neck where it met your shaven skull (which you sometimes decorated with a jaunty little Afrikan cap), but no, Xal, I never did expect you to do this bad thing now how am I ever to get my sorry teenage ass back to the kapital where I belong. Xal—I hesitate to mention—but the locals are giving me the eye—you know—appreciatively, sort of quantitatively, sizing me up—just like how we sit in a bush & look over the little children before we bundle them into the boat for their wild ride back to the kapital days & days later. Xal, you have hurt my feelings. You have gone & caused me to have a problem here. How could you do it Xal?" Easy, I found out. Just takes a little practice, like sexual intercourse with domestic animals that tend to jump, or anything else in human experience. Just takes practice.

Of course teenagers don't know about that kind of stuff & they just have to learn. They must be taught. Thanks Xal you have been a help.

When the stevedores finally loaded the last sack onto the ship and dispersed into the docks at twilight I knew I was in trouble. I started worrying in my stomach & in my head. Visions & blindness might have been a consolation to me then. Instead there was just the dirty river slapping against the sides of the boats, the stinking docks, the boats turning into black hulks on the silvery sheen that reflected the flare of red orange sunset over the jungle. My invitation was growing stale, my welcome was running out, I felt, as the last of the dock workers grabbed their jackets, heading into town in twos & threes. "Where you from, ese?" some squat indio smirked as he went by. "Nowhere," I just shook my head. I seemed to be lacking my backup now when I needed it, but the little barrel-house indio and his friends kept moving. I didn't want to be the last person at the party so I followed them into town. Maybe I could find Xal on my own. Even tho he had expressly told me, "Wait right here & watch this empty sack of useless items, empty bottles & broken musical instruments till I get back, be sure you don't move from this spot or I will break your jaw. Okay kid? Got my drift?" Maybe he'd just forgotten. Maybe he'd fallen asleep. Maybe the poor guy was in trouble and it was up to me to save him! Yeah, that was probably it! He sure would be glad to see me! I'd wade right into the bad guys doing bad things to poor Xal, I'd save his ass, he'd be grateful ever more he'd shake my hand man to man he'd slap me on the back & tell me I did good, he'd even start thinking about paying me. The trouble was that the first waterfront dive I walked into, the way they looked at me as I came in the door made me feel like the skinny kid I was, & what was I supposed to say when they asked—as the red-eyed sodden meat-face did—"Who the fuck are you?" Anyway before I could figure out the right answer, he turned to me, his friends had all turned to me, ready, & he snarled, "Get the fuck outa here!" "Anybody here know Xal?" I asked. "Why am I still looking at you, motherfucker?" the man with the swollen red face whined, swiveling heavily off his stool to a standing position. I put up both my hands & went out the door. There were only two more bars on the adjacent streets and it seemed like they all had the same guys in them. I don't know what their problem was. Bad day at work, shitty jobs most likely. They didn't speak Nahuatl so I don't know what they were saying exactly, tho I'm sure it wasn't pretty, I thought it must be some Miskitu version of the brush-off I'd gotten before. Xal didn't seem to be in any of the nearby bars, even tho I knew he sometimes popped into them as soon as we hit a town, as much to sample the local news and vibes as to get a drink. So I walked the little streets more or less systematically from the waterfront up the slope into town, the muddy streets littered with the trash washed by daily rains into piles & clumps against the walls & steps of the buildings, everything smelling like rotten fruits & vegetables, the sewage from the black puddles standing in the empty lots with oil cans & dead dogs lying half out of the water. Then it started to drizzle. Then I noticed that three guys were following me. Then I started running. Then I thought I lost 'em zigzagging thru some alleys, jumping over a fence & running thru some empty lots toward the river. I could hear 'em calling, friendly-like, "Hey Mexika boy. Where you going? We just want to talk to you." etc. I headed in some roundabout way — I didn't want them following me — back to the river. I went up a rickety flight of wooden stairs, across a balcony strung with wet laundry as gray as the rain, running past an open window where something sizzled and popped in a pan with the sharp whiff of fried egg, my footsteps spattered across the creaky wooden balcony teetering off the crummy building, I thought the guys chasing me were right behind me, I heard a shout, "He went up there!" Someone bellowed at me thru a screen door as I went past in some language I didn't recognize one bit, I went over the railing that threatened to break away in my hands & shimmied down a support post into the yard below piled up with stacks of rusted zinc roofing, pipes & pieces of scrap metal, machinery of various kinds clumped into rusted scaly unusable iron, boxes and crates of glassware and stuff falling apart in gray stacks of garbage, I scrambled atop some dead washing machines & heaved myself over a board fence that waffled back & forth & couldn't support my weight. So I had to jump to the ground in the weeds below and that was mean and nasty. Cuz under the grass & weeds & everything green in the gray drizzly rain, everything lush and smelling of the voraciousness of Life which gives it its *freshness*, supple & green, there were more piles of trash, boards & other stuff & I landed on all fours & fell sideways into a board full of nails. I was screaming out before I could make myself stop, I was giving them a fix on my location with a sharp yelp as several nails (I found out) penetrated my shoulder & one pierced my ear for me & dug a slight groove along my temple *hooked like a fish on a jig line.* "Shut up," I told myself. But I'd already blurted out a stupid noise. I had to figure they were coming, that they knew where I was. Everything was soft & quiet, the drizzle gently dampening the lush mounds of grass where I lay with the pain screaming silently into my body. I jerked myself to standing, all the nails pulling out of my flesh except one — it came out of the rotten wood as I stood and I had to extract the brittle rusty thing with the fingertips of my right hand & fling it aside with an exhalation, step lightly, carefully thread my way between the clumps of grass & debris (nails went thru my sandals a couple more times but without drawing blood as I proceeded out of the trash heaps with care) *my shoulder locked in a stiff triangulation of searing complaint;* I pinned my left arm to my side to try & minimize the feeling. So it was, listing to the left like a leaky vessel, I disappeared between the trees & silently ran, slid, stumbled, got soaked to the bone & chilled all the way thru from the cascades of water that showered me as I brushed against the weeping tree limbs, slipped & fell hard on my ass, got up & ran on, bloody, the blood running down one side of my face like military paint in the wet, my white cotton trousers black with mud & filth. I hung by one hand from the top of the two-story-high slanting seawall & dropped down, sliding. At the bottom of the wall several stones embedded in it emerged to hit me hard, a punishing pounding as I fell to my knees into the mud of the riverbank. I pulled myself to my feet with my good arm and leaned back against the slick wet stones of the seawall & listened for any sounds of pursuit. Tried to catch my breath so I could hear something over the pounding of my heart in my ears. I heard a boat bell clanking across the water, the wash from it slapping the wet black banks of the vile stinking Uxumacinta. I walked back toward the lights of the town along the mudbank, realizing I'd somehow lost a sandal somewhere cuz every now & then I'd step on things I could feel in the sole of my foot, things that would crunch like broken glass or fish bones, something that crunched like rotten cans. I tried to navigate the wide mud flats by using the reflected lights from town shimmering across the sewage seeping from pipes that jutted out from the seawall. Sometimes I'd step into a deep hole that looked like a shadow & sink into disgusting soupy black water up to my knee. I walked back & forth across the mudflats for hours. There was no getting past it, I realized, a couple hours before dawn. This was the spot where Xal & I had anchored the boat. I walked in a wide circle around the mudflats, around the idea that I inevitably homed in on — the boat was gone. Xal (Sandy) had done left me.

Ah, youth! The memories! Life! More memories! It never stops! I seem to recall that I stood there for a long time in the dark mudflats, with the lights of the town at my back. I tried to figure out what I'd done wrong. I couldn't. I was caked in mud, shivering as much from the puncture wounds as from my wet clothes, caked in stinking mud against my skin. Holding my left arm against my body with the other, listening to the lap of the river and clank of a distant boat bell.

I wonder what I was thinking then. *How long does lockjaw take to set in?* I know what I always used to say in the situations that I used to keep finding myself in. "Shit!" I used to say. "Fucking shit. God damn fucking shit." I used to say that a lot.

Of course the next morning when it was light I took a hard look at the surrounding jungle & immediately gave up the idea of trying to bushwhack thru the impenetrable mangrove thickets emerging from the black water. The river was the only way out; I had to stow away on a barge. I picked one out, swam out to it & grabbed on. It hadn't even left the dock yet when a guy leaning over the side to smoke a cigarette looked down & spotted me hanging with one leg over a rope, I was just hanging there, hoping my fingers would last till the tug moved away from the landing. The deckhand's expression didn't change. He just tossed his cigarette away & vanished from sight. I sucked air, dropped into the river, and tried to swim for it. I headed toward the pilings, thinking I might lose them under the landing. But I couldn't swim worth a damn, the cold deep currents pushing me around. I had to come up for air & a dinghy came up alongside & something hit me on the head really hard.

So I woke up with my wrists trussed to my ankles behind me. Sold into slavery, plus the insult of the low price to some overseer whose test for sturdiness consisted of first pinching your ribs to see if you had any body fat whatsoever & then hauling off & slugging you in the gut to see if you'd double up & fall over. I didn't; I hardly even bent over; I just hung my jaw open and gasped for air like a fish, trying to clear flashing spots from my vision. I passed that test. I did some time on an overseer's cotton plantation. He sold me down the road. Then I did some time in the cane fields. I lost the tip of a finger to a machete; I lost two bottom teeth to the beatings. Broken jaw. Crushed larynx. Separated cornea. Nearly lost an eye. I carry the scars of that time like the map of a whole 'nother country I hadn't even dreamt existed. Learned me a whole new geography that didn't exist in books. So this is what life must be like in Sierra Leone, Afghanistan, Burma, Sudan, Southside Chicago, Kambodia, Ciudad Juarez? Took me till my eighteenth birthday to figure out how to get off that shitty Mosquito coast. I killed a couple guys, some overseer and some slave who was just in the way, a little guy who would have just slowed me down, he begged for his life & I turned him around so he faced away from me & choked the life out of him & took an old leaky rowboat & headed north toward Mayan country. The overgrown Mayan country was looking good by then. You can bet I was weeping by the time I set eyes on the looming green Yukatan. That whole experience sort of soured me on the whole pochteka lifestyle. After that, I couldn't see myself making a mercantile career out of it. I ain't got a good head for business; there's some aptitude there I just don't have.

2 things about that time that I seem to keep with me, recalling now & then without thinking about them: the first is awakening once again in the pitch black of the barracks chained to the next guy, awakening in the fetid impenetrable humidity on the floor of the barracks, beaten & wounded, beaten for being wounded, my whole body a broken terrain of agonies, shifting waves of ripping pain like sheets of rain hitting a body of water in sunlight, my hand with the missing fingertip throbbing. Realizing that I was awake, that it was not a nightmare, that it was actual awakeness even tho I could not see a single thing, just the flare or lunging about of my own mind in the blackness for something to see, think about, recognize; calm-

ing my mind, ignoring its questing for something to latch onto beyond the sensations of damage, I wondered whether the dark was total & complete becuz of lack of light or was it some damage they'd done to my eyes? Had I lost my sight? My eyes swollen, half my jaw, the aching, loose molars. Then I had a thought that consoled me thru the miserable night. I reviewed the little fantasy again & again in my mind's eye, I pictured to myself what I would do with him when I caught up with Xal. "Xal, Xal, Xal, it's been such a long time." Xal would not have grown any more loquacious in the interim. "So?" Xal would say, gruff & indifferent as ever, not inclined in the slightest to show any recognition or any concern at all upon seeing me, except perhaps an almost imperceptible millisecond of hesitancy when he'd asked, "So?" I had seen it — or thought I'd seen it — becuz my stare was so intent on him. "So, Xal, when you sold me down the river," I'd repeat, *"when you sold me down the river after I spent all summer working for you for nothing,* they beat my ass to the bone for weeks & months trying to break my spirit, Xal. I still have headaches & nightmares. I nearly died, you fuck." I wasn't sure if Xal would shrug or just turn away, not even bothering to answer, already thinking about his next deal & no more concerned about me than he would have been about a gob of spit he'd hawked over the boat rail. Maybe Tezkatlipoka would murmur thru my lips, tap Xal on the shoulder with my fingertips, "Wait a minute, Xal, I'm talkin' to ya. I got somethin' to tell ya. I learned something during the time I was gone." And this was the good part of the fantasy that always made me feel happy inside. "Eh? What's that?" Xal would get around to asking. "Karate," I'd say, grinning as I snapped his head back with two punches before I knocked him flat with a front kick with the ball of my foot sinking deep into his diaphragm, knocking him flat on his ass so that he slid back on the seat of his pants, all the air out of him, and the shock of that landing causing him to wonder what was happening, Xal would be looking up at me quizzically, his curiosity aroused perhaps for the first time in decades. Then an inkling of what was about to happen would come to him and he'd plead, gruffly still, but undeniably pleading, "Don't kill me." "No, Xal doesn't need killing," I'd say, or something wittier if I could think of it at the time, "you'll live as well as you may," I'd explain as I disabled him with more blows to the face & body before I began removing his eyes with my fingers.

It didn't matter to me later when I learned that any dreams that come out of the slave quarters at night never come true. People like Xal would never be at the mercy of slaves in this world, but what does it matter if retribution is never to be ours? We leave it to Tezkatlipoka. We have the consolation of our thoughts when we need them; they were a great comfort to me in the insufferable darkness of the nights in the barracks on the Mosquito coast.

That turned out to be one of the lines on my resume that got me my present position, Keeper of the House of Darkness.

And the 2nd thing I'd remember about those days: after the incessant beatings, after killing two men with my bare hands to make my escape, with my chest drumming & the adrenal psychosis wearing off, I wrestled that shitty little barque into the surf & paddled north with a broken paddle as the calmness came upon me. I entered the vast ocean, it surrounded me with its repleteness, it was slopping & crashing into the crappy leaky little craft so that sometimes I had to stop paddling & furiously bail, scooping out water with both hands. The seawater rose over my ankles but I paddled & bailed, bailed & paddled as the sky grew dark, the clouds rolling off the headlands & bringing rain down on the sea. I knew I was irretrievably alone & vulnerable to the waves, so far from home that no one was likely to ever hear the circumstances of my disappearance when the rinky-dink rowboat went down, but exhausted as I was by labor, travail, illness, & beatings, my solitude seemed one of the best things that had ever happened to me. I was—at best—starting out at the beginning of a long, difficult, trouble-filled journey from which I might never return in this world, and what enabled me to paddle with feeling, to bail with immediate passion, paddle & bail & move on up the coast—slowly, inexorably the boat moved north, swell after swell, wave on wave—was the happiness that solitude amounted to in me. They'd tried to trap me & could not; they'd tried to break me & could not; they'd tried to kill me & I was alive. The day had darkened; night was falling with rain on the rolling ocean as I paddled north in a leaky little boat. I suffered from some kind of immaculate and perfect happiness; my arms were hardly responding, the long muscles of my triceps, biceps & forearms slack & throbbing with exhaustion, my shoulders shrieking distress at each sculling, but I dragged the paddle thru the rolling swells till I was afraid my numbed fingers would lose it over the side; I leaned forward, sobbing & gasping to catch my breath, bailing, paddling again. Till I was far, far . . . gone up the coast. . . . The soft chilling drizzle drifting out of a sky of black clouds drenched me like a blessing. The entire ocean of the planet was mine alone, the sky fading behind black clouds in the twilight, all of it was mine. I have not felt the same vast euphoria suffusing everything before or since as the man paddling the boat north along the coast toward the distant dream of the Yukatan. I was making myself free & I knew it, every shredded breath I took that cinched a hurt in my side moved me farther north; this was how being free felt, lost & alone on the sea, up the darkening coast.

I walked thru the corridor past the kill floor when Cuzatli (Weasel) pushed a steel cart full of hogs' heads thru the plastic swinging doors with a bang, so I stepped aside out of his way, and a blast of swirling humidity enveloped me, clouds of steam scented with blood, and I peered up into the rolling forest canopy, a drizzling wind blowing leaves all about me.

In the distance a river emptied in the sea.

13

SOMETIME late in the afternoon I dropped a dime in the pay phone in the yard by the Soto Street gate near the Tacos Oaxaca truck parked beside the so-called lunch tables and dialed her office; I left a message for Nita at the number she'd given me on her card. They said she was out in the field but they'd make sure she got it. "Tell her I got the signatures and I'll be waiting for her at the diner," I said. "Where?" said the voice. "She'll know where I mean," I said. Earlier Zahuani had leaned the mop against the wall, pulled a piece of meat out of his back pocket, like a red kerchief made out of nearly translucent tissue. He poked two holes in the flesh and lay it over his face. His living eyeballs peered out of the raw meat like a casualty in a burn ward. Rolling his eyes as he stuck his tongue thru the meat, he moaned, "Oh, Maria! Ooooooooohhhhhh, baby, come on!" Wagging his tongue back & forth, he looked at 3Turkey and me and said, "That's my Love Call." "Great," 3Turkey said. On the nite shift, as I recalled these words of wisdom from the day shift, I sniffled, wiping my nose on the sleeve of my white coat. I coughed into my white mask. I wuz freezing. I had to get out of the chilling room, if just for a moment. I shut the steel door behind me, the sound reverberating along the empty concrete corridor.

"Hey! Hey Zenzón!" I heard Weasel yelling as I hit the door, but bam, it slammed behind me and I was in no mood to go back & find out what he wanted. I was outside and it was a new day. If he was sucking up information for Max, Weasel was gonna have to do it on his own time. I was

done with the day, the day was done with me; the sun rose south by southwest in an indefinite sky. After 2 shifts I was feeling sick as a dog, an Aztek
dog, a Mexican hairless ixquintle raised for food on the outskirts of the
kapital in acres of kennels made of reed basketry on vast wastelands of dust
& pollution, bitter alkali dust that rises on a dirty breeze like the whimsy
of emptiness, which can make the little dogs nervous, so before they kill
them to fry or boil with epazotl, with cebolla, with cloves, you might see
the emaciated perritos staring at you with their eyes that like to pop out,
trembling and shaking. They might look & feel a little bit crazy like that,
sensing with their ratlike tails curled about their scrawny hindquarters that
they're about to get the knife. Somehow they know all about it even tho
they are only a senseless animal. That's why the dead Aztek wants a ceramic
ixquintle in his funeral spot, cuz it represents the Mexican hairless wisdom
of the universe, overlarge black swollen eyes, tearful & trembling & wise
like that. Which is to say that my nose was runny as usual, I had to wipe it
a bit on my sleeve as I exited the plant thru the side door along the loading dock, early in the morning, the sun slanting long shadows the length of
the old concrete dock, never used any more, bits of litter from the street
blown into corners with piles of fine dust like ash in obsolete loading bays
shuttered & closed forever, the trucks on Soto roaring by with a clatter, the
sun shining on everything in a very merry way. Surely it was semi-normal
to be feeling a bit under the weather like this as I skipped down the steps
to the asphalt and took to the street, I felt chilled to the bone & somehow
sick, basically ill in my spirit in spite of the fact that I wuz winning! I had
the roll of CIO union petitions under my arm, they were filled out to a T,
it was a masterstroke that would crash down on Max's head like the point
of the Pyramid of the Sun, I could foresee it all now—Max would be
beside himself, his haste & fury at always being overlooked in the Handler
family's closed advancement process that he allowed himself to secretly
dream he was a part of would be shown to be totally stupid, a sheer delu-
sion, Bob Handler would be mostly oblivious to any of it, certain of his
own selection in part based on the superior production statistics he got thru
the good luck of following on the heels of a hard-ass, of being cast in the

role of good cop without even applying for the part & without even being aware of the whole bad cop scenario really, part of the whole reason why everybody liked Bob Handler was becuz most of the time he was never a threat, he never really had any clear idea what was going on. "Can't we all just get along?" he probably would've murmured with silky smooth cluelessness had he any inkling of the iffy violence seething beneath the surface of day-to-day affairs that would, soon enough, erupt in vicious murder, high cholesterol, bad blood in the bologna, indigestion for the many, flatulence for a few.

Knowing in large part that *all that was ahead* becuz of second sight or second thots, Aztek wheels of circular reasoning & circles of time spinning in *the windmills of my mind*, calendrikal destiny shaky as the grit blown against the side of my face by jam-packed morning traffic as I walked on the sidewalk along the high wall of the plant in the shocking light of morning (at least, I found it shocking), the silly mural of pigs playing in a children's book picture of barnyards and pastureland sandblasted into opacity by the glare of the rising sun, I tried to walk normally. I can walk normal in an earthquake if I have to, I can hold my hand over a flame without screeching like a blue macaw, I can wipe my nose again on my sleeve & blink jaundice-eyed at the brilliance of sunshine on all hard surfaces of the orangish-blue industrial landscape. I can be sick inside, chilled to the pinche bones, you pack of weenies, & *maintain*. I scooted along the broad sun-stricken hectic avenue to the corner and hitched up my pants with one hand, thumbed the button for the crosswalk, shut the blare & gnashing of gears out of my ears, and leaned against the pole, fingering the roll of petitions. If Nita arrived ahead of me —

A semi blasted his air-horn at some fool in a pickup zig-zagging across the railroad tracks right in front of the grill of the truck, and I was roused from queasy misgivings & squinting dimly at the prospect of a pickup truck bouncing across the tracks fishtailing in my direction with a sudden clatter, feeling thoroughly washed up, I was about to remove myself behind the pole when the little pickup truck bounced in front of me & on, swerving into traffic. If I'd leaned over to tie my shoe, my brains would have been splashed in the gutter. My crackly eyes were scoured by particles of day-light, rinsed by waves of exhaustion as I crossed at the crosswalk, leaving my fate to a couple of painted lines that had existed more evidently than now. The Blue Hen Diner had an abandoned look, bluish windowpanes tinted by a gray film of dust, nearly opaque or flatly opaque under certain light, the same "Yes, We're Open" sign leaning near the door unmoved day in day out, faded blue letters on the dirty glass casting "Ostrich Burgers" unread-able across the crenellations of dusty booths. The interior was cool; I fled along a hallway to a rear booth, slumping in the corner . . .

Waitress.

"Coffee."

"Can I get you breakfast with that? Today's specials are chorizo & eggs and blueberry pancakes."

"I'm waiting for someone."

But who showed up was Cuzatli, slouching in a shuffle along the wall, walking like a cholo under the signed, faded black & white photos, their frames screwed into the wood-paneled wall, forgotten stars of yesteryear. Who was Red Whitaker or Tommy Crosby, do the teams they played for still exist? Weasel sniffled, wiping his inflamed nose on the sleeve of his Pendleton just like me, we all have incipient walking pneumonia from being locked in freezing high-ceilinged rooms double shifts back to back. I was making myself sit upright (already having stashed the paperwork for Nita below & out of sight, at my side) surely I did not look pleased as Weasel scooted into the booth opposite me. It wasn't his looks that caused his mother or whoever to name him Weasel but his manner—grinning at me across the little table as the waitress leaned her head around the booths to call out, "I'll be right there with a menu. Coffee?" I nodded and held up two fingers, Weasel nodding gratefully as his grin faded from one side of his face leaning his head to one side watching me askance thru his glasses (a vicious scar that gave the impression it still hurt biting into his skull like a dark zigzag thru the right eyebrow behind black Raybans, emerging onto his cheekbone from the corner of his eye, everything must look submarine in the diner behind dark glasses like that, I must have been staring at him like a moray eel waiting for him to get to the fucking point—but I knew he'd make me go down that road first), he said, "So this is your office, eh? So this is where the big decisions get made, so this is where you head honchos hang out." Before I could speak I sneezed violently, "Bah! Fuck!" grabbed a napkin, snorted and blew my nose into paper that immediately started disintegrating. When I could see clearly again Weasel was daubing his nostrils with a balled up napkin himself. "Max is gonna kick our fucking asses with these double shifts," he shrugged. "My old lady loves it tho, I gotta say. I'm out of her hair, never home, and she gets to spend the double paycheck. What the fuck, we needed a new roof anyway." I was in no mood to chitchat with Weasel about home improvement. I wanted his seat vacant for when Nita showed up. I didn't want anything we might have to discuss made common knowledge among management, giving Max a heads up, tho I was sure he already had some notion, which must be why Weasel was weaseling about at present. It wasn't becuz of the marvelous hash browns outlined in orange grease from the chorizo & eggs on thick warm ceramic plates that they served in this place. I had to think of something to get him out of here. "Weasel, look—I'm meeting somebody." His grin went a bit slack, the dark glasses glinted. "What? Oh, hey," he held up his hands, "enough said. I'll be out of your hair before she gets here with the coffee." "You never did tell me how you got that scar," I said. "What scar?" he said glumly. Then he chuckled. Then he leaned across the table (the edges of the puckered scar caught a little light from the distant windows & disappeared behind the sunglasses—I wondered vaguely if the story behind the scar, which had somehow spared the eye but not the eyelid, was unpleasant enough that asking about it would give him that much more impetus for leaving), lowering his voice, he confided, *"At first things didn't seem so bad, like I said. I mean, I just did what I saw other people doing. I tried to fit into this so-called civilization; I bought khaki pants, I wore a white T-shirt, clean & pressed, I shaved my head & took out my lip plug, people looked at me funny cuz I had this hole in my bottom lip but so what, I wore some little silver women's earrings instead, I was adjusting, I thot, I picked up a driver's handbook from the DMV & was learning about the chaotic, almost completely useless transport system they have here in this city. I mean, at first I thot I was doing fine. I had infiltrated their city & no one was the wiser. I got reports that my komrades were being killed or captured, but I seemed to be doing fine. I sent them advice in code, just like we had been given. I had tried all those fighting tactics & they seemed to be working fine for me. I had fat taken out of my midsection & injected into my penis, I had plastic surgery to remove my garish Aztek tattoos & sew up my lip plug hole, I bought a lifetime supply of seaweed algae & multi-vitamins, I worked out in a gym with a personal trainer, we became good friends, I confided in her about my anxieties related to my sexual & financial confusion (she personally advised me to stay out of the bonds market becuz the return wasn't high enough till the next recession, but to masturbate often, which did help), I bought lots of CDs & listened to all the kool musik they have, Alternate, Rap, Jazz, Rock, Hip Hop, & Latin, man all that musik is really happening & groovy [snaps his fingers], I really got into that scene, I went to lots of clubs & stuff, I met really kool people, la gente, ese, la vida loka, vato, me entiendes? Know what I mean, karnal? Con safos. I called the psychik hotline once a week, got thirteen credit cards, I maxed them all cuz I was leavin' this fucking place soon enough, I signed with an agency that provided extras & actors for commercials & porn videos, even if I didn't get that many calls it was a fun way to make extra cash, I made money by taking part in experimental studies at universities & medical centers, taking drugs & tests, engaging in computer sex, virtual feelings & sentiments, massage therapy, colonik therapy, made money mailing envelopes at home, earned a living calling up women from the ads in back of the street rags, slapping them around & ripping them off when they showed up, had some fun with their security escorts, I mean, everything was going perfectly okay, I thot. But then I started getting these feelings! My trainer called them panic attacks! To me they felt like an immense lake of loneliness! I felt so terribly alone, you can't imagine! I was living in a world, after all, where our civilization had been destroyed for centuries, wiped off the fucking map! Our ideology(s) had been absolutely erased, obliterated, corrupted beyond recognition! It all began to have severe corrosive effects on my personality. The warrior inside me began to fade away, began to crumble. My discipline became lax. I began to make mistakes, killed some of my victims by accident, my car got towed in a no parking zone, I got tickets for jaywalking & walking around with my zipper down, cut myself shaving, dressed sloppy, had bad dreams. Things began to go terribly wrong at some point. I couldn't perform dur-*

ing porn videos, lost my job, stopped getting outcalls. I tried to keep the cash flow regular thru the scam I was running ripping off women in the escort & outcall business, but my heart wasn't in it, I looked so bad that the women were suspicious soon as they set eyes on me, so that income dried up too. I stopped going to the gym, put on fat. Got diabetes, heart arrhythmia, cold sweats, catatonic episodes, spells of weakness & dizziness. My ideology was suffering. I considered—please don't think too bad of me, consider that I was cut off behind enemy lines, komrade—I considered joining some Christian church. Just for some company! The ideology didn't appeal to me, I swear! I swear. Huitzilopochtli is my witness. I struggled to remain true to the Revolution. But I was falling apart. Then I met **her.** She was my soulmate. Her name was Bertha. Okay, I admit it, we met at a Unitarian church picnic. But before you give me that look, Keeper of the House of Darkness, sir, consider that in the Unitarian church our beliefs as indigenous peoples are respected, I mean sort of, to some extent, at least, till we actually try to practice them. I mean, face it, their whole civilization that they got going for them—all of them Europians, whether Anglo or Afrikan or Asian or Indian—all of 'em think one thing then do Another, say one thing & do Whatever they need to get by, which, you know, involves rubbing two cents together to make a small feeling of warmth inside themselves, some piss-ass whiff of inspiration to blow against their shriveled desiccated spirits, but it doesn't get them far. I mean, the last thing they want is some blood & guts act or action that cuts to the Heart of Existence. Heart! I mean real hearts, like Aztek hearts! You were there, you know what I mean. But **she** was different, Bertha I mean. Sure, she was good in bed & all that, she squirmed underneath you, yowled & scratched like a cat, but it wasn't just that. She had some indefinable spiritual mystery about her that made me feel good. I don't know what it was, what it consisted of, that quality. But she had it. She wasn't like the rest of the Christians, I tell you. Then she was gone. She left me. She said that I wasn't really the person who I pretended to be, that I had issues I needed to work out, that I was an angry person, sometimes she felt as if I was a stranger. She said during my sleep I spoke in strange languages, described hideous tortures, she grew frightened of what she saw behind my smile at times. She said that she didn't believe she ever knew the real me. How could I tell her? Anyway, she said, she planned to move to Las Vegas & get a job as a blackjack dealer. She had always wanted to work in a casino as a black jack dealer, and now her sister had offered to get her a job at *the Sands, with free training. Imagine that! Free training! She was so happy. Bertha was so happy — she said, maybe we could get back together in Las Vegas after we had gone thru a "kooling off period." She thot it was quite likely, quite probable that everything was best this way. She kissed me long & hard, goodbye, you'll see, she told me, everything's going to work out fine. Me, stupid, stupid, stupid, I let her go. Well, soon I found myself in worse shape than I ever was. I felt as low as any human being can get. But I decided to take a chance, get together some money & move to Las Vegas to be with her. I convinced this friend of mine, Bobby, a black guy who lived in my apartment building, an ex-con who was working as a security guard at a bank building downtown, where he sat in the lobby all evening, hating his job, that we could do a few little robberies on the side, stick-up jobs, just to net us seed money for other legit projects. I was gonna grab the cash & hop the next bus to Vegas. Bobby didn't really wanna get mixed up in anything like that, but he did it becuz he liked me, he knew I was some kinda amateur, he thot he could take care of me. Wouldn't you know, wouldn't it be my luck, the first place we try to job, we went in disguised as short order cooks, wearing filthy white aprons & big chefs hats to throw off suspicion, just in case, we pulled out our pistolas, waved 'em around & told everybody to get down on the floor & shut up, we wanted all the cash & wallets & no one would get hurt! My nerves were fucked up by that time tho, I mean right away, the waitress bangs thru the swinging doors with a load of breakfast plates on each arm, lets out a scream & fuck everything to hell, if accidently I didn't jerk the trigger when she screamed, she shrieked, I thot at first from fear — bang went my little .38, bangbang right in her direction — I knew a split second later I'd shot her, she threw all the breakfast specials all over the floor, carne guizada, huevos rancheros, pigs in blankets, poached eggs, spinach omelettes, cups of coffee, black, half & half, cream or sugar, bowls of oatmeal, glasses of orange & grapefuit juice, splish splash, crash boom, all of it hit the floor — the waitress shrieked my name! It scared me, she knew right off who I was ("Cuzatli!" she shrieked), my finger twitched, I accidently shot her again; I screamed helplessly as she went to the floor. I recognized her in that second, "Bertha!" I was screaming. "Bertha you said you went to Las Vegas!" Bobby didn't know what the hell was going on, what was I shooting at? Bobby started shooting at people too. Anybody. He must've thot someone was shooting at us. I think he plugged a couple people by accident, while he was grabbing the receipts out of the* cash register. The weird part is how it all took place right here, late one nite, Weasel said, jerking his thumb over his shoulder in the general direction of the register at the end of the counter lined with stools. All that kash got Bobby excited, but I didn't care. Bertha was holding her belly as she hit the floor, sliding in the broken egg yolks, salsa picante, spilled coffee, tomato juice & blood, all the time looking up at me, wondering why I had shot her. She was saying my name as she went down on her side, her eyes already losing focus. I'll never forget that look. I went down on one knee beside her, I was trying to think of some way to save her life, when some big fucker got up out of a side booth & hit me. My baby was dying in front of my eyes & this motherfucker was slapping me upside the head! I didn't want to look at him, I didn't want to deal with him, but he'd slapped me hard. When I turned to look at him, the son of bitch stuck a water glass into the side of my face. The glass shattered against my cheek, entered my eye socket & I lost vision on that side immediately. I knew he had blinded me on the right side, I could feel stuff hanging out on my cheek dripping down my neck. I don't know . . . I guess at that point, sir, I turned & ran away . . . I knew I'd killed my baby . . . I heard the cops on a bullhorn behind me—I guess Bobby had turned the other way & had bumped right into them, I couldn't stick around to find out . . . I mean, I heard them say turn around with his hands behind his head, then the shooting broke out . . . By then I was already a block away, running fast, I grabbed some guy out of his car at a stop sign, jumped into his Studebaker & put the pedal to the floor. I was doing all of fifty thru a red light when I got broadsided by some car that thot it had the right of way just cuz the light turned. It smacked the rear wheelwell of the Studebaker, spun me around 380 degrees, I lost control of the vehicle at that point, I ran over two little kids on the way to school & some old lady—I plowed into some parked cars along the sidewalk. Must've busted a gas tank. Next thing I knew, the Studebaker was bright orange inside, the whole hood engulfed in flames. I couldn't move, my ribs were busted up inside from the steering wheel, my leg was messed up & crammed under the dash against the gear shift. By the time I had extracted myself, the steering wheel had scorched my hands it was so hot, I couldn't breathe for the smoke & my clothes lit on fire. That's when I got all burned up like you see me now." He shook his head in remembrance of that terrible misfortune. Weasel raised his voice a notch, "That's all behind me now. That's why you got to live klean. Just live klean. That's all you gotta do." "You got that right," I nodded in agreement. He had me pretty much convinced.

"Just live klean."

She delivered our coffee. I watched Cuzatli sip from the mug and said, "Really, I gotta meet somebody." He gave an understanding nod and hefted his cup o' java as if to signify he was just about done, just one more sip of caffeine for the road. I would have been internally cursing a blue streak but I am like a Zen buddhist of absolute self-control so komplete I could pour gasoline on myself & light myself on fire like a monk in orange robes in the middle of the street if I so choose, so I emitted a hiss, uttering, "Fuck!" To which—again—Weasel lifted his left hand and waved it at me, as if in surrender, scooted to the end of the seat, was about to rise to go (coffee cup in hand) when he abruptly turned back to face me, as if noticing something of utmost importance for the first time in his life, he asked, "Where'd you get such an excellent wristwatch? Is that Swiss Army or something?"

No time to tell Cuzatli the story about the high quality Leica 35 mm with a nice Zeiss lens. "I got it from a dead Nazi," I said.

Weasel was nodding appreciatively, eyeing my wrist like he expected to wear this watch soon himself. I checked the time; 9 A.M., I really thot Nita would be here by now.

Weasel slurped a last sip from his mug and gave me a farewell nod. "Well," he said. I looked at whatever was left behind the sunglasses.

He moved off, walking around the booths and sat down on a stool with his back to me. When he put his cup on the counter I noticed the pie rack above his head; inside the glass case the mirrors reflected the whipped topping of the lemon meringue, the caramel crust of the pecan pie, and the lipstick-red strawberry glaze at an angle down over the counter so that by glancing at the pies in the mirror I could see the black coffee in Cuzatli's white mug. That meant if he looked straight up, he'd be looking at me. But of course he just sat there drinking his coffee and pretending to peruse the menu.

14

M
E and Weasel sat that way for the next several days. At least that's the
way it seemed. It felt like I was sitting in the corner booth he on a
stool at the counter coffee cup steaming & sweaty glass of ice water and we
did not move at least for three days. Sun went up, sun went down, Nita
never came around. I would drink one cup of coffee after another till I had
a full pot I could empty in the cramped ammonaic urinal at the end of the
hall of the Blue Hen Diner. Before leaving the yard at nite or early dawn
I'd stop at the payphone I must've been an object of commentary I kept
leaving her messages; they said she was on her way, she got the message this
time, really she knew all about it, she'd be there in just one hot minute. Each
morning, Cuzatli & I, the two of us sniffling like the mangy dogs that run
the morning streets of the cities, would step out of the plant underneath
the high wall with laughing frolicky pigs painted on it, usually it was me
first hitting the steel door & Cuzatli following along some distance later as
if not following at all but *just happened to be* a regular at the Blue Hen Diner,
eatery of choice kitty corner to the meat packing plant, paper napkins atop
greasy hash browns with ashes & a cigarette butt decorating the affair. Daily
blue skies, smoggy, sun like to poke your eye like a lit cigarette hot sunny
glare runny as an egg on tractor trailer trucks parking lots industrial flats of
the City of Vernon railroad tracks deep concrete embankments of the L.A.
River bits of brown foam or froth floating on a couple inches of limp water
in the moatlike channel behind the plant, waiting. Traffic revving, heavy
trucks rolling across the tracks shaking the little stucco building, dead flies

riding the fans spinning soundlessly over snowy whipped Himalayas atop the golden meringue reflected in the glass case beside the strange brightness of strawberry where Weasel's eyes would have met mine in the glass if he wasn't wearing those black shades like a blind blues musician, the tilt of his head inclined to a full view of my situation such as it was, no Nita, anyway, just Weasel who might give me the nod if he caught my eye. But I might not acknowledge him with the rubber-banded roll of papers beside me.

So Cuzatli & I we sat and watched and waited.

Sun shining hard outside the dusty windows as big trucks rolled by.

I got to know the 99 cents special chorizo & eggs intimately. "Flour tortillas or corn?"

Early one morning I was waiting for my dinner breakfast special before heading home to bed when a shadow slipped out of the raw glare of sunlight. A thickset young white guy totally bald with shaved bullet-head and round metal frame eyeglasses glinting on his nose pushed thru the glass door of the diner and became a silhouette against the glare from outside, but I'd been keeping an eye on the door and had spotted him. Some time ago a motorcycle had zoomed by on Soto, the avenue mostly obliterated by glare. I blinked as my eyes readjusted to the interior dimness as the guy, in black leather motorcycle jacket and motorcycle boots strolled along the wall with the fotos of beisbol players and slid in the booth opposite me. I was certain Weasel was taking all this in from his usual stool at the counter, taking several kinds of mental notes in 2 or more languages, snapping black & white psychic snapshots & diagramming the scenario for later full reports. But I didn't give a damn. "Isaak Babel, Huitzilopochtli, I don't believe this! It ain't Day of the Dead yet, Isaak, what the hell brings you to L.A.? Last time I saw you was what, Moscow, 1937?"

Isaak gave me his shy grin (which was just this side of a grimace—just this side of a sly grin), tossed his leather gloves onto the table and shook my hand.

From her station back by the counter, the waitress leaned her head quizzically in my direction and I held up one finger. She nodded in reply. Isaak rubbed his bald skull, pink skin damp with perspiration.

"You shopping for Indian motorcycles? What brings you to L.A.? Shit, I heard you were dead!"

Isaak shook his head; again his little close-mouthed smile. "I got no bizness here I can go into. But that's not important," he said. "Nita told me where to find you."

"I'm on my coffee break, taking a break from the House of Darkness stuff, just for the moment. Care for breakfast? The specials here aren't half bad. I'll order you something."

Lowering his voice, Babel said I should remember what he was telling me for later: "The pharmacist, offering me a room. Rumors of atrocities. I walk into town. Indescribable terror & despair . . . They tell me all about it. Privately, indoors, they're afraid the Poles may come back. Kapitan Yakovlev's Kossacks were here yesterday. A pogrom. The family of David Zys, in people's homes, a naked barely breathing prophet of an old man, an old woman butchered, a child with fingers chopped off, many people still breathing, stench of blood, everything turned upside down, chaos, a mother sitting over her sabered son, an old woman lying twisted up like a pretzel, four people in one hovel, filth, blood under a black beard, just lying there in their blood. The Jews on the square, an agonized Jew showing it all to me, a tall Jew takes over from him. The rabbi hid, his whole house was taken apart, he waited till evening to creep out of his hole. 15 people killed, the Hasid Itska Galer, aged 70, David Zys, the synagogue caretaker, 45, his wife, his daughter, aged 15, David Trost & his wife—the ritual slaughterer . . . At the home of a rape victim . . . In the evening—with my hosts, like a prison, Saturday evening, they wouldn't cook till Sabbath was over . . . I go looking for the nurses. Suslov laughs. A Jewish woman doctor . . . We are in a strange old-world house, once they had everything—butter, milk . . . At night, a walk around the town . . . Moonlight, their life at night, behind closed doors. Wailing behind those walls. They'll clean it all up. The fear & horror of the inhabitants. The worst of it is—our men nonchalantly walk around looting wherever possible, stripping mangled corpses . . . The hatred is the same, the Kossacks just the same, the cruelty the same, it's nonsense to think one army is different from another. The life of these little towns. There's no salvation. Everyone destroys them . . . The girls & women, all of them, can scarcely walk. In the evening—a talkative Jew with a little beard, used to keep a shop, daughter threw herself out of a second-story window to escape a Kossack, broke her arms, one of many . . . What a mighty & marvelous life of a nation existed here. The fate of Jewry. At our place in the evening, supper, tea, I sit & drink in the words of the Jew with the little beard, wistfully asking whether it will be possible to trade . . ." (Isaac Babel, *1920 Diary,* translated by H. T. Willetts, 1995, New Haven: Yale University, pages 84–85)

Indeed; I nodded; I had heard similar reports before of course. "It's perfectly true, I know just what you were about to say, Isaak, that the Jews of Eastern Europa were wiped out during World War 2 by Nazis, but that has nothing to do with us of course it is true that nothing like that could ever happen to a great people like the Azteks, cuz we are just too great and powerful and we look way *too kool* with our black war paint and special hair cuts, lip plug, ear plugs, feathers, all the crucial stuff. It's a fact that the Aztex are not a wandering tribe like the Jews, well, all right, we used to be in ancient times but OK, we're over that now. Still, it's worth a thot—before calling on your men to lay down their lives in the morning and they stare at you with eyes red-rimmed, shivering sleepless in the cold under a milk-white sky tremulous like the Northern lights over the Volga—think on Tezkatlipoka's image of the world as smoke blowing away in a mirror, and consider that the Fate of Others that you so clearly describe may be ours, the mighty and marvelous life of the world vanished in cold morning light. I mean, imagine if the Spanish had conquered the New World, as was their plan, imagine that we all ended up living in the shitty Old World of their imagining. What a world that would have been. This world, for all we know, might be fleeting as all that, might vanish in the blink of an eye."

Poor Isaak, fretfully scratching his right arm thru the leather jacket or nervously rubbing his bald pate with his thick fingers. I looked at him & couldn't think of anything good to say. I was glad when the waitress brought his coffee.

Oh, Maria.

He slurped his coffee, but Babel wouldn't stay for breakfast. "I know you got your work cut out for you, that House of Darkness stuff ain't easy as it's cracked up to be."

"You're telling me."

I knew he had come a long way, with a longer way still to go, so I urged him to eat breakfast, but he wouldn't eat. "Come on Isaak, eat your chorizo. What would your mama say?" He was too restless, too much distance left to cover. "Thanks for the coffee," Babel said, "That was good," giving me the uptight little smile that made me feel that I was half-forgotten already, he was thinking of something else, something ahead in his future that was separate from all of the rest of us, slapping my shoulder with his gloves as he scooted out and stood by the booth. "Watch your back. Remember what I told you," Babel said, moving off thru the empty tables and pushing out the glass doors, vanishing like a ghost in the sunlight. After a moment, the motorcycle roared and then faded into the distance.

Bleary after another day done, another chorizo & eggs dinner before heading to the quiet of an empty house to sleep, I had wiped my nose & tossed my napkin on the plate, dipped my fingertip in the orange grease pooling to one side and, with a couple of returns for additional ink, wrote a neat two-inch N on the linoleum tabletop. That was when Nita walked in, sauntered the length of the counter, stopping behind Cuzatli who had glanced up as she entered and was now studying her ass over his shoulder as she waved & smiled at me—Weasel doing a half-turn on the stool, stepping down for a better view—she was standing at the table looking at me rub a circle of oil into the tabletop. She slid in opposite me, looking a bit flustered, setting her sunglasses atop her dark curly head, apologizing profusely, "I am so so sorry. You don't know what a hard time I had getting here today. I hope you got my message. Please forgive me." While she was excusing herself & apologizing some more (wasting time jinxing everything 4 ways I thought), Cuzatli had called to the waitress, "I think I'll go for a change of pace today, Marta—I'm gonna have breakfast in a booth today like one of your higher class of customers," and brought his cup of coffee over to sit at the booth next to us, facing away.

Nekok Yaotl, Enemy on Both Sides.

Telpochtli, Young Man.

Tezkatlipoka, Smoke in the Mirror.

"I need some coffee. Would you like a refill?" Nita asked, the skin of her face flushed and moist. I lowered my voice, sighing, "We got a situation to deal with." I pointed my finger like a cocked pistol directly at the back of Weasel's head. Nita followed my eyes, glancing behind her and nodded. She too lowered her voice to a whisper. "Listen to me, Zenzontli, listen. As Keeper of the House of Darkness, your steps from here on out echo throughout overlapping levels of reality and akross chronologies, parking lots, destinies & pork loin chops." I replied, "I have some theories! I have plans! I have some half-formed notions, mutated adverbs, scabrous adjectives, vacuous schemata of values, nostrums, commonplaces, pablum, whatnots; I am assembling all of these into a mighty, tremendous, interrelated, dialektical Toltekan Totality of Practice. I am practicing a lot. All my blasted motes and wads of ideas will be screwed together with a mighty torque! As the Spanish put it, A Mighty Fortress is My Lord. He is My B-29. I expekt to write a Book." "That's what I thought," Nita said, not unsympathetically, as she gestured to the tall thin waitress—who leaned over, placed a cup before Nita and poured us both full. I caught a whiff of a steamy dark aroma that conjured something like a vast territory of hormones, contoured by domestic order and kleanliness. It was a feminine thing that impressed. Nita's eyes glowed darkly with sorrow and sympathy, but at the same time there was the trace of a smirk, it seemed to me. Her wiggy curls splayed out from her head like she'd gotten hit by a minor tornado just before she walked in the door. The blast of hair gave her credibility as far as I was concerned as a left-wing spokesperson of underground organized divisions of labor. The coffee was too hot and I could feel it burning my tongue and palate; I drank some more in the hopes that it had somehow cooled faster in the cup. It was an error. Nita raised one eyebrow & flicked her eyes rightward in Cuzatli's direction, setting her cup on the table between us, steamy as a fresh road apple. "You don't have to explain," Nita said, "just nod whenever I'm in the neighborhood of a right answer. In flashes of clarity between long dark stretches of Amerikan loneliness in your soul, this is sort of some of your lines of thinking on the subject. Your mentality has creaked along like a broken-down rural bus on deserted stretches of volcanic Mexikan high desert at night, has come under attack by bandits in the dark, is blasted by gunfire, and when the hulking vehicle finally heaves itself into the solitary yellowish light of some lonely way station in the vast night, the driver is simply happy to be alive. Even tho he doesn't know if the bus, once stopped, will be able to continue on." Weasel glanced about coldly, as if casting about indifferently for someone he knew. He seemed to sniff the air, waiting for word one he could understand. I smiled angrily and nodded at Nita. I slurped skalding coffee. I wouldn't be able to taste anything for days. With this kind of woman you never knew if every detail of your encounter had been planned—not only planned but rehearsed for the appropriate effect—down to the cellular oxidation of your taste buds by the skalding caffeine. "You figured you were in trouble with some sector of the Party, some figure in the Party, you thot there was some bullshit bureaucratik conspiracy to amputate you and the House of Darkness from access to the Party hierarky, possibly becuz of your previous support for Party trade union positions puts you into conflict with current "market reforms" in economik policy headed up by Minister of Labor & vice-tlatoani Xalatoktli (Sandy Alluvial Soil) and his neoliberal market reformers who—furthermore—you suspect of having ties with the Mafia. All this disavowal of the Subconscious is right up your Alley. You could attend to such matters with your eyes Closed; in fact, isn't it Standard Operating Procedure to go into such situations half-blind? The better to allow the Subconscious access to totems, gods, nahuales, images, homologues, Ghosts in the Machine, vibrations, all under the color of sleep, blues, aquamarines, far margins of peripheral vision, glimpses from the corner of the eye once seen, then lost?" "If it were just that neat and simple," I began, but she cut me off again: "All right, we'll give you that much. House of

Darkness, thru a house darkly, with its Roads of Mud circling elliptically across the Empty Spaces to Cities of the Red Nite, metallik noises clanking, voices speaking to us out of the Past, déjà vu as *Tonal Indicator*, dial tone and lines blurred and faded by *Distance*, I know, that doesn't sum up the territory you're required to survey, but put it that way for the moment, House of Darkness does not equal the Subconscious. That's what you're going to say. Just cuz you're so anti-Europian like many macho warriors feel they must be to carry on the anti-imperialist wars, okay, and the theories of that Spanish Jew, Sigmund Froid, giving everyone side-splitting headaches in the Autonomous University Department of Psychobabble and Effrontery." "You really place any Materialist faith in the Idealist wampum of this Doktor Froid and his pseudo-scientifik S & M Predilectivity?" "Let's just say that when you get to a certain stage in Life, that you learn to keep an Open Mind. A Mind is A Dangerous Thing to Waste. An Open Mind is worth 25 cents on the Amerikan silver dollar with a bald Eagle grabbing laurels & arrows of War. Would it surprise you that the Amerikans are supplying $100 million of their ill-gotten gains in Lend Lease War Bonds to subsidize the Aztek Socialist Imperium's contribution to the war?" I snorted, "Pah! The Amerikans! Surely you don't take them seriously? We Aztex shouldn't even bother to take their genocide-tainted money laundering. Doesn't the Council of Leaders, the Tlatoani, the Speakers of Both Houses, our Party realize that the Amerikans poison us with their Vacuity? Precisely, it's precisely becuz of their Anglo-Puritanikal boringness that the Amerikan empire befuddled itself with torpor and stagnation, the Amerikan economy shriveled like a fig dangling between a leper's legs, the only interesting thing the Amerikans do is kill each other in massive numbers like *Kolombians*, but even that is tinged with boringness and boredom and futility and dubious idiocy of repetition, cuz basically they show truly limited aesthetik imagination (again, so often the basic simple *error* of bad poetiks!)—99% of yer average killing of Amerikan-on-Amerikan violence is all with handguns, knives, nylon stockings, baseball bats, cars, curtain cords, hammers, gasoline, blunt objekts, ice picks, wire or clotheshangers, choking with bare hands, sticks, kneeling on the viktims neck & pulling some fabrik taut with all their strength, an axe, rocks, rope, tire irons, but mostly knives and pistolas. You read their newspapers and that's all it is, 10,000 in Los Angeles, plus celebrity gossip *bullshit!* That's why the Amerikans can't never get anywhere in the Real World. Cuz in the Real World you gotta have more going for you than just some itchy trigger finger up your nose, you gotta have a Vision. This is exactly why the entire Karib Nation threw themselves into the sea rather than become like the Amerikans. That kind of Nation of Boredom is a Fate Worse Than Death! All they can do about it is make movies and sit like zombies in kavernous movie halls. Churn out recycled pop versions of Mayan rock & roll to brainwash teens into thinking that buying a record album is Doing Something." "I'm disappointed in you, Zenzontli. From you I expected more independent thinking than that. That's just the Party line they taught to you in school and you fell for it. Zenzontli, I know you of all people as Keeper of the House of Darkness know both the virtue as well as the necessity of looking at everything from two sides, or three sides, or 4 & 1/4 sides, to be exact." Nita continued: "I'm not engaging in some collegiate debate with you, Zenzontli, Darwin versus Zhdanov, or Huitzilopochtli versus Coyolxaukee, or the rights of sacrificial victims to copyright their own death songs and academik claptrap. You and I are beyond sophomorik contretemps. Are we not scientifik warriors on the frontiers of ignorance? Are we not at war against the sunlit world's tendency to turn into its opposite, Huitzilopochtli's dialectikal law which turns Victory into Defeat, rare understanding into kommon sense, kommon knowledge and then—at every level—turning enlightened principle into blind dogma? Am I not your prime ally in this subversive struggle of darkness against light, vision against blindness, the unknown against the Past & the Known, over and against what's intolerable and unbearable in this World?" I looked at the wobbly backside of Cuzatli's head and nodded, "Sure, I get that much. I'm not so sure as I'd go so far as to adopt these untested and mostly discarded ideologies, poetiks, raggedy koncepts of the churlish and unhappy cultures of all types brought into the kapital by boats of commerce and airships of our armed forces." "Our Party has this deal figgered out to within a hair's breadth of a cat's eye," Nita said. "I wouldn't want to stymie a good thing once it gets going, cuz why fix what ain't smoking?" I asked rhetorically. "Why shoot a dead horse once it's down for the count?" she said nonkomittally. "Why cast chopped liver after clam juice?" I added. "Why smack a boondoggle between a rock and the ptarmigan place, my daddy once said," Nita demurred. Then a light seemed to go on above her head (I myself heard the chiming tonalities of a vibraphone); she perked right up, leaning forward with her elbows on the table. She slapped my leg underneath it & I felt the sharpness of her fingernails retracting, arching her eyebrow as she exclaimed, "Why lock horns with the dog that bit you, your mama and the horse she rode in on, Kamikaze? Know what I mean, Stonewall Jackson? How's about hitting the side of a barn with a flat cow, eh? Snort that ramen pork noodles and snorkel it." "Gotcha where the sun don't shine, cowboy," I said, winking at her: "We're communicating now, can't ya tell." "I got you eye to eye on this one," Nita nodded; I knew I had her earnest support, by the look in her eye as Weasel scratched his head, sipping ever so solemnly the black dregs of cold caffeine. Distaste was forming in his uneasy grimace. "We don't want our own heads so far up our own asses we got to collect lizard's piss roaming the Wild West, Smoky," she warned. "For every eye that offends thee, burn fiddlesticks into ploughshares and split the difference," I agreed. "Absolutely," the Representative of the Congress of Industrial Organizations of the Western States said without hesitation. "Am I radioing you loud 'n clear, Kimo Sabby?" I asked—just making sure—adding, "Are you suggesting that this house may be bugged and we shouldn't speak of certain things openly?" "You couldna heard me say any sucha thang, Pop Tarts," the union & poarty organizer narrowed her eyes. "All right, all right! Don't get struck by a needle in a haystack on I-95," I said, trying to sound casual, "It's, like, whatever you say, Chappaquiddick." "You sure you're following me now, booger-meister?" Nita asked. I nodded; I was serious: "I know exactly how you're signifying-monkey, Kitchen-Aid! So blow it out of your ass one time for the Gipper!" "Let me get this straight, Each One Teach One," she grumbled, "You got more up your sleeves besides something that penicillin can't cure?" I nodded again, admonishing, "You only gotta repeat it just once, Ford Pinto Upsidedown. I just wish I had some more teen blood in this mug, Stinky Punks." "Hot twatty doodles, Margarita, I mean Marta, get the man some more Tlaxklalan or Spagnik blood and don't be so slow as a snowstorm in July, why dontcha?" "Way to go, Akhmatova!" I grinned, "You ain't twistin' off a cold witches tit and tossin' it over the back fence on a freight train like a black bat out of hell when you put it to 'em like that, lemme tell ya. I'd lay an ice cube against your left eye on that, Pencil Neck!" "I appreciate anyone's mouthwash hitting the wall at 60-miles-an-hour more than you might know, Chum the Waters," Nita Yahui (Tonantzín in her own right, Aretha Franklin Pantomime & child ballerina — a force to be reckoned with citywide) was assuring me: "You betcha the buppy Beamers, Buster Brown, Wet Dream in Stitches, North Carolina." "You ain't rooty-toot-tootin, Scotty Tissue," I growled: "We talk like this, they play the tapes backwards and get sinus headaches, cherry-plum visions of the devil dancing on the Ace of Spades, feel a blow straight to the diaphragm on a heavy metal Wednesday?" "Porky Pie, did you hear the man?" "I shorely did, yodel-lay-hee-hoo," Cuzatli muttered. "Wakantanka," I went on: "Bust that joint on a week of Sundays, Doodly Squat, I'll lay five to one a bitch in heat ain't gonna lay down for no horny toads spittin' blood in her eye once they sniff a whiff of our plan to bait and switch the Pea Game on this one, Everyready Battery." Nita pointed her index finger directly at my heart and murmured grimly: "All dressed up in a blue moon, Tuesday's Child, nowhere to go if the tree falls in a forest with your dick in your hand, no one to blame but yourself when the chips go down, fly up, stick between your teeth, Sweet & Sour Sauce, don't bite those nails." "My nails don't look that bad," I said. "Bug-eyed Bejeezus with Shit on a Shingle, Pizza Face," Nita shook her head, "Don't you know nothing? Let me put it another way. Why drown all your kittens in the same sack on a rainy day when you can wear concrete galoshes to your own funeral, find yourself staring up thru the dandelions hog wild on a Month of Sundays in the Windy City? Don't be such a Knuckle Sandwich, Spaz Attack!" "You straighten me out like no one can, Sin City! I got no one to thank for my troubles, Registered Voter

& thanks anyway, Lon Chaney. I'll let you know how it turns out any which way but *chingao*, Apply Pressure Here." "You're a whole hell of a lot smarter than you might seem at first glance from inside a pin-hole camera, Water Closet," the young woman conceded. I flushed, embaressed at her appraisal in spite of myself: "I just try to hold up my end of that tin lizzy of ours with one hand in someone else's pocket as the other romper stompers on a pontoon bridge pissing sideways in a hurricane wind, Come Again. Besides, when everybody else takes one step backward and you're standing in front by yourself, you raise your hand and say, 'I volunteer to tear you a new asshole, Que Chula!' Nothin' to it, Dudes & Dudettes!" "Ah, I was your age sometimes when I wished upon a star like that," Nita sighed huskily, giving me this piece of her mind: "Enjoy them pepperonis while you got 'em, Stagolee. Twisting in the wind wasn't built in a day, not when your wad's shot, one's swingin & the other's hangin, *one*. Not one time in Bakersfield in a pussy-whipped six digit figure!" "Waitress!" Weasel croaked, as if stirring to the life right toward the end: "Jeezus Huitzilopochtli Christ gimme some more coffee I'm begging you for the very last time! Bring the check while you're at it!" Cuzatli called as if squeezed by desperate circumstance to the front of the diner. I had to agree completely and told Nita so: "Tort Lawyer, if you can't afford it, the court will appoint your mama to the bench, Silence is Golden, so suck your stiff upper lip Hannah Barbera, this is gonna cross your heart stick a needle in your eye Bite the Bullet, High & Lonesome." "Furthermore, you got every chance in West Oakland, Itemized Deduction My Ass, Tony Lama. Kiss my pimp jumpsuit times ten," Nita added, staring pensively into the middle distance: "Argentine Military Junta Decrees Amnesty For Itself, he ain't gonna know ten ton of bricks from a duck's waddle, that's thinking! I just wish we had the rundown on the inside track, Green Teeth." *This was good. This was very good.* "The time is now or whatever, Caca on My Shoe," I replied: "Once this toothpaste gets out of the tube we'll be laughing on the homestretch all the way to a sticky place, Child Custody Guidelines." Nita placed her hands together thoughtfully (Marta, having returned to the middle distance with the coffee decanter, tossed a miffed sidelong glance in Weasel's direction), finally suggesting, "Red-blooded Aneurysm in a New York Minute, Chop Suey I. C. U., what's left won't amount to beans over tubular bells and cleat marks up & down the fat girl's stretch marks . . . Cellulitis, Beef Jerky . . . Debt Adjustment . . . Sizable Percentage . . . Climatology . . . Slipping & Sliding . . . It's all there, anyone can see, Bumblebee! Drop a dime on that call, Jap Mama-san." I thought about it before I nodded, saying, "I'll lick 'em fast as I can stick 'em, one-two-three, Last Call. You're the best field rep & backup that anyone could ever ask for & not get slapped with a subpoena, War & Peace." I slurped the last of my human blood and patted Nita's firm brown hand. "Now that that's all worked out," she exhaled, "I can breathe EZ across Seven Seas, Haiti Slant Eye & Pass the Coleslaw, cuz when they get the jump on what's coming the suits will cream in their jeans, lisp twice & lean to the left before they find themselves rarer in the mind's eye than an All Points Bulletin, Ciao Bella." I paused to review the landscape and fix its terrain more clearly in my mind. It was a dark picture with new light oscillating upon it. Nita's suggestions were knitting into an image for me now. "Sock me on the Jaw, Starkers!" I said softly. "Myocardial Infarct. Stolichnaya Appellate Court," Nita warned. "How about a thousand for my van?" I reminded her. Nita rolled her eyes. "Well, fuck me," we heard Weasel mutter to no one, talking to himself again.

Nita & I shook hands amidst diesel fumes drifting over the sunny side-walk outside the diner. Unseen inside submarine flat unreflective plateglass, Weasel was probably giving us the eye. "I won't be late next time, I swear," Nita crossed her heart, turning on her heel and walking off with the paper-work in her bag.

15

A FEW weeks later LAPD detectives Anglo Dick and Negro Slim entered the Blue Hen Diner as if diving into a very murky pool indeed, pausing a moment for their eyes to adjust to the interior dimness before moving with all deliberate speed thru the tables to me, sitting in my usual rear corner booth tapping the coffee mug with my finger. Dick drew himself up before me as if to study the centipede in my hair before he flattened it with a brick, a twitch in the corner of his mouth as he said, "Show me some ID." Slim positioned himself in clear view to Dick's right, hand on hip casually inside his jacket, glancing along the empty booths to catch Weasel's upturned gaze in the pie case (Cuzatli instantly decided his coffee, which he always took black, today must have a full dose of sugar), and turned on me a gentle frown. I leaned left to pick my wallet out of my pocket; "Keep one hand on the table," Dick growled & leaned toward me. Slim shifted his weight from one foot to another, hand now on the butt of his Colt 45, all this so I could place my wallet on the table. There! "How about the ID, you fuck?" Dick was saying, as I took out my library card, my Payless Shoe Discount Card, a pawn ticket for a Soviet medal from the motherland, an old grocery list, an empty but worn dues booklet for the John Reed Fan Club, an IOU from a shoeshine boy, and a photo of my mom wearing a sunhat, circa 1935. As I reached forward to flip what I thought must be my driver's license from the pile, Dick struck a stunning blow to the side of my face that threw my hair all in a tizzy, a rabbit punch that sent my coffee in a spray across the table as the cup rolled away, and I leaned far left in a half slouch, one hand to my face, tears squirting in my eyes (Negro Slim unmoved, watching me with a soft dark stare), as Dick picked up the card between thumb and forefinger and glanced at it, tossing it into the coffee on the tabletop. "Let's go out back where we can talk," Dick said, jerking me to my feet and pushing me ahead of him and his partner; he took one arm and Slim the other as they shoved me thru the backdoor of the Blue Hen into the dirty, blind daylight.

"Just sit here a minute, you'll be all right," Weasel was saying, leaning into my face much closer than I'd ever seen Weasel in my life—up close his one good eye shone with a fearful intelligence: "You might need a couple stitches on that mouth. That eye doesn't look so good either; plus, I think they broke your nose. Whoa, come on—sit up, now, sit up. Can you sit up?" He stuffed my license and personal papers in my shirt pocket hanging slack; the shirt hung lopsided—seemed nearly torn off. Glimpse of a splash of dark blood down the front of my white T-shirt. "They're looking for Max, aren't they?" I worked my mouth in consideration of a reply to Weasel—thanks for heaving me back into the booth where I belonged— but my mouth seemed to be filling with blood from a cracked tooth that moved about when I tried to staunch the flow with my tongue. "I know, fucking Max rips off the company and disappears and they take it out on us. Like we'd know shit about it, or hang around here if we were in on it. Say, did those LAPD motherfuckers say anything about me?" Sometime later, I was holding something burning alongside my mouth and when I pulled it off my face and looked at it there was a chunk of ice wrapped in a bloody washcloth in my hand and Weasel was nowhere to be seen.

I lost a molar on that one. Sitting in the corner booth in the back of the Blue Hen every morning after, I'd have to try to drink my coffee with the good side of my mouth (the side without stitches), sometimes feeling the hole in the gum with my tongue where the tooth had been. By all accounts it seemed Max was really gone for good too, and Weasel stopped following me to the diner. When the union certification vote was scheduled, Weasel made himself scarce, telling 3Turkey he was going on vacation; Zahuani told us Weasel told him somebody in his family had died in Mexico and he had to head south to take care of bizness. So we wouldn't have Weasel to push around anymore—maybe he wasn't coming back, but nobody wuz crying about it. Bob Handler put me and the crew back on single shifts while management considered who might replace Max as foreman. Maybe a couple other guys involved in shady deals took the opportunity to quit. The cops came around every week asking questions. Somebody had to know something. Anglo Dick & Negro Slim kept telling us, "Either the easy way or the hard way." But what could anybody tell them? What did anybody really know? Major players disappeared or weren't speaking & I wuz just making it up as I went along. I had actually tried to give the pinheads a few existential pointers myself, but they thought I was fucking with them & went for my testicles. That was their last chance. One afternoon on the kill floor I could make out thru my smeared goggles & bloody steam the inspector-in-training, Maria, with her white labcoat and clipboard, watching me from the landing. What was that about? While 3Turkey, Zahuani, Nakatl and the rest were chowing down carnitas tacos from the Tacos Oaxaca truck, I put a call thru to Nita Yahui at the Macarthur Park office and told her that the certification vote was definitely going our way, "Everybody's voting union. I don't know who it is—I got some ideas but I got to find out for sure. Somebody is spreading the rumor that Max actually never left the plant, that he crossed me so I paid Weasel $900 and Max ended up in the sausage grinders for hot dogs. I'm gonna find out who is saying that shit & give them a good talking to. Meanwhile, the rumors seem to be working in our favor, at least for the time being. People feel compelled to vote the right way. There's no middle ground in the House of Darkness." "What?" Nita said, "Say again?" "I said there's no middle ground in this vote." "Good," she said, then she wanted to talk to me about meetings about industrial concentration, citywide organizing, immigrant rights, organizing the disorganized & throttling kapitalism with the prosthetik arm of the people united who would never be defeated. "Fucking glad of that, I am too," I said, hanging up the receiver, sucking on the empty hole in my gum, I turned around & jumped straight up in the air. FDA Inspector-in-training Maria was standing behind me as if waiting for the phone the whole time. She smiled shyly and said, "I hear your name is at the top of the foreman list." "Ah, that's just what I need. I need to work longer hours at this place than I already do. Longer hours and harder work, that's just what I need." Maria chuckled. "Anyway, that's what they're saying," she shrugged. "I was on that list once before," I shrugged myself, "but hey— who is saying that?" "You know," she tossed her head toward the main office. I frowned at her. Which one of us was denser and dimmer, her or me? With her cute smile, she was certainly giving me a run for my money. There had to be more behind those nice dark eyes than the smoke I was seeing there now. I looked & there didn't seem to be any more to it than what she'd just said—which itself was just a repetition of something she'd apparently heard in the office. That's all there was to it, & to her? I didn't buy it for a second. So what if she was some girl with some college & never liked to get her hands dirty. There had to be more to Maria than that— had to be more than that to anybody; I was peering intently into her eyes when she laughed & looked at the taco truck. 3Turkey was checking us out; he'd be talking to me about Maria later, that was for sure. Zahuani leaned over cackling as he said something to placid, smiling Nakatl—he was probably describing some act involving Maria's female elasticity right at this moment. "Anyway, I just wanted to say good luck with that," she said half over her shoulder as she turned to go. "Good luck, maybe we'll be working together," she laughed as she walked toward the smokehouse.

THIS DEPARTMENT HAS WORKED 184 DAYS WITHOUT LOST TIME.

*Between you & me, they didn't have to notify **me** safety begins **here** by the door the Chinese & Vietnamese women go in & out of, Safety is practically my middle name, I know there's dangerous machinery in operation at all times caution is advised, it's a big plant with several tall buildings sporting steaming towers in the industrial nite, the warm blurry steamy industrial nite as we pull the graveyard shift* *like the rest of the secret armies of the night who make your city run when you wake up in the morning with a headache on the couch & your TV talking the same old shit, the trucks hauling hogs in & boxes of packed meat out the front gates at all hours, the Aztek calendar spins down thru the years, the stone of the sun indicating multiple overlapping cycles of time, on one level I saw myself like Officer Broderick Crawford of the California Highway Patrol standing beside my 1949 cop car saying 10-4 into a microphone as I pushed a stinking cart full of evacuated stomach contents, offal & byproduct to the waste disposal unit—but on another level shortly afterwards I could be hosing down the area with the high-pressure hose, recalling standing on a freezing Russian airfield while the wind rocked the transport plane, propellers whirring so the engines would not freeze, kicking ice crystals into your face like gravel, while on a whole other level I was much younger like dark lithe Sabu in his clean but questionable loincloth running thru the jungle scene filmed at the arboretum chased by a tiger calling out to Bwana Bwana White Man oh save me! from the delirium of endless labor in the chill room, tons of hog carcasses congealing and sighing at me in the freezing air as I jumped up—suddenly awake after falling asleep, shouting, "Para bailar your mama!" as loud as my useless throat would allow; on another level I was like Charlie Chan pointing out to the loud blustery open-hearted gringo cop the error of his not-so-subtle ways trying to kick me repeatedly in the nuts tapping my overlong Fu Manchu fingernails together sinisterly as if I was about to pick my own brain thru my nose—instead of doing like I do, following from the top of a ridge of bluffs a man below in the marsh thrashing his way thru the underbrush, following him silently from the ridge above as he crashed thru the tangled swamp of thickets, reeds and alligator pools, making his way north along the overgrown coast to a point where it met the river, his desperate haste and escape route both signaled by a white egret frightened out of a tree, flapping up above the bright greenery of the swamp, circling and rising into the afternoon sunshine shimmering on the ocean's vast blue—or, maybe I was the one being followed, what about that, I'd turn, shivering, sick and sniffling in the chill room, hands too numb to work, to feel the clipboard or the pen, and see Max watching me thru the tiny window in the steel door, watching me lean against the freezing wall to take a breather, maybe close my eyes for a moment, checking the window again, no one there—had Max been there or not? The corridor empty, swabbing it again, wondering if Max would appear to check up, walk thru the wet hallway to make me go over it again & write more absurd commentary in my personnel file, working fast to get it done, and why were there animal tracks smeared down the hallway around the corner, looking up again at the shiny film glimmering along the linoleum, but on another level I had to be more than ever sneering at Fate like Humphrey Bogart in Treasure of the Sierra Madre after asking, "Brother, can you spare a dime?" and—spurned on the streets of TJ—nevertheless spots two bits & puts his foot on it—sneering cold-eyed when 3 Turkey is gone with the dolly with the last load of gunked-up filters and the freight elevator opens onto the roof level but it's not 3 Turkey returning, it's Max watching me on my hands & knees on the roof screwing on the cover for the filter unit on the smokestacks, filthy with the black grease that comes from handling the stacks of filters, reeking with the stench of the blackest burnt bacon, Max standing at the edge of the building four stories above the yard smoking a cigarette staring off at the night lights as if unaware of me finishing up the job, wiping off the surface with a rag and throwing it and the Philip's head in the toolbox and walking into the freight elevator, punching the "G" button; rubbing my nose with the back of my hand and smearing black grease across my face, realizing that Max had not only been smoking a cigarette but he'd been holding an adjustable wrench in his hand, maybe I should check on exactly what Max had to do on the rooftop at the same time I happened to be completing the last assigned job of the shift, so I hit the "2" button and took the stairs back to the roof, arriving to find the cover plate for the filter unit askew and smeared with black grease, it had been removed and not very carefully replaced— maybe it was the perfect time to ask Max what was going on—so I ran down the stairs to get ahead of the elevator, catching it in the perfectly immaculate corridor of the third floor vibrating with a refrigeration hum, thumbing the down button, and when the elevator halts I find I have the Philip's head in my pocket somehow (I thought I tossed it in the toolbox) but Max doesn't bother to say hello or even look at me or meet my eyes, just smacking a big adjustable wrench against his palm sneering to himself and punching the "G" button, saying, "Meet me at my office at the end of your shift," (I swear I heard him say) so what if the LAPD dicks Anglo & Negro said I was reported sometime that nite in the vicinity of the sausage grinders (shaped like cement-mixer-sized triangular funnels with three circular heads with large interlocking teeth for the grinding of equal amounts of pork, beef and fat* dumped into the grinder in huge batches from stainless steel tubs) for the wieners, which are extruded into natural casings to hang like candles on dry racks that are wheeled into the ovens & baked, but I denied it, there were workers already there, I wasn't assigned to that area that nite and I don't remember being sent there on an errand say, unless I had returned a stray steel tub that had somehow found its way to the kill floor, maybe filled with things like hogs heads but on another level I doubt any of that had ever happened really, nobody would ever know for sure if Max ever hefted the adjustable wrench in one fist as if he knew exactly the best use for that thing, or if, surprised, he shot me a steely glance cold as the fresh white froth of the morning ocean, and then pop, after a popping sound the Philip's head protruding from his skull was lifted, so a fountain of blood splashed on the wall as he dropped spinning down into a corner, pure speculation all of it & certainly the fact that 3 troops of Boy Scouts at the Dodger game Thursday nite suffered severe gastric distress, colicky burps, stomach aches & poisonous farts doesn't mean there wuz anything wrong with those footlong Dodger dogs, I know there wuz some complaints from the old lady of Pasadena who complained she fed Farmer John all-beef weenies to her poodle & later found it floating in the backyard swimming pool feet in the air its belly swollen many times its normal size with putrefying gases so the skin appeared almost hairless & transparent, so what if it looked like a float from the yacht harbor, that is not a scientifik indicator a Mexikan was in those hot dogs, no matter that Tony Franciosa & Angie Dickinson were spotted on Fairfax Avenue at Pink's consuming large quantities of chili dogs hand over fist when their whole party fell out in simultaneous fits of projectile vomiting & blasts of outrageous vile farts so their movie careers tanked & you only saw them on stupid cop shows on late-nite TV ever afterwards each of them wearing some strange wigs like Ernest Borgnine or Lee Marvin in drag—you just can't eliminate the fact that hot dog stands like Pink's never really clean out the age-old katsup & mustard bottles, on another level you can understand why some immigrants from China thot these all-American hot dogs taste kinda weird really, we Orientals may not truly like the weenies of the West we shall stick to the time-honored ancient cuisines of Asia, that's just the way it goes, hot dogs are not for everyone, on the other hand, without any hesitation on my part I must point out that my freezer at home is packed with Farmer John products of all types even smoked ham hocks and I not only endorse wieners as dietary items of *a healthy modern lifestyle but I usually eat them cold out of the package from the open fridge without bothering to cook them at 2 A.M., they're good like that. In my freezer I keep a stash of packages of hot dogs dated to the exact date they say Max disappeared, which I may consume with relish & lick my fingers. You may kick me repeatedly in the face behind the dumpsters of a diner on Monday & Tuesday too but if I don't know what happened to Max I don't care if you found his shoelace dangling from the mouth of a toddler choking in Barstow. I don't have all the answers, please would you stop kicking the face.*

I can't hold it against the cops. Christians, sub-atomik physicists & alcoholiks alike, they're seekers after a simpler world with easier answers. We adults must accept that complications have set in. Sometimes you could glance in the mirror surprised to find out you got a brand new look, your face might be re-arranged, not always for the better since stitches stick out like hog's whiskers & confused looks flit nervously across a bruised & blackened, squinting face; other times you look in the mirror in the cramped restroom at the end of the hall and see nothing but smoke. The world is some shifty joint where universes intersekt & spin away into new directions like car crashes on the Golden State Freeway at the intersektion with the 101. Aztek calendrikal science denotes numbered interstices in cycles of death & rebirth for transitions to new seasons, new epochs fraught with risk, danger, pollution, smog advisory & wind warnings, leaving a funny smell on your hands. Somebody played Russian roulette with reality, everything turned out kinda funny, nobody told us this (One Reed) wuz happening—now it's time to start again. That's why I am telling you, so when your life goes thru the spin cycle and is hung out to dry in a smoggy breeze, you can look inside yourself while you push a mop bucket down long corridors where the meat sways; if it stinks of burnt flesh & there's a massive racket like machine guns, you can survive inside the House of Darkness—get a real job for a change. All while peeling skin like Xipe Totek off a new life. Me, these days I find that I have a purplish interior life. From inside looking out, it looks black-and-blue with the violet shading of broken capillaries. Sometimes it's shot through with pitch-black shadows, tendrils of hanging vines, the febrillating light through the giant figs over-hanging the avenues of the kapital, the occasional blinding glare on the paving stones, slanting in across the broad empty plane of the mind with the sudden lateness of the afternoon itself. "What does it mean to be a man?" CIO field rep Nita Yahui asked me at some point in her harangue of encouragement (by phone of course, since she's too busy to meet at all lately), urging me to attend nite classes in Marxism-Leninism so I would understand the Forces of Production, the Four Tezkatlipokas, Dark Night and the Wind. I was certain she'd go on to declaim my duties to myself as super macho, killer elite (fixer when the fire hits the fuel line) party activist. She just sighed when I allowed how I was mighty busy and I tried to guess ahead to what else she was going to say so I could prepare in my mind the korrect answers, as my wife long ago used to suggest. Well, in my purplish inner life, I *am* a *man* . . . I truly feel I am a man, and sort of a monkey too. Part of me is a man who sits back — as I was sitting back in my slatted ceiba lounge chair with its maguey-fiber backing, ocelotl throw draped across it, rocking back in it gritting my teeth against the coursing fire (very like a steel metro train thrust through some wobbly sponge-tunnel in my skull) that I pictured sending bubbles of methane gas up through the latticed interstices of my skull-bones, to lodge underneath skarred patches of my long-haired skalp. Part of me is that Man, seemingly relaxed with a giant pain in his brain marked by a small "oh" like a small look of surprise one might draw across one's face before looking down to find a blade, or spike, or something that has pierced some flesh, body part or limb, protruding through the skin before your eyes. Part of me seems to be a man with a Giant Pain as if one's head has been sliced klean off and instantly replaced by a kokonut with a splitting headache. A hairy kokonut with sweet milk that aches. Yeah. Well part of me seems to be a man reclining in a certain position in space, defensively thinking toward a plausible space where — perhaps somewhere outside of Tukumkari or Mazatlán — where pain has entirely vanished. But we Aztek big men, we warriors all the way Jack, bear that note and notion like it was nothing, light as a feather, a feather drawn across the wrist of an arm whose hand has been summarily chopped off by the Islamik klerik in charge of the thieving teenagers at some Central Juvenile Facility in Muslim Afrika. Hmmph, we might say at such a moment, we Aztek big men, jack, black belt Aztek warriors to the core, heart thumping etc., while the beads of perspiration spring forth on our brow like human aspirations appear on the horizon which serves as the brow of the gods themselves. (One less hand for thievery & nose picking invokes the oft-necessary interior ritual called Setting of Priorities.) My inner life teems, it seems, with the sunshine yellow of the sago palm planted within the brain's vegetable pain, I figure, yellowish as fatty tissue and green with its fibrous fronds thickening at the stem with something of a vegetative surly determination! My inner life resounds at such a juncture with the clackity clack of dry fronds and palm bark. *What is it to be a man?* (Why should anybody have to be asking me such a question at a time like this? Can't they see I'm busy? Even the guy who runs Spanish Torture Services, some fleabitten small business outside the Market District, called to ask advice, which I refused him—"Do you think information on Spanish torture is free? Pain costs money! Time is money! Pain is Time!" I cried—he whined something about rising rents in the gentrified areas outside the Eastern Market and blubbered one complaint after another about his life, and summed up his whole hopeless inutility with that question. I hung up. Private enterprise! Doctrinaire idiots! Privatizing their own goofy asses! "What does it mean to be a man?" my ass. If they had a clue they wouldn't have to ask such a thing.) Though, once you think about it, something in my mind feels like a monkey. Besides the man—who I acceded was there, holding his headache in his mind like a skull within the palm of his hand, frowning at it as if conversationally at the graveside, sputtering about the slings & arrows of prissy fucking History—there seemed at the same time to be a monkey scampering back and forth inside my inner life. Sneaky little bastard. As if looking for an exit from the dark purplish bruise of a jungle garden that was my soul, sort of squashed and bleeding at the edges by circumstance. Frothy, between the steel teeth of concertina wire, glinting with loamy thickening of coagulated thot. Something that can make a monkey nervous. Of course, I am a Scientifik Monkey, a true believer in

Aztek Socialist Sciences and Teknospiritual Advances, and if they say we are descended from primates, and that Ketzalkoatl may not actually have "stolen our bones"—as we happen to define "bones" in 1942—(I can accept that)—during Ketzalkoatl's psychedelik travels in the Underworld, from Miklantekutli ("Big Daddy of All of the Dead People and the Place They Got Throwed After The Shit Hit the Fan"); instead, they tell us all now, that mythospasmology may simply be inaccurate Theory for the actual processes of evolution where humans, Azteks mainly, achieved pre-eminence in our current victorious Form. Epitomized by *me*. Reclining in my comfortable rear-corner diner booth with a cup of Java and a Fucked Up Headache that makes my saliva taste like metal. Like I might have metal teeth, which I do. Some new ones. I might even think this was the mechanism of my doom & permanent exile from Aztlán except that I've existed in this kondition so long it has become second nature. Perhaps that's what accounts for the flakes of blackened silver along the raw, sore, scabby roots of my inner life, sunk as they are into the infant-shit-yellow paste of my psychological clay. The shadow of a monkey there, wavering there, flickering back and forth like a moth caught in a web. I mean, sometimes I sense a monkey spirit. I could be mistaken. That's the trouble with one's inner life. Monkeys could be playing around with it. They'll fuck around with your stuff if you let them. You'll be looking for something in your inner life, some truth about your situation, in this world or some other level of existence somehow, then you'll have to take care of some other Business, and when you turn around, when you go back and check your inner life again, just watch, the monkeys will have fucked off with something. Some part of your interior life will be fucking lost cuz of the monkeys. I don't know what you can do about that.